For the ten little legs in my life.

Finch Henry's
AIR FISH

E. HEROLDBECK

Paperback ISBN: 978-1-6720-3100-4

ACKNOWLEDGMENTS

With endless thanks to Martin, Clare, Vicki, Cath, Wendy, Kate J, Vince, my editor Lesley Jones, and especially to Bid, for all of your enormous generosity, help and encouragement. It has been so very much appreciated. Thanks also to Monty Python for allowing me to quote your work. Finally, I would like to thank Anil Seth, Professor of Cognitive and Computational Neuroscience at the University of Sussex, for his remarkable and fascinating work that helped to shape my character Boff's description of reality.

1 DEMOCRATISING THE ANGELS

PART 1

Finch had never been in a church this size. It was clearly ancient in places. There were familiar cold stone pillars bearing the calligraphic graffiti of long-dead choir boys, and enough space to hold a town. On entering, this was a regular, if almighty church, a cathedral perhaps – Finch had never seen one – but this was different; where the east window should have been there was an architectural glass structure replacing parts of the roof which undulated and swept in an irregular curvature that drew up into apexes and gliding arches like nothing Finch had ever encountered. The glass construction was interwoven with the original fabric of the building and bowed down to ground level creating an extended area of soft light at the front of the church, immersing the space in a diffused radiance.

Sitting roughly in the centre, as Father D'Myno had suggested, Finch made a show of reading the order of service to calm his nerves but the words were not getting past his eyes. This was all new. He felt like an imposter. After all, he was just sitting in, waiting for D'Myno to take him on to the AU base, but the priest clearly wanted to show him something and had stressed the importance of observing this service. Finch had spent most of his life cloistered within the religious school back on the island, so entertained some vague assumptions about the imminent proceedings. He had learned, though, that the mainland was unpredictable, volatile even; it seemed able to deliver irrational, life-threatening situations followed by encounters with highly enlightened, reasonable people who rejected the dangerous hedonism he had seen just minutes earlier.

The guests were entering through ancient wooden doors, passing an easel that held a large portrait photograph of a young woman. She was in her thirties and posed happily for the camera. To Finch, the image looked like the cover of a magazine. Cursive script spelt out 'Juliette' across the base of the portrait. Now there were all manner of hats and outfits arriving, the extreme colours and styles far beyond those that Finch had witnessed on his native island. They looked frivolous, extrovert. People greeted each other with twin kisses and polite shoulder hugs, attempting to summon the names of second partners, stepchildren and friends not seen since the last wedding a couple of years ago. Tissues were being offered and coats removed as people excitedly took their pews.

Self-conscious and sitting alone, Finch cast his attention back to the order of service. There were familiar prayers and hymns but with some alteration in places. Finch did not understand much of the terminology used to describe the ceremony itself. After some time, everyone was finally seated. Children, who seemed explicitly focused on a beautiful yet anachronistically modern pod-like structure at the front, were now being hushed by their parents. The chamber that drew such attention was constructed of curved glass and lit with fine bars of white light that seemed integral to the structure itself. The pod merged into the glass extension, subtly protruding from it, separate yet unobtrusive.

Ethereal music began. To Finch, it sounded deceptively unstructured as the choir filled the space with soaring notes that lingered before fading, the acoustics imparting a haunting drift to the sound. Finch was considered a musical prodigy on the island but he now felt a sting of wonder that there was so much more to learn here. Perhaps it was this that Father D'Myno had wanted him to experience first-hand.

The guests strained backwards for a glimpse of the bride. Silhouetted in the light from the doorway stood a woman in a full-length, off-white dress of flowing translucent fabric that held the sunlight. The music changed and she began her journey to the front of the church where Father D'Myno waited. Multiple lengths of spectral, air-light fabric floated behind her as she passed, as though in slow motion or underwater. She carried a cascading arrangement of wild-looking flowers and grasses, and her loosely waved hair was twisted up in places, tumbling free in others. It too was dressed with wild flowers. There was a natural, bohemian freedom to her appearance that Finch had never before observed in a bride. She looked radiantly joyful, though visibly nervous and overwhelmed by emotion. She beamed through tears at the faces she recognised on her way to the altar.

Father D'Myno led the gathering in prayer and song. There were stories of Juliette's good deeds and her achievements. There was mention of family and friends and the eternal bonds of love. Finch had never before been to a wedding where the groom played such a minor role; he couldn't even be seen from where Finch was seated and there had been no mention of him yet.

Following a blessing, the bride walked past Father D'Myno and slowly entered the glass pod where she lay down on a simple, altar-like bed. She rested the flowers on her chest; her dress, hair and the long bouquet poured freely over the bed's velvet-draped sides.

Three vast cinema screens had somehow emerged while Finch had been absorbed in the unfolding scene. He could not see how, or from where they came. The technology on the mainland was fast and bright. Finch had been stunned by it at first. Now he was prepared to be astonished at every turn by what appeared to be actual magic, but was apparently 'just tech'. The screens showed live images of Juliette lying on the bed from different angles. The doors to the pod drifted shut silently, emitting a subdued electrical beep once closed. Finch observed the guests as they watched the screens intensely, becoming respectfully quiet while the choir performed another, increasingly stirring composition.

2 THE OUTMODED GHOST

Playing his cello in another cathartic craze – this island could make Finch boil with fury and frustration at times. He was seated facing out of the great arched window of his otherwise spartan room in a cold, dank wing of the church lodgings. The stone walls were eternally wet and the meagre furnishings gratefully rotting, as though keen to escape by disintegration.

He was forced to share a room with Akton, a heavy-brained thug whom Finch loathed. Akton's presence was not an improvement on the surroundings and his hobby of random violence did not benefit anyone. To Finch, Akton was simply non-stop ugly. Finch was not the best choice of room-mate for Akton. If anyone had been able to look up into the window where Finch so ferociously played, they would have noticed, if they could catch a glimpse behind his erratically swaying fringe, that he was wearing a bold smudge of poppy-red lipstick. This was not something Akton would appreciate.

The lipstick had belonged to Finch's mother who had passed away on the island several years previously and whom Finch still missed enormously. Until recently, Finch had lived with his grandfather, but things had become difficult with Grandad's increasing age and they were forced to face the inevitable parting of ways when he had stopped recognising Finch on occasion. So Finch, who had finished his A-levels two years earlier, had remained at the church school as one of many assistants in order to stay close to the local 'home for the elderly' where his grandad now resided. Finch loved his grandad dearly and found his state difficult to accept, visiting at every opportunity. He was intrigued by the swinging shifts in his grandfather's attitudes and opinions and chose to focus his attention on them, rather than become engulfed by the impending grief that he could almost smell in the air of the place.

Matt, as Finch's grandad was known, had been a Founder, part of the first generation that came to the island in its newly recognised state as a separate entity back in the twenty twenties. Matt was younger than the majority of Founders, having been born in the nineteen seventies. The larger body of founding members had been elderly at the time of separation and were no longer around, spared the bleak reality of their legacy.

Although Matt had always outwardly cultivated a strong sense that this move had been the right one, Finch now detected that his grandad harboured conflicting views on the subject. Recently, when they'd been fishing together, Grandad had muttered about 'That discovery' and 'This wasn't the plan'. These murmurings had become more frequent, though his grandfather would avoid elaborating further once quizzed. He would just mumble vague statements such as 'We'd good intentions,' and 'We just wanted *normality* to continue, not *this.'*

It had been during the big clear-out for his grandfather's departure from their decrepit cottage that Finch had discovered his mother's old make-up bag. He couldn't resist experimenting. He'd spent most weekends in the tiny island cinema watching anything they'd been allowed to show, and he was fascinated by the monochrome glamour of those old-fashioned movie stars. He'd seen all the films repeatedly, especially the colour ones. The island rarely received new pictures and when they did it was more of the same, but still a world away from Finch's mundane existence.

Now, bowing his cello with gusts of violent energy, Finch was at once enraged and utterly desperate for something more, although he couldn't begin to comprehend what was so troublingly absent.

Finch's thoughts turned to Father D'Myno, who had recently returned to the school. At least he brought fresh life. D'Myno was a unique case, having been allowed to come and go several times now. No one who left the island would ever be allowed to return, but D'Myno had somehow managed to do so, becoming something of a legend as a result of this inconceivable feat. D'Myno had also earned the boys' respect with his undertone of irreverence and readiness, encouragement even, for the students to question the unquestionable. He was probably in his forties, so decades younger than the other tutors. His appearance was slightly anarchic, his greying hair clipped clean to his head on one side. This was unheard of and absolutely not in the book of style options offered by the island barbers. It was a source of ongoing bewilderment that the headmaster allowed D'Myno in, let alone for repeated visits. All the elderly tutors made no secret of their disdain for him and openly directed barbed remarks and dagger-laced glances towards him, but Father D'Myno seemed not to notice, or perhaps care.

D'Myno had been paying Finch special attention recently. Finch had been experiencing episodes which no one could adequately explain, and these were becoming increasingly difficult to conceal. Finch had always felt future events physically – a sensation of something wanting his attention, almost tugging at his sleeve until he was forced to acknowledge it. The situation would then inevitably unfold before his eyes as an event he had already sensed was happening. He saw movement in the air that others were clearly not aware of – crystal-clear eddies and currents, motion that could swirl up then wink out silently – a performance purely for Finch's eyes. He heard odd noises and wafts of conversation that seemed exclusive to his senses.

These profoundly disturbing occurrences completely absorbed Finch, and left others perturbed by his trance-like state. He was convinced he was dying or going mad and sometimes, frequently in fact, it was all too much. Father D'Myno had been present during several of these episodes and had attempted to broach the subject with him, but Finch was not ready to admit he was going insane. Insane people left, never to return. No one knew what happened to them.

Finch was aware he shouldn't be abusing his cello like this; it was too risky. The concert was tonight, but the tempest in his head demanded release – Grandad's desperate condition, the likely probability of his own insanity or illness, the guilty feeling of applying the lipstick. Then there were Akton's clumsy, demoralising fists, the satisfying pain of the cuts on his arms and, worse still, these dank, miserable quarters he was now forced to call home.

The door slammed. A deep silence enclosed Finch as the last notes from his bow faded. Akton, also an assistant, had returned from his duties. Finch didn't even breathe, acutely aware of the approaching footsteps. As Akton passed he casually knocked Finch's head forward with the palm of his hand, as though for fun. Finch glared at the floorboards. He knew the lipstick would add fresh fuel to Akton's propensity to indulge his vile nature. He also didn't care. He'd had enough. Akton was a lowlife. Finch genuinely pitied him and the regularity of Akton's petty savagery was wearing away his reserve.

Something shifted and it now seemed pointless avoiding him any longer. Finch stood and turned, looking straight into Akton's eyes. Predictably, Akton's face fell into a malevolent, greedy grin at the sight of Finch's red lips.

'What …' began Akton.

'Lipstick, actually,' Finch interrupted, in his deepest voice.

'You, fag boy, queer …'

'Oh, fuck off, Akton, you *irksome* little prick.'

At that, Akton launched himself at Finch, who had predicted the move. Finch, for the first time, raised his arm to punch Akton, defending himself against the oncoming assault. Akton moved and Finch's punch met with his neck, causing him to collapse, coughing and gasping for air. Finch had never hit back before and Akton was looking up at him with shock and indignation, almost as if Finch had hurt his feelings. He stood up and staggered out of the room, hunched over and clutching at his neck.

***

Regardless of how apprehensive he felt, Finch knew it was time to leave for the concert. His arms had stopped bleeding from the new cuts he'd inflicted having acknowledged the gravity of his situation – of actually injuring Akton. He'd be in serious trouble and was dreading the call to the headmaster's room for the inquisition and eventual punishment. It was time to go – he must get it together. Finch put on his robe and carried his cello across the cobbled courtyard to the church where the audience was assembled ready for the concert. He stood to the side of the stage, watching the choir perform. Father D'Myno perceptibly stalled when he caught Finch's eye, causing him to become horribly aware of his own ill-prepared state. Finch suspected he probably looked exactly how he felt – wrecked, distant and shaken, and tried in vain to flatten his unruly hair, but D'Myno continued to look horrified. Remembering the lipstick, Finch hastily rubbed a wrist over his mouth to remove any that remained.

A pang of shame slid in sideways, suddenly

prominent and bringing with it the guilt-laden realisation that D'Myno had worked so hard to convince him to perform on this occasion; he had actively nurtured Finch's musical talent at every opportunity, seemingly under the impression that he was extraordinarily gifted. Finch glanced at D'Myno, now intensely aware that he didn't want to let the priest down. Something was wrong. He beheld a frantic D'Myno desperately gesticulating something, then holding both hands up, palms towards Finch, just as he felt a shove from behind and found himself on stage. He had missed his cue. Father D'Myno covered his face and Finch felt his stomach leaden. This was not going to go well. He was in no condition to perform.

There were audible mutterings at Finch's appearance as he took his seat and prepared to play. The ensemble behind him began the introduction and Finch sat poised and ready. He glanced fleetingly into the faces of the audience, only to discover that they were wearing expressions of concerned revulsion at such dishevelment and the lack of respect it conveyed. Finch immediately regretted looking – that had been a bad idea.

The room gyrated. Finch began to shake from his core and felt as though he might actually vomit, now, in full view of all these people. He froze. His vision distorted. He was aware of a fast, swirling movement in mid-air above the audience. *Oh, God. Not now*, he thought. Everyone seemed to have slowed down. The noise around him altered as though the pressure had shifted and left a sucking, backwards sound between his ears. His attention was drawn almost hypnotically to the distortion that had expanded above the heads of the now motionless audience. Blinding veins of liquid light erupted through the whirling vortex like unstoppable cracks that seemed to make space for an expanding swell of gentler light at the centre. Emerging from the light, a face, one he knew so well: his mother. She was there, smiling warmly, beaming a blast of support and compassion at Finch, so potent that it nearly knocked him off his chair. Her eyes were gleaming with inexorable love and confidence in him, rendering him suspended in an expression of dumbstruck awe.

The audience, who had somehow stalled in time, began moving again and the music had returned. Finch noticed in his peripheral vision that his bow was now busy going through the usual motions of this piece and his hands seemed to be executing all the right movements. His eyes were locked on his mother's and his countenance had not altered. Instantly, as though glancing into a mirror, Finch saw himself from the perspective of the audience as if projected free of his body. He watched, intrigued. His physical self looked like a pale, wild-haired puppet whose body was frantically dancing while his head and face remained immobile, the remnant lipstick and fixed expression only reinforcing the impression of a troubling, life-sized marionette.

He observed Father D'Myno watching intently. As Finch's performance progressed, D'Myno fumbled through his robes to locate a flat oval object that he held out in front of himself, somehow casting a light back on to his own face. D'Myno hadn't taken his eyes away from Finch for a second, but was now looking into the space occupied by Finch's vision of his mother.

As the music drew to a close, Finch's perspective snapped back to his usual bodily position just as easily as it had left, and he became more grounded as the trance-like state gradually lifted. At the end of the piece there was an astounded silence. His playing had been utterly raw and beautiful. The audience seemed to be endeavouring to balance his soul-felt performance with his deeply unsettling appearance. A light spattering of stunned applause emanated from the back of the church before building to full appreciation, loud and fierce, as Finch paced back into the wings, keen to be anywhere else. D'Myno took hold of his arm as he passed.

'Finch? Finch. Stop. Are you okay?'

'I need to …'

'Finch, look at me. What *was* that? Come with me.'

At D'Myno's office he simply told Finch to sit, and returned with two cups of scalding tea.

'You're not in any trouble, Finch. I know you've been having … difficulties, with Akton. That's not why we're here. That was some performance. Just what were you looking at?'

'Something … she, the air … I … don't know.'

'What did it look like?'

'I … light, something …'

'You're not in any trouble, Finch. I want to help. Take your time. What did it look like?'

'My-my mother.'

'Your mother.'

'Yes.'

'Okay.'

'Okay?' Finch had not expected that.

'Yes. It's okay. I think I know what's happening with you. Sometimes – are you aware you're wearing lipstick? Never mind. Sometimes, certain people can see things others can't, like visions, or maybe people they've lost. Sometimes they see their surroundings from a different perspective as though out of their body, or they can predict things. I think something like this could be what's happening with you. Listen, Finch, your playing is beyond, well, it's really, seriously good, but we need to help you through this problem so you can focus. You're aware I'm able to travel between here and the mainland?'

'Yes. What do you mean, see people they've lost? People die and they're gone. My mother's gone.'

'Okay. Look, Finch – do you think you would ever want to leave here?'

'Leave?' Finch was still recovering, fuzzy-headed.

'There is a whole world out there, Finch. I know you're not in a fit state right now, but I need you to think about this. There is a concert on the mainland at the end of the year. A good friend of mine is part of the organisation. It showcases people with incredible talent, like you. I know it's a hard decision, to leave this place, but I would help you with the transition and you would have a much better existence, I promise you. Well, think about it. This place, well, it's not good for people like you. I've seen your arms, Finch. What is here for you?'

'I couldn't. Grandad would … No. No. I've got to …'

'Finch.'

The door slammed behind Finch and he was gone.

***

After service the following day Finch took his grandad fishing. Dreading the inevitable summons to the headmaster's office he was eager to be elsewhere, although somehow the torment of awaiting the inescapable reprimand was worse than simply receiving it. Perhaps Akton hadn't told anyone? But then, D'Myno had mentioned trouble with Akton, so he was clearly aware of the situation. Maybe it would wait until Monday morning.

Finch told his grandad of D'Myno's suggestion about the mainland concert, omitting the part concerning his 'visions'. Grandad said nothing. They sat for some time. Grandad's ability to concentrate had deteriorated and Finch had grown horribly aware that these trips away from the home were going to be out of the question soon. However, Finch needed some form of guidance. His head was close to shattering with the many questions and possibilities related to leaving which, while not an option, seemed the only option.

'This place,' his grandfather said distantly, 'it wasn't meant to be like this. Out there, they've caught the fish, son. They're not sitting enjoying the water, like us. I always felt, well, fishing – it wasn't really *about* the fish, but for them it *was*. And it's been a while – I don't know what you'll find, but I do know what's here, and since they stopped people coming and going, well, it's not the same.'

His grandad was referring to the island's development. It had been established, as far as Finch understood, by an extraordinarily wealthy man, Mr Monk, who headed up a political group and upon whose vision the island had been modelled. Monk had intended to create some kind of idyllic paradise. The story was vague, being unofficial and handed down verbally through family members. As a child, Finch would frequently hear sayings like 'It wouldn't have happened if Monk were around.' It seemed that the original vision for the island had become corrupted when Monk had died shortly after its creation, and his team of colleagues, the Council, took over. They had gradually shut borders, trapping the residents within, and enforcing stricter 'guidelines' in order to 'maintain control'. Finch knew not what they were hoping to control, nor why, and was largely troubled by the question of what was so bad on the mainland that this had been a necessity. Monk Island, as it had become known to its inhabitants, was certainly not a paradise, with its dilapidated buildings and ancient cars. It may have been a better place forty years ago, but nothing had improved in that time – quite the contrary; the place had gently disintegrated.

'Fishing. Well, that's cryptic, Grandad,' Finch responded, causing his grandad to let out a wheezy laugh.

'It seems I am increasingly cryptic, even to myself. Oh, Finch. As time is creeping up on me I don't know if I was right. It was *our* decision. It shouldn't have affected the kids like this. That's where they started going wrong. *Born into captivity* … No one thought about that.'

They sat silently for some time. Finch knew from experience that to press Grandad on this subject would permit no progress, and would simply shut him down.

'Finch, have you thought about going, son? It has to be better than this. If I had my time again, well, I'd do things differently – and your mum might still be with us.'

Grandad always seemed to intimate that the island had somehow been responsible for Finch's mother's death. Mia, Finch's mum, had died from an illness so Finch didn't understand this. Finch's baby sister, Hope, had devastated the family when she'd died in the island hospital at eight weeks old and Mia had never recovered from the grief, dying herself just a year later. That was how Finch had understood it, although the facts were nebulous at best; neither Finch nor his grandad had been able to visit his mother for the five months during which she was treated. When she died they still weren't allowed to see her, which was normal practice for some medical cases on the island. Hope's father, Luca, suffered some kind of breakdown and left Mia shortly after Hope's death, so he hadn't been around when she passed away. Finch's father had never been known to him as Mia had been just sixteen at the time of Finch's birth, and there had been a surrounding air of shame at such indecency.

'Oh, get out of it! Gone to the dogs. The edit, *my arse*,' Grandad suddenly blurted at no one.

'If I left, old man, who would tolerate your company?' asked Finch with affectionate mock horror.

'Oh, no you bloody *don't*! I am *not* your excuse to stay, my boy.'

Finch walked his grandfather back to the home and spent the rest of the day watching old Marilyn Monroe films he already knew off by heart at the quietly decaying cinema. It had been a while since they'd had a new showing, which was a big deal because the film would be screened simultaneously in the tiny cinema and on people's home televisions, making it an island-wide event and talked of for weeks afterwards. Marilyn Monroe, however, he could happily watch on a loop. There hadn't been any girls in Finch's life to date. The timing of his mother's death had been unfortunate – just at the time the other boys were discovering girls, Finch had been plunged into terrible grief. Marilyn, though, she always awakened something in him.

At the cottage they'd had a boxy old wooden television and Finch missed it. TVs were not allowed at his church lodgings. He'd particularly liked a comedy show called *Monty Python's Flying Circus* that at least brought some colour into his world, but there were only two short episodes that repeated. Other than that, the dreary broadcast schedule simply featured recurring episodes of harmless sitcoms and game shows. It was drab at best.

Finch pedalled his hefty old pushbike back to his church lodgings. Bikes were the main form of transportation since the general infrastructure had broken down, causing the island's car population to become diminished. Although the recipient of mainland government money, the island was now lacking the expertise to maintain the road system and its cars.

Everything on the island had become inert. There was no development. It seemed as though the only goods available were from charity stores. The place was somewhat random, charmingly picturesque in places and downtrodden in others. There were shipments of new goods sometimes, but these were strictly twentieth century, as per Monk's original agreement. There was a prevailing make-do-and-mend culture that only enhanced the appearance of a post-war era.

The place itself had once been a holiday resort offering typical British seaside attractions, but those beachside areas were now skeletal phantoms of their former selves – the many decades of relentless coastal battering leaving them wrecked beyond recognition.

***

Predictably, on Monday morning Finch was called to the headmaster's office. As he entered, he was curious to see Father D'Myno waiting for him alongside Father Vine, the headmaster. Vine was in his late eighties and an original member of the Council. Though frail, he remained venomous, seeming to harbour a bitter resentment towards the boys in the school.

At times of high stress, Finch tended to see clear, colourless patterns in the air around people, much like movement in water. Usually this emanated from them in waves of some sort, but Finch was unsettled by what he saw around Vine. Whereas he could see pulses of gentle waves emanating from Father D'Myno's head and upper silhouette, with Vine it was different. Vine had nothing, except when he moved; his movements left a rhythm of jagged cavities in the space he had occupied. Vine's patterns seemed formed of repeated diagonal juts like the edge of a venetian blind. Fading slowly, it was somehow more solid as though permanent, or perhaps dogmatic. Finch was preoccupied with this and as Vine directed his attention towards Finch, blades of sharp distortion sprang out, warping Vine's face and causing Finch to shift instinctively in avoidance.

'Come in. Sit down, Finch Henry. It has come to my attention that you injured your room-mate in an altercation. It was also apparent that you were in rather a state during your cello performance at the concert and made a mockery of us all. Have you anything to say for yourself?'

'No, sir. I'm sorry, sir.'

'Little good that will do you. It seems that powers above and beyond have intervened in your plight. Father D'Myno here has obtained a transfer for you to leave the island, for good. However much I dislike the government encroaching where they're not welcome, in light of your recent behaviour, I think it a viable option for you. You do not have to take it, but, given your recent conduct, I strongly suggest you do. Well?'

'I-I don't know, sir.'

'As you have completed your studies and were merely remaining as a church and school assistant, you have been spared expulsion. However, should you decide to stay, your room will no longer be available to you and your position will be filled by someone else. Is that clear?'

'Yes, sir.'

'There is only so much from which your musical ability will spare you. There are limits. Father D'Myno, talk sense into this boy. I have service.'

Father Vine left, leaving behind a slowly fading figure of barbed distortion as though he remained seated on his elaborate wooden throne. D'Myno pulled a chair up closer to Finch and sat down.

'I understand it's an immensely difficult decision, Finch. You've got a lot to think about. I know the mainland is a terrifying prospect for those living out their lives inside these … *sectors*. But listen, there are people that can help you with your visions and you won't be alone or feel trapped any more. I will take you to the AU, that's our Acclimatisation Unit, where you'll learn all about the mainland. We have a system in place to help island leavers to adjust. It's not that uncommon, Finch, and I will make sure you're okay. There is great work you can do there with your talent. You'll meet people you have more in common with. I never see you with anyone here. I know your visions have alienated you from the other assistants. That won't happen on the mainland, d'you see? You're meant for so much more than this. Well, think about it. I'm here for two more weeks. This is my last operation, tenure, here with you. You can go now. We'll talk again in a few days. Oh, and Finch, Akton is being moved to the Second Wing as we speak and, I'm sorry, but Vine wants you to vacate your lodgings within the month, so time is of the essence.'

Finch, confounded by the seriousness of this official development, stood up to leave. D'Myno was fiddling with a pen, as if holding back, maybe internally debating whether to go further. 'Finch, I wasn't sure about making any promises, but it's possible that on the mainland we can find some information about what happened to your mother.' D'Myno winced slightly as though he regretted the statement on some level.

'Information? She died. She was ill.' Finch noted the new forms of air disruption around D'Myno. There were larger, concentric circles pulsing from him as though he had so much he wanted to say but was holding back, and just alluding to it had triggered a sense of confident excitement in him.

'Yes. But there may be more to it. The rest of the world, well most of it anyway, doesn't function like this place, Finch. There will be records, perhaps some hope of closure for you.'

Finch had no idea what 'closure' meant; the island had gradually become a time capsule of largely mid-twentieth-century vernacular, but he understood the general essence and intention. However, he was distracted by this apparent reversal in hierarchy – it seemed D'Myno had influence over Vine.

'Father Vine said you are government?'

'I am, in a sense. This island, well, it doesn't hold any authority over me. The mainland *tolerates* this set-up under the Religious Freedom Act, and they're in constant debate about the rights of the Gen-Three Residents, the third generation, like you, and whether to open up the borders. I come here to find talented people. Vine doesn't have a choice. Well, anyway. Think about it. Trust me. You've really nothing to fear.'

Finch went back to his room, his mind like spaghetti, weighing up the aspects of this situation and trying to manoeuvre it all into some kind of logical sense. To Finch's relief, Akton had been completely moved out. On another day that would have been cause for celebration, but Finch was feeling desolate, profoundly worried about this new insecurity. He lay on his bed examining the patterns of mould on the whitewashed fan-vaulted corners of the ceiling and attempted to unravel the complications born of the last few days' events.

Of course, he could not leave Grandad, but one thought kept returning to him. D'Myno had described other people experiencing altered perspectives 'out of their bodies'. Finch had himself experienced this sensation a number of times, and again during the concert. It was usually glorious, and real, he felt. He would find himself up against the ceiling, gently drifting. He could see his physical self, down below on the bed. His large frame looked so long and his overgrown curly fringe splayed out over the pillow, the auburn of his dark hair against the cold, stony white of the bed sheets. Looking down at himself was the least interesting thing, though. The sensation was blissful – complete freedom, and a kind of enhanced awareness of everything – a sophisticated level of perception that afterwards made the island feel even more claustrophobic by comparison. Finch had always assumed these were vivid dreams. D'Myno could not have known about this occurrence because Finch had never told a single person. So maybe D'Myno was to be trusted about all of this – his claims that Finch would be okay on the mainland, and that he could find information about his mother.

***

After service, Finch went to see Grandad. He was met on the drive by Harriet, one of the nurses at the home. She was usually warm and motherly but now Finch found her distressed.

'Finch, love. I was on my way to find you. It's Matt, love. Come in.'

Harriet looked lovingly concerned for him, head on one side – almost a caricature of empathy personified, which was alarming for Finch. She took his arm and led him into the house. Finch was guided into the staff room where two whispering nurses quickly made themselves scarce. She sat down opposite him on an exhausted sofa that had seen better decades.

'I'm so sorry, Finch. There's no easy way to say this. Your grandfather has passed away, lovey.'

There was a silence as Finch tried to absorb the news. No. How could Grandad be gone? 'No. No,' he said.

Harriet's eyes were now overcast and weary, as

though she'd been the unfortunate purveyor of this sort of news many times and knew the reaction well. Perhaps she was gathering patience – an expectation that it would take a while to sink in, Finch wondered on a superficial level. But Grandad gone? No.

'I saw him yesterday. He was fine. We went fishing. Where is he?'

'He's still in his room, but …'

Finch fled, leaving Harriet yelling after him, rushing along behind. 'Wait. Finch, no! Don't go in there, love. Finch!'

Finch was through the door in seconds, halting abruptly as he laid eyes on the scene. Grandad was there on the bed. He'd obviously been sick in his sleep some time ago. There was a pot of white paint with a brush standing in it. 'Go' was daubed on the wall above his bed in huge letters over the old floral wallpaper. Then Finch's eyes dropped to the open pill containers. All empty. 'Oh, God.' He felt sick.

'I'm so sorry, love. We only just found him. We would've cleaned up in time if you hadn't turned up like that.'

Finch was still surveying the scene in shock, eyes darting from the pill containers to Grandad and to the painted message. He turned and fled again with Harriet shouting after him. Finch, whose world had so rapidly disintegrated, was now in even deeper turmoil. He had no idea how to navigate his way through this much grief. He ran back to his lodgings, weeping in disbelief at this disturbing new ordeal.

***

Days passed. Finch sank deep into an isolated, abject depression. He sat for hours, staring, never leaving his room, struggling to cope with the depth of upset and shock that had so engulfed him. He took to his cello as though it were a polished wooden lifeboat amid a dark sea, and was only vaguely aware of D'Myno's near-constant presence through his profound, relentless sorrow. There were times, while playing, that Finch would hear D'Myno arrive outside his door, but there would be such a delay before D'Myno made himself known that Finch was again lost in his music, defaulting to the remoteness of his own loss-drowned mind. Occasionally a thought arose through his grief and broke to the surface – perhaps D'Myno was touched by Finch's playing, hearing Finch's mood before seeing it, outside his door. Whatever the reason, Finch was glad for the company, though aware that he was not engaging with D'Myno to any normal degree. Eventually, D'Myno broached the subject of the mainland.

'Finch, there's something we need to discuss. I know this isn't a good time, but I'm leaving soon and I want you to come with me, away from this place. I've been unable to

extend my time here and I leave soon. Please, come with me.'
Finch continued to play as though no one had spoken. 'Finch, please talk to me. I need to know how you're feeling about this so I can make arrangements. It takes time and there are questi—'

'I'll come,' Finch interrupted plainly, eyes fixed on the strings, continuing to play.

'Okay. Good. I'll make the necessary arrangements then.'

***

D'Myno had assured Finch that he wouldn't need to take much – just sentimental things – because all other necessities would be provided. His cello was technically church property but D'Myno had acquired permission for Finch to keep it, having witnessed its importance to his survival. It would be shipped separately along with all of Finch's possessions, D'Myno assured him.

The day came and Finch was collected from his room by Father D'Myno, who was driving the brown Mark One Ford Escort he always used. Finch considered that it was in good shape compared with most of the vehicles on the island, which suffered from a lack of new parts, what with manufacturers no longer producing them. Everything on the island seemed moribund due to a lack of replenishment or maintenance. The place would grind to a halt eventually,

Finch thought. He was keen to think about anything other than his current departure and yesterday's funeral. The affair had been small and basic with just a few workers from the home and a handful of his grandad's remaining friends. Island funerals were tactlessly blunt. There was little to ease the suffering of grieving families, as though brutality would somehow minimise the pain, like ripping off an Elastoplast. Finch had played his cello at the ceremony, which was followed by a cold ploughman's lunch at the Red Lion. Grandad had been laid to rest, as planned, in the local churchyard.

Finch's departure was intensely unnerving for him; he had only ever known the island. Father D'Myno had told him of some of the broader differences to expect, like the omnipresence of 'technology' and the many different religions and races, not necessarily all understanding each other, but generally getting along reasonably well. This was vaguely reassuring to Finch because if there had been some monumental difference, surely D'Myno would have mentioned it then.

They drove thirty minutes to the goods transportation dock on the other side of the island. Of course, there was no existing passenger transportation so D'Myno had arranged for them to hitch a ride on one of the cargo ships. The security was not nearly as stringent as Finch had expected. It seemed slightly lackadaisical, as though no one really cared any more if an islander wanted to stow away. Perhaps, like everything else here, it had lost all drive and direction in its own little bubble, and forgotten why it had cut itself off to this extent; maybe it had simply become as forgetful as Grandad had in his old age. Finch merely had to show his birth certificate after D'Myno stated, 'He's with me – Finch Henry,' to a woman at the barrier they drove through. Perhaps this was because they were used to D'Myno's comings and goings, Finch thought; they all seemed to know him well.

As D'Myno handed back the car keys to a man in a kiosk, Finch breathed in the diesel fumes perceptible in the strong ocean gusts and studied this industrial-looking section of the island with its crane-like structures. There were two small ships unloading containers with a winch and rumbling baritone engine noises below the squawks of gulls. The sun had just set and the place was lit by strings of white lightbulbs and the faint glow of coral street lamps. It had already stopped looking like home.

They boarded a cargo ship, all metal underfoot and steep, narrow staircases. There was a lounge area where they found a table and chairs. The journey to the mainland, D'Myno said, would only take an hour. Finch said he'd had no idea they'd always been so close, to which D'Myno added, 'Close only in miles.'

Their plans, D'Myno explained, were to head north to the Acclimatisation Unit in the Yorkshire Dales, which would be a few hours' drive. The concept of driving anywhere for more than half an hour was alien to Finch. Once there, he could get a good night's sleep before being introduced to the unit properly and embarking on his induction.

For the first time in Finch's company, D'Myno was wearing regular civilian clothing and was without his robes. Finch found it an odd sensation, the obvious lack paradoxically becoming a presence in itself. D'Myno looked slimmer and taller, the cut of his casual blazer defining him more sharply. He removed a fine gold chain that had been around his neck underneath his shirt and allowed the chain to pour free of a gold ring that he slid on to his finger.

'Island rules,' he said. 'Vine does not like this ring.'

'You're married?' asked Finch, already feeling somehow better for being removed from his predictable island existence, despite the last few weeks' myriad ordeals.

'I was, a while ago.' For a moment, Finch saw a flash of his own grief reflected in D'Myno's eyes.

D'Myno poured them each a cup of steaming coffee from his thermos flask. He pulled an oval-shaped piece of clear polished glass from his inside pocket and it lit up instantly, like the screen of a television.

'This is a device, Finch. Everyone has them. You use it to make calls, just like a telephone on the island, but we don't need the cables.'

Finch took it silently and D'Myno allowed him to study it for a few moments, seemingly aware that Finch had a lot to take in. Its sides were smooth and rounded, and the glass itself was almost entirely transparent but for a barely visible network, a fine linear texture within the glass. Finch passed it quickly back – his touch had instantly sent some symbols rushing around disconcertingly. Solid-looking elements of the screen had emerged and were hovering over the device, fanned out and suspended in mid-air a few inches above the glass. They looked like colourful three-dimensional logos or objects, slightly glowing and evenly lit throughout. There was a tiny old-fashioned telephone, a camera, and others that Finch didn't recognise. They appeared to be actual physical objects, bobbing slightly as though floating on water. D'Myno reached out and touched one of the logos, causing them all to dive back into the screen, becoming two-dimensional again. Finch took a deep breath.

'Don't worry – it's meant to do that,' D'Myno reassured him. 'It responds to your touch. That's how it works.'

'What *was* that? Everyone has these?'

'Yes. That was just holo-mode. 3D. It's like

interactive light. Probably best to look at it flat, like this, for now. It's not just a phone. It's also a camera, a map, a TV, a computer ... Finch, these aren't new – they existed before the Edit. Sorry – that's how the separation of small islands became known, so I mean when your island became separated from the mainland. We call it the Edit. Anyway, the Founders of the island rejected these devices along with all forms of computer, which are kind of more complex versions of this. They were trying to keep the islanders "innocent" by restricting information. You're going to find it an adjustment, Finch. The island was behind the rest of the world at the time of the Edit and has only regressed, if anything, so there will be much that will surprise you.'

'Good grief. What else? I know it's what the AU is for, educating me, I mean, but I'd like to know what to expect when we get there. It's not all flying cars like Chitty Chitty Bang Bang?' asked Finch, sardonically.

Visibly relieved that Finch seemed to be lightening up, and clearly aghast at the reference, D'Myno laughed from his gut. 'They showed *that*? You poor, poor things. Anyway – no. Definitely not. And there are drones, yes – not exactly cars, but people do fly in them – like taxis, and they deliver stuff.'

'Oh, okay. Wow ... So, what else, Father? Humour me. This is ... well, it's all a bit unnerving.' Taking the device off the table again, Finch added, almost to himself, 'Yeah – definitely not designed by Caractacus Potts.' It suddenly buzzed in his hands, startling him. Finch had inadvertently answered the call and a voice could be heard.

'Seb. It's me. D'you have the cellist?' asked a mature-sounding Englishwoman with a haughty, cut-crystal accent. D'Myno took the device out of Finch's hands and lifted it to his ear.

'Finch? Yes. I'm with him now … Okay. Why? Okay. Get Gustav to send over the details. It's not all that convenient – is there no one else who can cover? Don't you think that's a real baptism of … I'm not sure. Okay. We'll be delayed to the AU, then. One night in Winchester – the usual. Yes – it's staffed by people. Make sure Gustav updates the AU – he knows the drill. Okay. Thanks. Will do. See you later.'

D'Myno sighed as he returned the device to the table. 'Sorry – that happens sometimes. Change of plan. We're taking a slight diversion. Someone has dropped out of a service and I need to cover. It's in Winchester tomorrow so we will stay over tonight and head on up to the AU tomorrow, after the service. It doesn't make too much difference.'

'So, you are actually a Father, then, D'Myno?' said Finch. 'I wasn't sure.'

'Yes, but I also work with the government. Anyway.

Please call me Sebastian, or Seb. We're not on the island any more, Finch. I'm not your tutor, just your guide and guardian, and hopefully friend. Okay … what to expect. Well, the world is more open-minded now, mainly. On the island, you've been living "under protection" as they originally termed it – meaning no internet – so, that's no new information. No technology that could access any information. You see they, the Founders that is, wanted to keep existence as it was at a certain point in history, and if you all had access to the internet – which is a source of information available to everyone – from devices like this, then their manifesto would become redundant and it would corrupt their attempts at denial, or *maintenance*, as they called it. It wasn't as strict at first but, after Monk died, it all became quite fundamentalist and freedoms were removed in order to maintain control. I doubt your grandad would have signed up for it if he'd known.'

'So, we have been deliberately living in some archaic age with no new information, to be, what – happier? But it's the mainland I'm interested in, not the island, so what's this about it being more open-minded?'

'Well, on the mainland, there have been decades of focus on the acceptance of minorities, like homosexuals, same-sex relationships, that is, and transgender people, so androgyny, or men that like to present themselves as women,

44

for example. Again – this was the case pre-Edit when the island split away, but the Founders, probably unintentionally, rejected it as they did with most modern notions of equality. Men can marry other men on the mainland, and women can marry women, Finch. It's totally normal.'

'Is that why we split away, then?' asked Finch, although his mind was busily trying to process this unbelievable information and piece together a picture of what to expect.

'No. The island's social regression was a kind of accidental by-product – I don't think it was intentional. Probably more to do with the era they naturally fell into having rejected technology, which was a fairly intolerant one, an era they felt comfortable with because the older Founders grew up in it.'

'So it was this *technology* they were rejecting?' asked Finch. He had never really known that the island had deliberately cut itself off to this extent. There had been a certain level of subtle propaganda and fear-mongering relating to the mainland, but this was taken for granted by most of his generation. He just felt restricted and was increasingly aware of this now he was leaving – like the sensation of hearing a never-ending noise that only becomes noticeable by its absence, once it ceases.

'No. Listen, it will all be explained at the AU – and

the service tomorrow. They will do a better job than me. I know you're going to be so glad you made this decision, Finch, trust me. But Finch, if you wanted to wear lipstick on the mainland, people will barely notice.'

***

It felt as though they'd only just departed when the boat docked. On leaving the ship, Finch was reassured by the familiarity of the dockyard surroundings, which were not dissimilar to those he had noted on the island, albeit on a much larger scale.

Sebastian led Finch towards his low, sleek car that looked entirely made from one seamless, high-gloss, dark material – lights, windscreen, everything. It had beautiful curves and sculpted grooves in its liquid-seeming surface and, on some subconscious level, it summoned the notion of a black puma stalking its prey. The car flashed multiple lights as they approached, dazzling Finch. There were no visible headlights, but as it flashed, a laser-fine line of intense white light appeared, spanning the front width of the car at the level of regular headlights and curving around the sides over the wheels. It may not fly, thought Finch, but it's unfathomable technology compared to the island cars.

Finch lowered himself into the soft seat that hugged his frame, forcing him to recline a little. Sebastian started the car simply by handling the steering wheel and it awoke with a purr. The windscreen came to life in a similar way to Sebastian's device. Symbols, journey information, and glowing markers that seemed to show directions were superimposed perfectly on to the road they could see through the windscreen, even from Finch's perspective as a passenger. They glided effortlessly out of the car park.

Now they were on a main road, Finch noticed that the painted road markings were brightly glowing completely of their own accord, and not simply reflecting the light as had been his first assumption. The speed seemed hair-raisingly fast, yet the car was almost floating along with very little noise. Other traffic was swishing past, equally sleek and beautiful, most vehicles appearing virtually abstract in form. The roads were long and sweeping with many lanes of graceful traffic. Some cars appeared to have no driver at all, or a sleeping passenger in the driver's seat. Sebastian reassured Finch that these self-driving cars were now very safe and more common than regular cars, although he preferred to drive, likening it to meditation – without any explanation as to what meditation was. But Finch had other questions. 'Can you tell me about the AU? How long will I be there? And what about after that?'

'The process usually takes about three months – that's the process of learning about the mainland, how it functions, understanding why the Edit occurred, dealing with the psychological side of leaving the island, things like that – nothing to worry about. You can stay on until you're comfortable leaving, but there will be work you can do with your talent, so you mustn't worry about that. You'll be fine. I think there are already plans for you.'

'Plans?'

'Yes – but I can't say more right now. You'll need to trust me. The talent I've seen in you is astonishing, Finch, so don't worry, please. It's nothing you can't ha— Fuck.'

Sebastian was cut short by the shock of seeing an oncoming swarm of several glowing white vehicles, like flying motorcycles, heading straight for their car at high speed. They were still on the motorway and these hover-bikes appeared to be playing chicken with the approaching traffic at ground level. It was just a second or two before they were alarmingly close. Sebastian quickly pushed an obviously placed button at the centre of the steering wheel that read 'AUTO AVOID'. There was a slight jolt as the settings adjusted. The tech took over and dodged each bike systematically as it tore towards the car at reckless speed.

Finch found himself with his arms up covering his face, instinctively expecting impact. Then they were gone. There had been little noise and, on the screen showing the rear view, Finch watched other cars manoeuvre to safety successfully as the bikes continued their kamikaze joyride.

Then it happened. One car, two bikes and nowhere to go. The car was fine, but the bike on the right hit the barrier and spun out of control. There was an almighty white explosion and that was all Finch could make out as the scene diminished behind them.

'Fuck. Are you okay?' Sebastian was clearly shaken, yet relieved they'd managed to avoid catastrophe.

'Think so,' Finch said, not even sure. 'I think one of them died. I saw it crash, on that screen.'

Sebastian pulled over and made a call on his device whilst pacing beside the car. Finch heard drifts of what sounded like a police report. 'Jet bikes – about nine of them. One fatality so far, but the way they're going … Yes – looked like Rouletters …' He climbed back inside the car, muttering, 'Death Wishers – unbelievable. Selfish dicers don't care about themselves or anybody else.'

'Why would they *do* that?'

'Don't worry now, Finch. The important thing is you're okay. I'll explain later. We're nearly there. I've reported them. The emergency services are on their way, including the police.'

Finch was trembling, mentally rerunning the experience, attempting to extract some kind of sense. From what he had glimpsed, the bikes had glowing white transparent sections and fluorescent pinkish-white fire escaping at the rear. The people riding them seemed manic to Finch … crazed. Some wore no helmets so their long hair could be seen, thickly plaited, and they were all roaring and grinning – whooping as if it were some kind of sport. They wore long beards and bikers' leathers, but with additional glowing sections at the chest and over the top of the legs, like armoured panels. He thought one of them actually had horns – maybe on a helmet. The bikes were literally flying, mainly at the same level as a regular motorbike with occasional increases in height to the level of their car windscreen.

A sense of relief settled within Finch as they entered Winchester, leaving the motorway behind. Sebastian took a route through the comfortingly old part of the city, as he put it, allowing Finch to take in the sights. Everything was bright with illumination – shops, bars, restaurants, churches – it was all was glowing. There were several shops offering untranslatable services that Finch could in no way decipher. He noticed people who seemed to be on a night out, drunk and staggering, others walking dogs, eating food in the street. It was frenetic and the people looked extreme to him – their hair, their clothes. It all seemed chaotic, threatening even.

Sebastian pulled into the underground car park of the hotel and parked among other beautiful, sculptural objects that were barely recognisable to Finch as vehicles. He explained that Gustav had booked them into the oldest hotel he knew – one he'd booked on many previous occasions when Sebastian was with a Leaver. He added that the modern alternatives were more tech-centric and that this hotel would be an easier introduction for Finch.

Once in the lobby, Finch took in his surroundings. It was a place of mid-scale, period grandeur that combined the original details of the Queen Mary building with a clean, bright aesthetic. Sebastian helped Finch check into his room and seemed well acquainted with Syrus, the man at the front reception desk, asking after his well-being. When Syrus stood he seemed hugely overweight, and he was stretching and clutching at his lower back. Finch's train of thought was interrupted when Sebastian mentioned that Finch should have been allocated a 'Leaver's room'. Syrus raised an eyebrow and gave Finch a lingering look of sympathy, saying, 'You okay, honey? You're free now. Spread those wings, honey. It's all over.'

'I … will… Thanks. Honey,' Finch replied, wearing his best half smile. Finch's politely dark sense of humour had evolved partly out of necessity – survival even – and it was now more at home than any other aspect of him. Sebastian declined Syrus's offer to talk Finch through the room facilities, saying he'd do it himself as it was rudimentary stuff here, just the voice control in the bathroom and a few other basics.

The room was clearly designed for comfort. Finch found it to be a luxurious version of what he'd been used to on the island – all sloping floors and irregular angles due to the age of the building. It was neutral in style and the large sash window of his room overlooked the back of the hotel and a clutter of outbuildings. The room seemed equipped with everything he could possibly need and Gustav had even requested a cello. It was modern compared to Finch's, but he was touched at this level of consideration. Sebastian set Finch up with instructions on how to order a room service dinner, and left the hotel to buy him some appropriate clothing for the following day's service. He took Finch's only outfit for size, leaving him in a hotel robe – Finch wondered whether this was a move Sebastian regularly deployed in order to deter Leavers, should they feel inclined to go exploring. They would be far less likely to do so in a hotel dressing gown.

Finch was playing the cello when his food arrived. It was just a steak sandwich and fries but it was the most delicious meal he'd had in years and the flavour was a new sensation. He climbed into the huge bed between the freshly pressed sheets and slept, though his sleep was troubled at times. The question of whether he'd made the right decision in leaving was prominent in his mind. The crazed bikers had shaken him severely – what else was he to expect? He thought about Sebastian. The painful days following his grandfather's death had been eased because Sebastian had spent so much time with him, making sure he was coping, ensuring that he ate and slept, and just being there for him. Sebastian was someone he could trust. Besides, what had he actually left behind? No family, no friends since his visions had ostracised him. No girls – that had never even been an option for Finch. He was in his twenties now and had no prospects on the island apart from his music. He knew that logically he'd done the right thing but what had he walked into? Trust Sebastian, his mind reassured him, and everything would fall into place – that was what the AU was for.

Finch awoke having slept a few good hours. D'Myno arrived early proffering a suit, a large box containing shoes and a few other garments all folded neatly in a structured paper carrier bag. 'Try these on. I think you'll like them,' he said as he left to prepare himself for the service. Finch decided to take a shower before looking at the clothes. He experimented with the voice activation control, seeing what it could understand.

'VC – shower on.' Steaming water immediately pelted down. 'VC – flush toilet.' It flushed. 'VC – 'ello Polly! Pooolleeee!'

'I'm sorry, Finch, I didn't get that. Please repeat it,'

responded a woman's soft voice in an American accent, causing Finch to halt, surprised at the VC's level of sophistication in addressing him so naturally.

'VC – this parrot is *no more*. It has *ceased* to *be*. This is an *ex-parrot.*'

'*Monty Python's Flying Circus*, Finch? Would you like me to play some for you?' Finch had not expected that.

'Yes – er, VC – yes. Please.'

The computer played the famous Dead Parrot sketch through the audio system while Finch showered. It was different. There was an extra line: 'It's expired and *gone to meet its maker*!' Finch asked for a replay, bemused at this addition. Though he thought it odd, in the big scheme of oddities that he had so far encountered, it didn't register as important.

Finch found the outfit uncomfortably starched and fitted compared to the island's pre-loved sartorial offerings. There was a mid-greyish brown suit that felt natural to the touch and was beautifully stitched in places; a pair of dark brown leather boots, minimal in detail and well-structured with a wooden layer to the heel; an off-white plain shirt; and socks, underwear, a belt. No tie. He left the top button of his shirt undone and stood looking in the full-length mirror. He did look good. Better proportioned, incredibly smart. He negotiated his curly mop into submission with the comb. The church had been quite strict on the boys visiting the barbers regularly, so his hair was smart enough when combed.

Sebastian and Finch ate breakfast together in his room. Finch was aware of being slightly protected from any outside influences and, as he mentioned the extra line in the *Monty Python* sketch, Sebastian's eyes flashed a look of annoyance and he abruptly stated that it was time to go.

Once in the lobby to check out, they found that the receptionist was the same man who'd checked them in when they'd arrived the previous evening – the owner's partner, Sebastian had mentioned.

'You haven't worked all night?' enquired Sebastian, looking concerned.

'Oh, no. I've just started, honey. Sharmi has flu. Not sure how much longer I can go, though. This one's just about ready to have me horizontal now.' He rubbed his belly gently with both hands, smiling happily down at it.

'I have a Leaver with me,' Sebastian reminded him. 'Not been to the AU yet. Speaking of which, there was an issue with the VC – it allowed *access*. He listened to some *content*. Make sure that doesn't happen next time, won't you?'

'Oh – I'm so sorry Mr D'Myno. I'll let the techie know. I hope it wasn't anything too problematic?'

'No, I don't think so. Still, no problem, but please get

them to ensure it won't happen again.'

'Will do. Again, apologies, Mr D'Myno.'

Finch had been sitting on a nearby sofa, listening, and when Sebastian returned they left for the church, walking at quite a pace.

'Was that a ... man?'

'Yes. Why?'

'He seemed, well, pregnant?'

'Oh. You noticed. He is. Very. He shouldn't still be working. It's normal here, Finch. Science developed ways to allow men to carry IVF babies to term. It may seem crazy to you, I understand, but there is much more equality now as parental duties are more evenly distributed – there are many benefits.'

'Wow ... is that why the Edit occurred?' Finch thought this a sufficiently divisive issue to explain it.

'No. The Edit was an attempt to deny one single scientific discovery that people struggled to deal with. You're about to understand, Finch. Come on – we need to be there now.'

They were progressing quickly towards the enormous church through extensive public gardens. There were large groups of people sitting still on a vast lawn with their eyes shut. 'They're meditating,' Sebastian said, as though predicting Finch's next question. 'It's a mind–body exercise to gain enlightenment and well-being. They're trying to improve themselves. It's a great thing to do – they'll teach you at the AU.'

3 DEMOCRATISING THE ANGELS

PART 2

Juliette, the bride, reminiscent of a pre-Raphaelite painting, lay on the altar-like bed with her flowers and dress cascading over its velvet-draped sides within the glass chamber. Finch could see her on screen, the hushed sound of hissing air below the other-worldly choir composition. He sat at the centre of the cathedral, observing the array of emotion among the guests – some clearly rejoicing, others openly weeping. Many were videoing the screens with their small devices. Finch had momentarily taken his eyes off the screens. He caught up. There were two of her.

Juliette was there, on screen – both versions of her. The second Juliette was drifting upwards, a blurry form as though watched through a shimmering, gentle waterfall of light. She was waving, smiling and looking at herself and her surroundings in absolute wonder. She turned and entered a circular, wobbling, spinning distortion that had developed in the air behind her, a rotating liquid bubble finding its own form as though fighting gravity. Finch recognised the distortion immediately as the air eddies and whirlpools he had sometimes seen in his visions. He noted that the guests could also see the phenomenon on screen. He wasn't mad.

Other human-shaped forms could be seen greeting Juliette lovingly as they quickly retracted and dissolved together into the swirling tunnel and the fading image was replaced by crossing bands of earthly reality, supplanting the whirling aperture. There was a joyful cheer from several of the guests through overwhelmed tears. Finch could see that, for them, she may still have been in the pod, but she, the she that mattered, had gone.

The service continued with one last prayer for Juliette's onward journey, and the living funeral was over.

The crowd filed slowly out of their pews, blowing their noses and making polite chit-chat about how beautiful it had been, in that truly British way that firmly avoided any real comment on the enormity of what had just taken place. There was talk of getting a drink at the reception, and arrangements regarding who was travelling in which car.

Finch remained alone after the crowds had gone. He

sat, dumbfounded, not knowing what to think. Father D'Myno appeared, and while dabbing his face with a hand towel, slumped down on to the pew.

Finch was entirely astounded by what he had just witnessed. On the island there had been no concept of anything existing post bodily death. Even the Monk Island Bible was beyond bleak, lacking any mention of the non-corporeal, so he had no framework on which to pin this bizarre experience apart from his own visions and gut instinct.

'She's *dead*?' asked Finch. He hadn't taken his eyes off the pod and the screens still showed the image of her body.

'Yes – in a sense, Finch. She's been *released*. It was what she wanted. Juliette was extremely ill. She had planned this for years, as many do these days. I'm sorry, Finch. I didn't think a living funeral was the best way to explain this to you, but my superiors were of the opinion that actually seeing it would help you to validate your visions and to understand more easily. I wasn't allowed to warn you. In this world, Finch, life after death is *fact*. It has been scientifically proven repeatedly ... What you saw on screen was real. We are *energy* having a *human* experience. That's what the Founders of the island sectors were trying to edit out. That's what caused the Faith-Quake in the twenties.'

Finch said nothing. This had magnitude he couldn't even begin to contemplate. His entire world had just shifted into a completely new place. His questions were so numerous that he knew not where to begin.

'Do you understand what you saw, Finch? Was it similar to your visions?' asked Sebastian.

'Absolutely. I saw her leave. And yes. The tunnel – it's the same,' he said, in astonishment. 'They could *all* see it on the screens.'

Two people in clinical-looking outfits entered the pod and busied themselves around Juliette's body. Sebastian seemed to be allowing Finch some time to absorb the information, watching as Finch stared at the pod in disbelief.

'Worst wedding, ever,' Finch said, finally meeting Sebastian's eyes, his coping mechanism present and correct.

'Come on – you've had a shock. Let's get you to the AU where they can explain everything to you properly.'

4 THE EDIT

Finch slept much of the way to the Yorkshire Dales where the AU was situated. The relentless emotional overload he'd weathered recently had left him exhausted. Thankfully he felt comfortable enough in Sebastian's company to rest, despite his inward anxiety at the prospect of further motorway travel, that they might encounter more 'Death Wishers'.

Finch awoke to Mozart's '*Requiem*'. It was the gentler, *Tuba Mirum* movement that he so adored. Sebastian had increased the volume of the audio system, Finch assumed, in order to rouse him from his well-earned slumber, aware that this particular piece was one of Finch's most loved. Seb explained that the AU was half an hour away and he was conscious that he should allow Finch some time to gather his thoughts before the next instalment of psychologically challenging information.

Finch watched the scenery pass as his mind caught up with recent events. The landscape, and it was just that, possessed a kind of regal magnificence. It was at once serious and austere, yet ruggedly beautiful. The sun was setting, causing the greens of the rolling hills to adopt a copper richness and the rocky terrain felt friendlier for the warmth of the evening light. The area was largely uninhabited from what Finch could see. They drove infinite, narrow lanes that meandered for miles offering no sign of civilisation but for dry-stone walls and the occasional sheep. There was something so acutely raw, almost brutally real about the landscape that, by comparison, tinted Finch's recollection of the living funeral with a surreal filter, a lens of dream-like impossibility.

At last there were signs of life. The area they were now passing was surrounded by a stone wall that had a tall clear glass addition at the top. Finch could see occasional glimpses of a very modern piece of architecture within. It spread wide and low in irregular clusters of rectangular blocks, showing off glass expanses and boxy, cantilevered levels – possibly post-modernism disguised as modernism, Finch thought. Form over function yet employing the visual language of the reverse. Finch had devoured the few architecture books he could find on the island, most of which focused on the twentieth century. This style, from over a hundred years ago, seemed somehow to have retained its integrity and continued to be drawn upon. The construction was contrasting – either whitewashed concrete, dark glass walls, wooden panelling or exposed vernacular stone. The visual narrative of juxtaposed materials and angled sculpture was enticing – Finch was curious to see how the inside worked and whether it was as considered as the exterior. As though reading Finch's mind, Sebastian turned on to a long drive that led towards the building. They had arrived at their destination, the Acclimatisation Unit.

A band of bright blue light moved over Sebastian's face before enormous metal gates opened to allow them through. 'Welcome back, Seb,' said a computerised female voice.

As they approached the building, an expanse of wooden panelling morphed into a glass wall as their perspective altered. It was as though the entire wall was wearing the same technology that had caused the screen of Seb's device to spring out into three-dimensional form. The appearance of the material seemed to change, depending on the angle from which it was viewed; what appeared to be wood from one angle was actually glass from another.

Seb parked the car underground and they took a lift to the vast main entrance which seemed to span the depth of three storeys. It had a white marble floor and a noticeable echo. A long slab of black polished stone formed the reception desk, and behind it, a simple silhouette of a flying seagull lit from behind and seamlessly flush to the wall. As they made their way towards reception Finch could see that a large section of the floor was actually glass and below it was a koi carp pond teeming with an array of beautiful fish, the water up against the glass. There were tropical-looking trees in pots clustered near the pond and modern sofas positioned here and there.

A young woman with white bobbed hair cut bluntly at asymmetrical lengths stood behind the desk. 'Seb! How are you?' she said through a wide smile revealing the most perfect teeth Finch had ever been dazzled by.

'Hi, Clydie, I'm great, thanks. This is Finch. Gustav will have checked him in with you.'

'Yes! Finch – we are so pleased to have you at last. Welcome! You'll be so happy here, I promise.' She spoke with a childlike, bubbly accent that was possibly Swedish; Finch wasn't sure, his knowledge of accents understandably limited.

'Thanks,' said Finch. 'This place is not what I expected. It feels … good.' He couldn't believe the words escaping from his mouth. But it did … feel good. He had envisioned a military-style set-up. Probably the word 'Unit' had given that impression. This place had a warmth – an

65

intelligence – he could feel it. Alongside this thought was the realisation that he was happily talking to a girl. That said, Clydie was so far removed from the island girls as to practically render it conversing with another species, which didn't present the same pressure, somehow.

'It does, doesn't it?' she agreed, as though she'd never really noticed until now. 'I've let Olga know you've arrived. She'll be down soon to show you around, introduce you, arrange your induction. She'll be your guardian, your go-to person while you're here.'

'I'm staying too, Finch,' Sebastian reassured him, 'for as long as I can while you're settling in.'

Finch was relieved to hear that. The ongoing culture shock of the last two days had been all-engulfing and Finch had a clearer mind now. He realised there were obvious questions he had yet to ask, so he could do with a trusted friend like Seb.

'Okay, Finch. Let's set you up with an AUID key. Come with me.' Clydie led Finch to a small room behind the reception desk, which housed a sizeable and complex-looking piece of tech. 'This is going to give you your ID techtoo, Finch. It doesn't hurt and it's not permanent. Put your hand in here.' As Finch obliged she turned his hand palm upwards, flattened out his fingers and secured his arm and fingertips with straps to restrict any movement. While interacting with a screen that Finch couldn't quite see, she said, 'Okay. You'll feel a slightly warm tingling. Keep as still as you can. It only takes fifteen seconds.'

'So, how was your journey, Finch?' she asked, filling the time with small talk.

'Oh, you know – flying motorbikes, pregnant men, a living funeral … Ironically, given all of the above, the realisation that I'm not actually insane after all. So … dull, really.'

Clydie laughed. 'I'm sorry you had such a harsh welcome. We are usually so careful to ensure Leavers get a gentle introduction – it's like time travel for most and that can freak them out! You had some bad luck, I think. You didn't take the subway dragon then?'

'The subway *dragon*?'

'Yes – you know, the dragons, flying around in tubes underground – you ride them, no?' She broke into laughter, and then so did Finch, relieved that she was clearly joking.

'Oh, thank God,' he said through a sigh.

'Well, time's up,' Clydie said. When Finch removed his arm he found a gently glowing patch of solid red light on the palm of his hand. It was shaped like the stylised silhouette of a flying seagull that he'd noticed behind the reception desk. It was utterly beautiful with its mellow illumination. Its very presence was mesmerising – how could he possibly have a glowing tattoo that he couldn't even feel? He moved his hand and ran his fingers over the seagull, expecting to detect its presence, but felt nothing.

'I know. Boggles the mind, right?' said Clydie as she watched Finch's speechless awe. 'You're one of the lucky ones – we used to put a tiny chip under the skin. Anyway. It will open doors for you. You just hold it up to the circular scanner at security doors. It will also change colour the longer you are here, so we can all see the progress each AU pupil is making. You know, so the newbies are obvious compared to those that have been here longer and started adjusting more, that sort of thing. It will go through the spectrum and, after ultraviolet, it'll finish on a bright white light in about three months. We will remove it when you leave. There'll be no sign it was ever there.'

'This place! Subway dragons are more believable,' Finch said, still preoccupied with his baffling new adornment. It was certainly a world away from the tattoos his grandad's generation seemed so fond of. His grandfather's body had been concealed behind multiple tattoos from the neck down, just like many of the elderly people on the island.

'Okay. Time for your body scan so we can print you some clothes.' Clydie looked serious.

'Really?' Finch said, at once realising he sounded sarcastic, erring on the side of disbelief.

'Absolutely. No, seriously. Sorry – I shouldn't have joked with you. You can choose the kind of clothes you want later. It's just the scan for now, as part of the induction.'

The scan took moments once he was in the scanner pod with the door shut. He didn't even have to stand still. Afterwards, Finch took a seat as instructed and awaited Olga. Seb had left in order to check in with his colleagues so Finch entertained himself by gazing into the palm of his hand at his new seagull.

'Jonathan,' said a woman's voice close to his ear.

'No … Finch,' he corrected her. 'Hi.'

'No. *Jonathan Livingston Seagull* – it's a book by Richard Bach. Essential reading in this place. Hey. I'm Olga. It's so good to finally meet you, Finch. Seb has talked about you for so long. We are all so glad you came, even if the circumstances were not ideal. I hope you're doing okay?'

Olga held out a hand for Finch to shake. Something about her over-familiar yet sincere approach had disarmed him completely. Her voice had a subtle accent that Finch could not place – Scottish perhaps. There was a gentle, rhythmic lilt to her speech and she sounded confident, well spoken. Finch got up to greet her and could now appreciate her in full. She did not look like an Olga. Her expression changed slightly when he stood tall and turned to face her, as though she was suddenly taking him more seriously. She was

69

strikingly attractive, and shaven-headed. Dressed in a slim suit consisting of a long blazer and narrow trousers, pencil thin, with a clean white shirt buttoned up to the top, Olga wore little obvious make-up apart from poppy-red lipstick the same shade as Finch's. Her eyes had immense warmth and compassion, and there was humour there, too. She seemed to be assessing him, her eyes darting about his person.

'How was your journey? I understand you had a run-in with some Death Wishers.'

'Yes,' was all Finch could muster.

'Well, let's get you settled in. I'll take you to your room.'

They proceeded to the accommodation block, passing many security doors at which Finch waved his seagull to gain access. 'So, how have you found us so far?' Olga asked as they stood facing each other in a spacious glass lift that overlooked the gardens.

'It's … the mainland. It's just nothing like the island. I mean – *life after death*. And – it's superficial, I know, but everything's so shiny – reflective. Even the people. Everybody looks, well, polished.' Aware that he'd nervously launched into a full-blown burble, Finch corrected his direction, returning to the question at hand. 'You're all really welcoming. And this place – it's just like nothing I've seen

before. I mean, I have a glowing tattoo that opens doors …
and Clydie … the only people I've met before with matching
hair and teeth are, well, best forgotten.'

Olga laughed as though she hadn't expected that.
'Well, lucky mine don't. Non-existent teeth make for a dull
diet.'

'I like it,' Finch heard himself say.

'Thanks. I felt like a change, and off it came.' She
beamed at him. Finch stood grinning back, watching Olga,
happily silent.

'You look so …' she began, her eyes studying Finch.
The lift doors opened, offering Olga the opportunity not to
continue.

'So …?' he asked.

'Oh, I'm not sure. I think you remind me of someone
– it'll come back to me.'

Finch's room was on the first floor within one of the
cantilevered sections. The entire end wall and part of the
floor were glass, allowing a view into the gardens below and
out, over many miles of rolling hills. The general décor was
ultra-modern yet comfortable, lightly masculine. There were
several trees in pots, but apart from that everything looked
functional and stylish. The large low bed was covered in a
linen blue-grey duvet and one long pillow. There was a
stylishly crumpled linen sofa suite in a dull blue tone and

interesting lamps with playful proportions and unexpected combinations of materials. The bathroom was glassed off, clean and bright, situated next to a smart but minimal kitchen area. Finch cast his mind back to his damp church lodgings. How could this place have been just a few hours away the whole time?

The wardrobe already contained clothes in what looked roughly like Finch's size. He could see trousers and shirts in neutral tones and casual fabrics. The palette consisted of dusty greys, blues and off-whites with trousers in shadier tones and a few pairs of darkest indigo jeans. Each garment appeared to be of solid colour and clean in design, yet relaxed. Olga confirmed that the clothes had been prepared for him, and weren't the worryingly abandoned attire of a previous occupant.

Olga gave Finch a tour of the eateries, the leisure facilities, the study areas and a rough timetable for what to expect during his daytime learning sessions. The schedule seemed to combine mind–body practices such as meditation and yoga with educational classes geared towards understanding the development of the world following the Edit – cultural, political and religious. There would also be therapy to deal with the adjustment, and tech education to bring the Leavers up to speed with how to function on the tech-centric modern mainland. Olga added that there would be some supplementary 'Si-Si' training relating to his talents, but that would come slightly later, and not to worry about it for now. Finch wondered when his cello would arrive.

***

Finch met Seb for dinner in a small section of the canteen that had been designed to feel like a restaurant and overlooked the gardens. Having arrived early, Finch briefly explored the area immediately outside the canteen to find that the garden offered an interesting and beautiful space for reflection. Given the landscape's limitations, the gardens were cleverly designed with natural-looking sweeping curves of tall grasses and foliage, occasional bursts of colour and a variety of shrubs and trees in hues from deepest burgundy to bright lime. There were rounded acers alongside spiky, architectural plants and plenty of height to create dividing sections, suggesting a sense of intimacy. The ubiquitous rocks that Finch had noticed scattered over the panorama had been incorporated into a water feature that flowed into the koi carp pond. Apparently the pond he'd seen under the reception's glass floor was predominantly exterior.

'So, on a scale of one to ten, how mind-blown are you feeling right now?' Seb asked with an understanding smile.

'There is a lot to take in – and it's so far removed from home. It's unbelievable that all this was so close the whole time.'

'That's how most Leavers initially feel. There is a process you'll go through – they'll explain it in the therapy sessions. It's very well understood and you'll be fine.' A waiter brought over a bottle of red wine and poured them each a glass. 'I've ordered you a pizza – hope that's okay?'

'Great, thanks. So, how many Leavers are here? This place – it's larger than it looks when you arrive. I think we took lifts that went some way below ground?'

'Yes, it goes down. Leavers? About two hundred at full capacity, but there aren't that many now. I think you're number forty-two, and there are a few other new arrivals too, so you won't be alone in your classes.'

'So is this actually what you do, Seb? Rescue islanders one by one?'

Finch saw a momentary flash of relief in Seb's eyes, as though he'd been pleased to hear the word 'rescue' rather than 'recruit', 'coerce' or even 'abduct'. Seb laughed and replied, 'In a sense. I am a priest, but I work mainly for the government. This is a government set-up designed to re-assimilate the pockets of, well, ignorance, back into contemporary culture. My training was as a priest, but I was recruited to help islanders from many different sectors because I can easily be accepted into communities, depending on the prevailing religion of course. Yours is not the only island – there are many others. I locate and hopefully "rescue" talented people for whom existence would otherwise be a troubled and possibly short experience.'

'You only help the talented ones?' asked Finch. He wasn't looking for confirmation of his talents; it was more that it seemed unfair on those suffering there, with no discernible gift to free them.

'No, of course not, but there are criteria that must be met. There isn't the funding to help everyone – just exceptional cases. Removals must be either outstandingly talented, a minority in danger of sorts, an individual desperate to leave, or gravely ill, and so on, but there is an emphasis on people who can bring something to the mainland and help us with our own development. We don't always achieve approval on removals – it's quite strict.'

'*Your* development?' Finch was forced to make a mental leap when considering that the mainland, which was so many light years ahead of the island, was still focused on its own progress and continuing to push even further forward.

'Ah yes. We may have tri-misters – birthing fathers, I mean – and the knowledge that there is some existence after this life, that there is so much more to us than just, well …'

'Meat machines?' offered Finch through a broad grin, entertained at his own crude way with words.

Seb laughed. 'Meat machines – yes – I like that.

Exactly. But we still have some way to go. There is so much we've yet to understand.'

Their food arrived and Seb seemed to steer the conversation towards lighter subjects, giving Finch the impression that he would get the information, but in the tried and tested format and not over a bottle of wine from someone whose speciality was not professional tact.

5 FAITH-QUAKE

The other Leavers weren't arriving for a day or two so Finch had time to collect his thoughts and begin to absorb the new truth that there was some conscious existence post bodily death. The grief at his grandad's suicide had been slightly eased by this, although he still found it an impossible concept at a deeper level.

Clydie took Finch through various inductions: the gym, spa, and the library, which, she explained, was rather a relic these days; physical books had become antique curiosities, collectables even, rather than a useful means of imparting or gaining knowledge. Any part of the mainland that had allowed the internet a free rein would have no need for actual books any more. At the AU, however, internet access was thoroughly restricted in an attempt to control the rate at which Leavers could access information, so books were back in service.

Finch spent his time using the leisure facilities, swimming in the pool, exploring the extensive grounds, sleeping, and playing his cello, which had finally arrived by drone. Olga had left him her copy of *Jonathan Livingston Seagull*, which he'd discovered at the foot of his door on returning from the gym. He loved the book and finished it within hours. In the evenings Finch ate with Seb and was settling in well, uplifted by his new beginning.

On the first day of class, Olga collected Finch from his room and they took the lift down to the lecture theatre. It was virtually empty but for three other recent Leavers and their guardians. Finch had expected a classroom with elevated seating but the lecture theatre was a circular room with black walls and a collection of rotating luxurious seats at the centre. The guardians greeted each other like old friends before introducing the Leavers to one another. There were two teenage girls and a slightly older man, probably in his late thirties, with a greying beard. They all looked on edge and exhausted.

'Finch, this is Raku and Tiatu. They're sisters. This is Robert. You are all new here,' said Olga. The Leavers glanced at each other's seagulls and mumbled nervous *hi*'s.

'Well,' continued Olga, 'welcome all. We are going

to show you a series of films over the next few classes that explain how the world has been shaped over recent decades. This first film is an overview. The following films will then focus on each area in more detail. If you have questions at any point just raise your gull and I'll pause the film as we go. This theatre shows 3D surround films, so the picture will be all around you and it will look as though it's coming out of the screen – this is nothing to worry about – it's just a film.'

The lights dimmed and the film began in three dimensions. This was incredibly disconcerting for Finch at first, but he soon became involved in the information. A man with a seasoned Shakespearian voice was narrating over historical film and photos that illustrated the concepts he was introducing.

'We now know, without question, that there is life after bodily death. How do we know this to be true and how was this discovery made? Let's go back in time and take a look.

'It's the mid-twentieth century. In medicine, CPR – that's cardiopulmonary resuscitation – has been discovered as a way of saving lives and is being used as a commonplace medical procedure. Patients are frequently brought back from clinical death, and they often have stories to tell. Science at this time is wary of such subjects and writes off the accounts as the result of medication or trauma, considering them non-scientific and absolutely not to be taken seriously. This is not a respectable area to study and it is viewed as fit only for eccentrics, fantasists.

'Decades pass and a body of anecdotal evidence is building. People who are brought back from clinical death appear to have consistently similar experiences. Many of them report that during this period of clinical death they observe themselves from a higher perspective as though out of their bodies. They will often describe their surroundings with astonishing accuracy, along with activities and conversations going on around their body, mystifying doctors and family members. Similarly, some even claim to travel vast distances in a single instant to see friends or family, witnessing their activities and convers-ations, again astounding those relations or friends when reporting these experiences back precisely, post-resuscitation.

'During the OBE, that's out-of-body experience, the patient typically sees a tunnel with a bright white light at the end. They feel this light draws them in, pulling them towards it and they start to travel through the tunnel where they eventually meet up with deceased relatives and friends or spiritual entities who define themselves as guides. These entities sometimes impart knowledge or new information the person does not know to be true until they return and have it confirmed. Commonly, this experience ends when the patient is told "This is not your time", or "You have more work to do on Earth", and they are instantly transported back into their now resuscitated human bodies. They also typically experience a panoramic life review where they relive every single moment of their human life, but from *all* perspectives, thus demonstrating the effect their actions have had on others, and actually *feeling* the emotions of people they have affected, for better or for worse.

'One regularly noted factor is that most of these patients report an indescribable, powerful sense of love and compassion coming from this white light, and they usually don't want to return to their earthly lives. They claim that this love energy is completely unconditional, and infinitely more potent than any love ever experienced here on Earth.

'Another recurring sensation, often reported, is that of hyper-reality. It is frequently recounted that the reality experienced during the NDE, that's near-death experience, is far more *real* than the earthly life the patient then returns to following resuscitation, rendering the patient's earthly existence the illusion.

'As time passes, more and more doctors and surgeons become convinced by their patients' inexplicable experiences. Highly respected medical professionals find themselves believing that these patients are indeed experiencing some out-of-body phenomena. Slowly but surely the need for investigation into this phenomenon becomes a greater necessity as an increasing number of serious people feel braver about speaking up and press for a scientific explanation.

'There are, of course, other theories that attempt to explain the more common symptoms. There is good evidence that the brain can produce the bright light and tunnel impression as it begins to close down, for example, but none of these theories can yet explain the OBE aspect that is so

frequently proven to be true. People can consistently demonstrate that they *are* conscious entities
outside of their human skins.

'So, it is the accumulation of reports from
reputable professionals that eventually sends
quietly curious tendrils through the cracks in what
had been an absolute refusal to research such
unconventional subjects, and open up minds
sufficiently to begin asking new questions. In fact,
prior to the Discovery, the reality of this
experience grew increasingly obvious, and science
had begun to appear almost dogmatic in its
determined avoidance, which, ironically, is not a
very scientific stance.

'With a wave of more enlightened people that
now *includes* scientists who have experienced
their own near-death encounters, science reluctantly catches up and probes tentatively into this
new field.

It is the development of quantum photography,
however, a technology designed to visualise and
study dark matter, by which the Discovery is
eventually made.

'Fast-forward to the early twenty-first century
and Q-Pho, as quantum photography becomes

known, is developed to aid the understanding of dark matter, and later its interaction with life. Designed purely to study the negative spaces within dark matter, it isn't *intended* to make such a discovery. There are, simultaneously, other studies seeking this evidence, so the news is welcome nonetheless, if only by science.

'Let's go to London, England. In a laboratory, Professor Sarah Gunthorpe and Dr Lia Chang are using Q-Pho technology to study the interaction between dark matter and living rodents. Dark matter becomes visible when using Q-Pho and has the appearance of fuzzy black rain, as you can see from this early footage.

'The Q-Pho camera accidentally captures the unexpected natural death of a lab rat named 02CMG and the phenomenal images that emerge show a clear departure of energy from the rat's body and the opening up of a wormhole through which the energy then disappears along with the wormhole itself. Though Q-Pho images are poor quality and grainy at this time, the visuals are undeniable. The wormhole appears to be a white-hot spinning tunnel with liquid streaks of light flowing from it. The rat energy emerges looking actually rat-shaped, before gently reducing into a glowing ball and being pulled into the wormhole which then closes shut like the aperture of an antique camera. Nothing is left but a flickering glow which lasts just a few seconds. Let's take a look at the actual footage. You can see quite clearly why this has to be taken seriously.

'Later, with human volunteer subjects, the same is seen again, and sometimes other figures can be seen around the bed of the dying patient. They too disappear into the wormhole that spirals in and out of existence around the time of death.

'In one famous case a patient, aware of the experiment and having left the human body at death, actually waves to the camera in energy form. Another, unaware the cameras are being tested, has a temporary out-of-body experience and is then seen conversing with another form. Later, she returns and describes in detail how she'd held a conversation with an entity she referred to as her guide, who had insisted she return and speak of the experience in order to enlighten the world. She conveys all this without any knowledge of what has been filmed. The discussions this patient held with her guide are now taken very seriously as they have clearly taken place, and this information helps to decipher some of the structure of the afterlife in a reliable way, especially as it is consistent with the accounts of many subjects who are interviewed.

'The unequivocal evidence is there. It is unbelievable yet undeniable. It is tested under lab conditions repeatedly and still it remains consistent and unarguably real. We are conscious energy forms, or souls, who inhabit the human form and vacate the body upon death.

'The announcement of the Discovery causes what becomes known as the "Faith-Quake". When serious, indisputable scientific evidence of the existence of a soul energy is published there is a dizzying readjustment of everything. It shifts and shakes destructively until it finds a place to sit among myriad existing religious notions and philosophical frameworks which, although largely based around the concept of the existence of soul, somehow manage to be completely unprepared for such a reality to be delivered.

'Perversely, religious establishments falter as to how to assimilate this into their rooted, naturally unbending philosophies. There is an element of vindication but, ironically, the new proof does not sit well. It isn't that the soul should exist that is contentious; the difficulty lies in it becoming the subject of cold, polarising science and being referred to in the scientific language of "energy". Science has encroached where it is not welcome. Worse still, it seems to render *faith*, in essence, redundant.

'Also problematic for established religions is that this new belief becomes all-pervasive rather than being the exclusive preserve of one's own particular religious club. Eternal life is now open to all, democratised. Murderers on death row who agree to be filmed by Q-Pho appear to have the same joyous experience as everyone else, and this causes deep discomfort for many religions. The fallout is immense and takes years to settle as the new thinking elbows itself some space at the head of the table and quietly refuses to move.

'So, the Faith-Quake's initial shock wave causes some unsteady staggering in the existential status quo. Post-Discovery life is described by one prominent religious author and thinker, Jess McCarthy, as like watching a film with no McGuffin, as Hitchcock might have put it –

meaning nothing to chase. We hadn't, she says, realised how much richness the absence of certainty had brought until irrefutable fact was delivered and we no longer could sit wondering what else was out there; we knew. It was as though the former absence of meaning had inadvertently provided meaning, and the delivery of a true religion had, contrarily, negated meaning.

'Immediately following the Discovery, there is a period where workers don't turn up, erratic behaviour soars, festivals of celebration spring up and sputter out. People roam the streets leaving their front doors open. Everything rocks and sways while the fabric of everyday life is tinted with a new colour, a colour never before seen. Nonetheless, eventually the shock matures and subsides. People are people and no matter how enlightened they become, they still need food and shelter, have bills to pay, family to support and careers to pursue. We may now understand that we are immortal energy but, while in this life, we need to keep our children in shoes and our hospitals open. Governments still need to run countries and people continue to require cars, food and technology. So eventually people go back to work and compartmentalise the information, a side dish to their normal lives.

'Let's look at the variety of reactions seen during the Faith-Quake. To recap, the specifics of the afterlife are loosely understood through anecdote, and not yet scientifically proven, but there *is* a conscious soul energy that leaves the body upon death and this is *fact*. With this blinding new light being shed upon existence, the shock waves of reaction are varied in their nature; there is a sizeable increase in people committing suicide, dubbed "Edgers". This is attributed to the significant rise in rash and risky behaviour, encouraged by the shift in the risk-to-consequences ratio, but, in reality, it consists largely of people who are already on the edge, now persuaded that last but crucial millimetre to take action.

'Factions form – outright denial and closed-mindedness for some, akin to climate-change deniers, aggressive in their determination to ignore blatant scientific proof. Ironically, often these people belong to the more demanding religions. Then there are extremists who decide to live hedonistically, dangerously and murderously because death no longer holds such power. There are also adventurers, dubbed "Death Tourists" and "Flatliners" after a well-known movie – those who undergo deliberate medical procedure to take them to the brink, then return complete with other-worldly experiences. There are conspiracy theorists who think the whole thing is a hoax created by sophisticated Russian or North Korean computer hacking which could fake the Q-Pho imagery.

'The level-headed majority, though, consists mainly of modern thinkers who take it seriously and carry on with their lives, but with a new background attitude of positive experimentation with life and a desire to do the right thing; now it seems there is more of a point, or less of a point, but with possible repercussions which are not fully understood in this existence. Despite the many instabilities caused by the Discovery, there is also, thankfully, a sense of wonder and elation to be found in the minds of many people. Of course, fear of grief and disaster is significantly diminished by the knowledge that there is no real death, but along with this reassurance come questions about our purpose while we *are* here, and whether this confirms the existence of a god, a higher intelligence, and if so, whose, and should we all shift our behaviour?

'In true human spirit, the news is barely digested before new questions take centre ground, such as the need to define and map the structure of the reincarnation process, and whether this also applies to other life forms such as plants or even bacteria.

'There begins a new focus on "energy workers", formerly known as sensitives, psychics, healers, dowsers, clairvoyants, remote viewers, and so on, as the Q-Pho images have proved these people are indeed opening connections through wormholes and manipulating or channelling energy. This is the next logical direction for scientific examination. Of course there are charlatans in all areas, but the truly gifted individuals who have natural ability are highly sought after to provide further answers through scientific experiment. Paradoxically, it had not been foreseen by any of these sensitives prior to the Faith-Quake, that science and a belief in the supernatural would ever become so inseparably intertwined, having existed previously at opposing ends of philosophical thinking.

'Hypnosis for past-life regression, considered widely to be whacky nonsense prior to the Faith-Quake, now undergoes a rebirth as it seems able to explain something of the structure of our repeated existence on Earth. Online media, which details myriad personal stories relating to such matters, allows the now curious masses to discover more and more about why we are here, resulting in a more spiritually conscious expansion of knowledge. Now that there is absolute truth in the near-death experiences of people, these practices of hypnotic regression become mainstream and lead to a better understanding of the life–death cycle and its long-term purpose.

'The acceptance of the concept of an afterlife grows more concentrated with a new generation who have never known otherwise. Known as "Second Wavers", the generation who are born after the Faith-Quake enter into a world where this knowledge is a given – they never have to accept grief and heartbreak. They become known as children of naïve wisdom. The world has now given birth to third and fourth wavers, all of whom know the Discovery to be simple fact, and take the knowledge completely for granted.

'So, dear Leavers, your question must be, how did you come to be born into a world where this knowledge had been consciously rejected?

'It is hard to understand that anyone would choose to reject the concept of eternal life. To the vast majority, it must be emphasised, the Discovery was a beautiful and uplifting wonder – a gift to assimilate into this earthly life. Yes, it caused a certain amount of disorder, but the phenomenal fact that we will see our lost loved ones again, and that life is infinite, brought enormous comfort and joy to most people. You, however, dear islander, have been born into a place that chose to discard this concept. We must now examine the reasons for this so that you may begin to understand your origins, and find your place in the modern world.

'As we've discovered, the world dealt with the Discovery in a variety of ways. Among them was denial. The crucial argument many religions embraced was one relating to religious faith. How could faith continue to *be* when knowledge had been delivered. What did this mean for the many religions for whom the *test* of faith was so central, so enduring? The Discovery had thrown faith into sharp relief against the new reality. This caused significant discomfort for those whose pondering of the nature of existence and a possible higher power was intellectually and spiritually richer than cold, hard, scientific fact.

'So, pockets of rejection formed. Sometimes these groups justified themselves by citing conspiracy theory, that the Discovery was faked for one reason or another, typically by foreign superpowers whose objective was to cause mischievous chaos, perhaps as a smokescreen – misdirection to divert from more important matters. Others rejected the Discovery based on the question of faith, or simply because they wished their lives to continue as previously without this intrusion of solid fact into their existential thoughts. There was also a refusal to accept that science should deal in such matters.

'The ensuing havoc, post-Discovery, did not help – the Death Wishers, Edgers and general chaos simply encouraged anyone with a leaning towards denial or rejection straight into island life, as the sheer volume of unpredictable and tumultuous reaction made the world more volatile, more threatening.

'In short, it became apparent that the first generation to encounter this knowledge could not accept it deeply or completely, even when wholly willing to do so. Their programming simply would not allow it, rendering them ill-equipped to integrate such information. This grew increasingly evident when the second wave demonstrated a total acceptance of the Discovery, which only served to highlight the unease that even believing members of the first generation felt when trying to truly, fully accept the Discovery.

'How did these pockets of denial become and remain so detached? Some *islands*, as they became known, developed slowly in a natural way and others were simply walled off, capturing those inside whatever their beliefs. This was more common in the Far East, however, and usually ended quickly in revolt. Frequently, though, the islands were self-declared areas of "retro-faith", thus self-consciously and openly stating that they wished life to continue without this information affecting it, to preserve or reinstate former notions of normality.

'Let's look at an example. The Isle of Wight, situated off the southern coast of England, is one of the largest remaining islands. This island developed, at first, naturally. It was later officially separated and governed by politician, billionaire and self-proclaimed visionary, Edgar Monk, whose religion was paramount to his politics. Monk was the architect of the island's conversion. Prior to this, the island's inhabitants were more inclined towards retro-faith, and mainlanders with the same inclination post-Discovery relocated to the island, understanding it to be of a similar mindset. It had become known as a haven of old-fashioned values, away from the new anarchy of the mainland. As the island's population of retro-faith supporters grew, those who wanted to remain within the contemporary world's philosophy, and were in favour of the Discovery, moved away from the island, and so it evolved that a natural majority formed consisting mainly of retro-faith advocates.

'Edgar Monk, an indigenous islander himself and avid retro-faith campaigner, argued politically for the island's separation from the mainland on religious grounds. The concept of religious freedom had recently been allowed to legally incorporate Designated Religious Areas. Since the world had dissolved into apparent disarray, this was thought a fair and sensible way to tackle the unrest. Eventually, permission was granted via local referendum, and the island was allowed official separation. Monk considered himself to be the Curator of the island and helped draft the initial trade and contact agreements along with guidelines for the island's interaction with the mainland.

'Less than a decade later, Monk passed away unexpectedly from a coronary event, leaving his group of councillors to run the island. Among the councillors were several who held more funda-mentalist views, and those individuals pushed for hard borders and stricter rules, which they achieved all too easily. They had been of the opinion that Monk's relaxed attitude towards the boundaries was too laid back and they feared contamination of their philosophical bubble, should people come and go at will.

'So, those who had left the island must stay out, and those inside must never leave. There was a substantial outcry on the mainland at this repressive move, but as the islanders themselves didn't object, the mainland opposition seemed redundant. The islanders might well have vetoed the move had they not already become significantly disconnected from world events – only accessing their local newspaper and having no internet access. All devices had been handed over on official separation at a "tech amnesty". The islanders at the time were ready and willing to reject technology in favour of a retro-faith modus operandi. Monk had created a strong and positive vision for the original islanders and he had their full support. They all understood that any remaining tech would be a threat, and feared that similar anarchy could ensue on the island in time if tech and internet access remained. This decision backfired when the move to create hard borders went largely unnoticed and unopposed by the islanders themselves.

'Thus, the island and the mainland evolved in opposite directions. The Isle of Wight, or Monk Island, as it became known, has inadvertently become a sadly degenerating time capsule, now largely populated by the second and third generation whose opinions on the matter were never sought. These generations are held captive and unknowing of the modern world.

'That, dear Leaver, may help you to understand how you came to be a captive on your native island.'

Olga stopped the presentation. There was an overwhelmed silence from the Leavers. She stood and rewound the footage. 'This part, I always feel, is significant to Leavers,' she said, as she restarted the film.

'In short, it became apparent that the first generation to encounter this knowledge could not accept it deeply or completely, even when wholly willing to do so. Their programming would simply not allow it, rendering them ill-equipped to integrate such information'.

Olga continued. 'As Leavers, you are effectively part of the first generation. This discovery is as new for you as it was for them. No matter how much joy and relief you may feel at this discovery, you will still encounter these feelings of non-acceptance. So, your next classes will focus on dealing with these – and the many questions you must have. We will go into more historical detail over this series of films, too. Later, when you have adjusted – assimilated the news and found a way to integrate it with your personal belief system – we will focus on introducing you to the modern world. You'll receive tech lessons, language respect lessons, tolerance and modern inclusivity lessons, personal counselling to deal with your particular issues relating to leaving, and spiritual enlightenment classes. Then there will be advice on how to operate in the modern world and classes in recent history to educate you on world events and current politics. But now we will give you some time and space to absorb everything you've learned today. There is a yoga and meditation class starting by the pond in an hour. Feel free to attend. You'll find the appropriate clothing and equipment in your rooms.'

6 MADE UP

At the yoga class Finch exchanged a few polite words with the sisters who now introduced themselves as Koo and Tia. They were from a different island, Finch was sure. Robert, who had chosen not to attend, looked slightly familiar – perhaps he was from Finch's island, which he now understood to be the Isle of Wight. Yoga was new to them all and there was some hilarity between the sisters as they attempted the positions. The others there were proficient and Finch noticed a variety of coloured seagulls on their palms.

Questions had formed in Finch's mind recently that required Seb's insight. At dinner, Finch waited until they were happily eating, small talk flowing, wine bottle nearly drained. 'So, how will Vine explain my absence to the other boys?' he asked.

'That's up to him – we don't have any control over

it,' responded Seb. 'I would prefer it if we did, though. I've heard stories to explain someone's sudden absence that I haven't found all that ethical but I think it's due to lack of imagination rather than malice.'

'Really? I don't expect many would even notice my absence now. My school friends all moved on to jobs on the island, but I stayed at the church after Grandad started forgetting things. I lost touch with most of them. I – what was it Clydie said – *freaked them out*, I think.'

'Clydie said that? In what context?' Seb asked, sounding concerned.

'We were joking about my journey here. She was just referring to the Death Wishers.'

'Oh, good … okay.'

'When I think about it, the church took me in – I had no other options. I suppose Vine was furious about Akton and the concert. He probably faked my death.'

'Probably. Or cited insanity. It's been known,' Seb confirmed, unwittingly. 'That would have been the most believable option following the concert.'

'My mum …' Finch began. Seb stopped. His hand, which had been raising a fork of coiled pasta, lost its impetus and landed back on the table. Finch noted his reaction and continued. 'Is it possible she left? I mean, when I think about it now – several months in hospital with no visitors, then death, and still, no one sees her … We were too devastated to question it, but this happens on the island sometimes. Is it possible that she left, like me?'

'I don't know, Finch. It sounds possible. It was before my time on the Monk Island assignment. The person overseeing your part of the island no longer works with us. When I mentioned to you that we might find information on her, well, what I meant was, now you understand about the Discovery, you at least know you'll see her again at some point – absolutely. I hoped that would bring you some comfort. Closure, we call it here.'

'Ah. It does help, thanks. I thought you meant that she maybe left, too. I suppose the Discovery does cast a new light, although I still find it too good to be true,' Finch said, inwardly disappointed that there wasn't more solid information now that he was on the mainland.

'Well, I'll ask some questions if you like. I think I can access information on previous Leavers. I'll look into it.' Seb appeared genuine and interested himself. 'So, how was today? You watched the first film, didn't you? Does it help you to understand?' Seb was changing the subject and Finch detected a sense that he shouldn't push it.

'Yeah – it's clearer now how all this came about. It's crazy, though, that such incredibly *good* news could have caused so much division and chaos.'

'Well, we're human while we're here, Finch. And humans are often idiots. What have you got on tomorrow?'

'Er … a counselling session, whatever that is, then *enlightenment* class?'

'Okay – counselling. It's nothing to worry about. You just talk about how you feel, really. The counsellor will guide you and help you to work through various issues, feelings you need to acknowledge – it's to help you process all the new information and deal with your departure from the island. The enlightenment class is about meditation, afterlife philosophy, developing any talent you might have towards being a sensitive.'

'A sensitive – like my visions, you mean?' Finch remembered mention of sensitives from the film and how they had gained new respect after Q-Pho had revealed many of them to be genuine.

'Yes. Everyone is encouraged to work on that side of themselves. Most people have some ability – not like yours, Finch. Yours is astounding. In fact, I need to tell you, Si-Si want to get you moving – train you up so you can work with them. I have tried to buy you some time, to take it easy, to adjust, but they are keen that you start as soon as possible. It's not ideal but I think you can handle it. You seem to have settled in really well and are taking the information on board as well as can be expected.'

'Slow down, Seb. Who are Si-Si?'

'Si-Si – spelt S,C,I-P,S,Y – like science and psychic. It's just the name of the department that deals with sensitives. Listen … I am conscious you need this information more slowly, so it will all become clear in time. There's nothing to worry about – just take it as it comes. I'll make sure they don't fast-track you if you're not ready.'

'Okay – thanks, Seb.'

'Now, what shall we have for dessert?'

***

The counsellor's room was a dimly lit, calm environment with moody hues on the walls and very little clutter but for shelves that housed what appeared to be a lovingly curated collection of antique books and objets d'art. There was a raised area hugged by a curved floor-to-ceiling wall of glass that could have been mistaken for a fish tank; it looked out into the murky koi pond like a submarine. Underfoot was long-pile dark carpet covering the curved steps that led up to a seating area, which accommodated one stylish reclining black chair, one plush rotating chair and a low coffee table.

The lighting was artfully subdued while managing to highlight various fascinating objects placed here and there, emphasising their punchy colours and textures against the quiet tones of the room. Glaring out of the brooding darkness was a theatrical Chinese dragon headdress, all tassels, pompoms and paint. There were curious vases and sculptures, all in gloomy tones but with some fiery streak or neon flash, given life by the lighting.

Finch had been guided to the counselling room by Olga, who before departing, had reassured him that it was nothing to be nervous about. He was to await Dr Lenny. Finch was aware of a background apprehension relating to the counselling session but his mind was largely occupied with questions he'd like to ask Olga. She thoroughly interested him, but he sometimes felt too self-conscious to communicate in the way that he'd have liked. She was a few years older than him, he imagined, and light years away in terms of the worlds they came from. He must have seemed like a child to her.

Finch had never met a beautiful girl with a shaven head before. All the girls on the island had emulated the glamorous look of the early to mid-twentieth century actresses they admired from the limited cinema and television offerings. Exposure to any kind of trend was non-existent, but fashion found a way in through the only available means. The island had developed its own sense of aesthetics along with everything else, based on what was available. Most clothing deliveries consisted of second-hand, usually older men's casual wear and the odd piece of sportswear. The island girls were not catered for, presumably due to a higher demand for vintage on the mainland, which may have left slim pickings for despatch. So, out of necessity, they had developed tailoring skills and would alter men's clothing to fit, or adapt casual-wear pieces into softly tailored suits. They were innovative by necessity and, combined with their screen goddess hairstyles, carried it off well. Olga, however, completely threw Finch. He had never before seen a girl who had chosen such a severe and masculine look and could wear it so well. It looked supremely confident to Finch, only serving to disarm him further.

Finch sat watching the fish, considering Olga and studying the pond from this new angle. The koi carp seemed designed for this room with their occasional flashes of colour against the darkness of the water.

Dr Lenny entered and sat down in the rotating chair, releasing a stack of cardboard folders on to the coffee table. The word 'Henry' and a number, '3008745', were printed on the edge of the folders.

'Finch, hi,' she said, looking up with an expansive smile. 'I know, hard copies – very old fashioned. I like paper – I can't help it.' She was, like the room, dark yet colourful. Finch guessed her origin as African, possibly some generations back. She was middle aged, slim, beautiful, and stylishly dressed in a simple suit of a closely tailored tunic and matching slim-fit trousers. She wore bright coral-pink earrings and her dark hair was in a tight bun at the back of her head.

'Hi,' Finch responded. 'I had no idea the pond was so deep.'

Dr Lenny laughed. 'You've no idea how appropriate that statement is to my job here, Finch.'

After Dr Lenny had been through some preliminary formalities relating to confidentiality and Finch's personal details, she asked, 'So, how are you today, Finch?' She grinned warmly at him as though knowing exactly how he was.

'Erm, fine thanks. Getting used to it all, still.'

'Go on.'

'This place – the mainland … The idea that my grandad's not properly gone, I suppose. There's been a lot to take in. The fish – is there anywhere in this building you can't see them?'

'Yes. Tell me about your grandad, and how you came to be here.' There was something about the low, soft way Dr Lenny spoke. It was gentle and considered. It comforted Finch. He sensed a trust, a kind of integrity, and felt more at ease.

Finch outlined the events that had led up to his decision to leave. He found himself describing his grandad's suicide as a sacrifice, and emotion finally overwhelmed him.

He wept for his grandfather. Finch missed him, and was still dealing with the cold horror of his loss, no matter what Q-Pho had discovered.

Once the initial swell of emotion had subsided, Finch moved on to relaying his eventful journey and attempting to outwardly balance his internal conflict – the shock and exasperation he felt at discovering that the island had *intentionally* locked itself, and its younger natives, into what now appeared to be a wholly bygone era. But that era was his normality. By contrast, the mainland was some kind of nightmarish future-scape full of reckless insanity and implausible science. It helped Finch to speak this aloud at last, crystallising his bewilderment into coherent thought and clearing his mind a little. Dr Lenny listened to every word and said nothing until they were nearing the end of the session.

'You know, Finch, our time is nearly up for today, but I want to reassure you – there is a set pattern of, well, grief, that most Leavers find themselves following. It is like any loss, but you'll find it can be the very loss of *loss* that is most confusing. It's different for everyone, but the process usually includes anger. This is understandable. There are people who made decisions on your behalf that affected your life and outlook significantly. There will be, at times, liberation and delight at the Discovery, and sometimes disbelief, denial even. There may also be a sense of non-belonging, as though you're not a member of either place – or time, if you like – given that the two cultures you've encountered seem many decades apart. You, like most, will find yourself working through this, and I will be here to help you navigate. You seem to have a good insight into yourself, Finch, and you have a mature, emotional intelligence, so I think you'll cope well. We'll see each other again in a few days, but for now, be kind to yourself and take it easy. You can go now. Relax – that is essential.'

Finch had a few hours in his room between the counselling and enlightenment class – a down period, designed to allow him space to reflect and gather his thoughts, should he be able to haul his mind away from Olga for any significant length of time. Frustrated by his quietly emerging obsession with her, he needed a distraction.

***

Finch looked curiously down at himself, sprawled asleep on the sofa wearing nothing but black eyeliner and striped pyjama bottoms. His bow was still in his hand and his cello lay on the floor with a broken string. He barely had time to acknowledge this out-of-body sensation before a knock at the door took his consciousness directly to the source of the sound, as though automatic. There he found Olga awaiting his response. When he failed to answer the door, he watched as she held up her palm and used her egg-shaped techtoo to override the lock and gain access. Olga entered slowly, tentatively calling 'hello?' in a hushed tone. On discovering Finch, she stood still, watching him breathe for a few long moments. 'Wow,' she muttered to herself under her breath. 'You are such a beautiful creature, Finch Henry, even in your sleep.' She turned to the kitchen, returning with two cups of tea, and sat down on the floor next to him. 'Finch,' she whispered. 'Finch, wake up.'

Finch, instantly body-bound again, roused, and on seeing Olga so close, leapt off the sofa and stood up without quite knowing how he'd arrived there. He remembered his mother's eyeliner and started to rub at his eyes.

'No. Don't, Finch, stop – it suits you,' Olga said, smiling and relaxed. 'Seriously, it's fine – loads of men wear make-up here. It's normal. You don't have to worry … Although …'

'Although?' asked Finch hesitantly, fully expecting the 'but' part of the conversation.

'Although your application – technique – could use some work. Come on – I can show you how to do it.'

'Oh. Okay – if we have time?'

'Absolutely. I'm early. I figured you might be a little, well, emotionally fatigued after counselling and maybe not so prepared for enlightenment class, so I came sooner than needed. Hope you don't mind – you didn't answer so I used my egg – we're meant to … Sorry, I know it seems a little intrusive …'

'No – that's fine,' said Finch.

'Now let's see, what have you got here? Ah, classic – a black kohl pencil. And liquid liner. All dried up. Finch, this looks like an antique. How old is this stuff?'

'It's … it was my mum's.'

'Oh, God – sorry, Finch. Of course. She … yes.'

'She?' asked Finch, puzzled as to where Olga was going with 'she' and what had caused her to stop.

'She must have been a cool mum.'

'She was. I suppose she was so young when she had me.'

'Right.' Olga said, taking control. 'Sit here. Now, let's start again – moisturiser?'

'No. Just this. It's all I've got.'

Finch sat on the bathroom stool in his pyjama bottoms with Olga tantalizingly close, her fingers on his face to steady it while she concentrated on removing the smudges before applying new eyeliner. Her breath on his face was so intimate as to make him panic. He was aware of her mouth just inches away and he could almost feel the pressure of her energy against his. He started to see movement in the air around Olga's jawline. She was pulsing slightly – waves of rippling light distortion flowing continuously from her, and the occasional larger pulse. It looked erratic.

Finch observed what was happening and tried to stay calm, to focus on what he was seeing while holding it within the background of his mind so as to prevent himself from becoming overwhelmed. He tried to remember what he'd learned. He knew now that the visions were not a sign of insanity and that, crucially, they shouldn't terrify him anymore.

Olga stood back for a better view of her handiwork. He could now see her energy more plainly. It was fainter on one side. It looked weak, low level, as though exhausted. A spattering of ripples occasionally escaped on that side whereas there were clear, bolder pulses on the other.

'Are you okay?' Finch asked.

'Yes – why?'

'Your energy – has something happened to your left side?'

'You can see something?' Olga looked suddenly distressed and Finch regretted mentioning it. The distraction of the conversation caused the vision to dissipate but Finch felt no relief at its withdrawal. He barely noticed, he was so concerned at having overstepped a boundary with Olga.

'Yes – well, not now, but I could. Sorry – I didn't mean to …' His deep voice was cracking as he attempted to explain. Finch could now see that Olga was trembling faintly as she returned the make-up to his mother's little washbag. She wasn't meeting his eyes and was clearly deeply uncomfortable with the intrusion.

'It's okay – please. It's fine. Let's go to your next class,' said Olga, as though trying to hold herself together.

'I'm so sorry – I didn't mean to intrude, Olga. I was just concerned.' It was evident from his tone that he was grappling to mend the damage he'd so obviously done. Olga stopped. She turned and took his face in both hands as though to gain his attention, looking at him with compassion. There were tears in her eyes and a forgiving expression that conveyed an understanding of how mortified Finch was by his own tactlessness.

'Finch, stop. It's okay. You haven't done anything wrong. I've been ill but I'm okay now, I think.'

Finch gently took her wrists from his face, pulled her closer and wrapped his arms around her waist. He was still on the seat and she stood between his legs hugging him back.

They proceeded to class saying little to each other, Finch acutely aware of the bond that had grown between them.

***

The enlightenment class was held in the garden. The other Leavers were already seated on the grass in a circle with their guides, having left space for Finch and Olga.

Olga introduced Finch to the tutor, Jude, who was possibly in his early fifties. Jude's long grey hair was tied up into a topknot, emphasising his receding hairline. He wore loose white linen trousers and a finely striped cotton shirt with an Indian influence. His eyes were surrounded by strong laughter lines and his deeply tanned skin was flecked with grey stubble.

'So this is Finch. At last, brother,' Jude said, cheerfully. Finch's proffered hand was grasped warmly by both of Jude's. 'Welcome, Finch. We are so glad to have you. Please, take a seat in the circle and we'll begin.' He gestured towards the gap in the circle and Finch obliged, quietly noting that his eyeliner elicited absolutely no response from Jude, although Koo and Tia seemed to be watching him, intrigued, and Finch found himself embarrassed to note their appreciative glances. He was distantly aware of his own strong bone structure and good frame. His mother had warned him that women often found striking features such as his, together with his auburn hair, extremely compelling. He had even heard the nurses at his grandad's home whispering about his 'gorgeous build' when they thought he wasn't listening. Personally he thought the eyeliner an artistic addition and liked how the combination of his flighty hair, strong bone structure and make-up made for an interesting play on his natural masculinity.

'Welcome, all!' said Jude. 'So, I see trepidation on some of your faces, but fear not. Let me explain. In this class we will be covering many aspects of spiritual enlightenment. We will start with basic meditation, some gentle exercises to begin developing any sensitive ability you may have. Later, we'll look at what we know to be fact regarding the Discovery, and the structure of the afterlife that we've come to understand. We will learn how this impacts us all as spiritual entities having a *human experience*, and how many diverse cultures have all assimilated this knowledge in their own way. You will find your own paths, as with any personal belief system, but I am here to impart the knowledge, to help you transcend and reach a higher level, to connect with your higher self, to understand the many facets of psychic ability and decipher your purpose on Earth. So, just another day at the office.'

Jude guided them through a gentle meditation, which involved the internal repetition of a mantra, accompanied by his softly directed visualisation. It felt to Finch like being deeply asleep yet conscious – blissful relaxation combined with an alert, clear mind. Jude instructed the Leavers to practise this twice a day.

Now they were open and interested, Jude introduced them to the idea of Reiki energy, a form of channelling healing energy that had been proven valid by Q-Pho. Jude attuned each Leaver by performing a small ceremony and taught them hatsurei-ho, a short meditation designed to cleanse the energy prior to channelling Reiki, that involved brushing the arms and stating positive intentions. Once they had been through the cleansing process, Jude encouraged them to connect with the Reiki energy and hold it in the air between their hands. As Jude demonstrated, Finch observed a heat-like energy radiating from Jude's palms. He was transfixed, then noticed the energy emerging from his own hands. His seagull was shimmering slightly beneath the waves of Reiki; the energy Finch was channelling wasn't nearly as powerful as Jude's, but it was there, just.

Olga was watching Finch as he gazed at his own hands. 'You can see the energy?' she quietly asked.

'Almost – I mean, on me, slightly. It's clearer in Jude's hands.' Finch looked at Jude's upturned hands, noticing as Olga and Jude exchanged glances, Jude's eyebrow raised.

'Can you always see energy, Finch?' asked Jude, casually.

'No. Just sometimes. Maybe at times of heightened stress, or, intensity.' Finch was immediately struck by how this would sound to Olga, given the encounter they'd just had, and consciously resisted the urge to backtrack.

'You are stressed now?' asked Jude, in a concerned tone.

Finch hesitated. 'No, I'm not,' he said, with puzzled wonderment as to how the Reiki was visible to him, given his tranquil state.

'Let's discuss it afterwards, Finch,' Jude said, glancing at the other Leavers. Robert, now beardless and better groomed, seemed uneasy during the lesson and consequently, it seemed, Jude was attempting to control the flow of bewildering new concepts he was introducing, seemingly conscious of pushing the group beyond their natural limit.

When the other Leavers had gone, Finch, Olga and Jude remained.

'So, tell me about when you see energy, Finch. How does it appear to you?'

'It's like water flowing … like what was visible on screen during the living funeral Seb took me to – movement in the air. It differs depending on the person. The Reiki looked more like heat waves rising.'

'Wow – you are incredibly lucky to have that ability, Finch. Anything else you've experienced? I'd love to know.'

'You say lucky. I thought I'd lost my mind. Other aspects – sometimes, time slowing. Stopping, actually, when I was performing at a concert on the island. I saw my mum appear and she helped me get it together.'

'Your mum, who has transcended? Sorry – that's another way we say passed away here.'

'Yeah … She was there in a spinning vortex like the one on screen at the living funeral. She looked … happy, and beamed, no – almost *fired* this kind of assurance at me, like I was unable to fail. I was held in her grasp of, well, utter *knowing* that I'd be okay. There was no other option. It wasn't just that – there was an all-engulfing, well, love? I don't have the words for it. It kind of took over.'

'Finch, wow, how wonderful. That's quite some experience – it sounds powerful. Let's go back. You said time slowed? How did you know? How did this manifest itself?'

'People, the audience, all slowed down and then froze. They just stopped, still. Then I sort of emerged from it and they were all moving again, and I found I was playing my cello without even trying.'

'Okay. There is a form of epilepsy that can create the sensation of time slowing – temporal lobe epilepsy – but what with the other aspects, I don't think we need to worry. I'll request that the doc looks at your scans just to double-check.'

'Scans?' Finch was slightly more accustomed to the futuristic realm he now inhabited, but the technology still baffled him.

'Oh, yes – when you arrived? Everyone has a full

body scan for apparel printing and they usually perform a health screen at the same time. They will have checked it already so doubtless you're fine. It's more likely you had a level-five connective experience, I think.' Jude explained. 'It's a highly sophisticated level reached by a sensitive. Some people spend their lives striving for that kind of connection and don't even scratch the surface, level one. Yet you're doing it by accident. I can see why they want me to fast-track you.'

'There were times I'd have given anything to be rid of it, so that's a new perspective for me. I think it's coming more easily since I left the island. But what does fast-tracking involve?' Finch thought it sounded unpleasant, especially as Seb had mentioned he was attempting to postpone it.

'Well, it's like today's lesson, but just with me, and we will see each other more often to practise techniques and develop your skills as far as we can, ahead of the others.'

'Okay. That doesn't sound so bad,' Finch said, thinking carefully.

'Go and rest, now, Finch. You've had a full day, my friend.'

Olga and Finch walked back to his room. 'So, *printing* clothes? What's next? *Sewing* me a glass of water, or *sculpting* me a Monday morning?'

'Tomorrow, my Finch. You've had enough for

today. Why don't we get together and you can look at the options – we can print you some then. I'll *grow* you an hour or two and we can *melt*, no … *knit?* a lunch of sorts. It's the weekend. How about we paint ourselves a picnic?'

Finch gave Olga a playful shove to the side and they both grinned as they went their separate ways.

7 THE SEAGULL

Playing his cello facing out of the glass wall at the end of his room, Finch wore nothing but his pyjama bottoms. Clydie had supplied him with replacement cello strings and he had just tuned up when he became aware of movement in the gardens below. It was Olga. She had a dog with her and was waving for Finch's attention. Finch waved back and signalled that he'd come out and join her. He staggered into his trousers and left his room, still buttoning up his shirt as he made his way down to the gardens.

'Sir, this is Finch,' said Olga to the dog, kneeling down to its level. The dog looked like a form of large spaniel, Finch thought, with similar red-brown colouring to himself, or it was possibly a red setter. Finch had never seen one so was unsure, but its name, more importantly, was *Sir*.

'Oh, wow – so, this is the boss of the AU? Pleased to meet you, Sir.' Finch performed a mock salute at the dog, whose reaction was a long, humourless stare.

Olga laughed. 'Tough crowd. And no, not the boss – possibly the owner.'

'So, *Sir*? Talk me through it, Olga. That's an exceptional name for a cat, but a dog? No – terrible. No wonder he looks so unimpressed,' said Finch. 'Saying that, he does perhaps look like a Montgomery, or maybe a Rafe?'

'You'll understand, in time. Let's walk – I know a good spot.' Olga reached for a picnic basket that Finch insisted on carrying as they walked. It was clear they'd arrived when Finch found himself at the brow of a hill, able to see for miles over spectacular rolling hills. A clearing within the foliage created a sense of privacy from which to admire the vista, and although Finch had never been in a box at the theatre, it summoned similar notions – a sense of enjoying an advantaged, cosy position from which to regard something magical unfolding. Summer had arrived and the sunshine was warm. Olga spread the tartan picnic blanket out.

'It doesn't fly or anything, does it?' asked Finch with bogus concern as he tentatively touched the corner of the blanket with his foot.

'We'll find out,' responded Olga, holding aloft a

bottle of what Finch guessed might be champagne. Sir had been surveying the view, but on noticing the blanket, came and sat right at the centre. 'Sir, would you mind? I mean, I'd be very grateful if you'd consider moving, dear boy,' Olga requested politely. Sir looked on. He wasn't going to acknowledge this appeal. 'Sir, move!' insisted Olga, but nothing. 'Sir. Come on – *off*!' Still nothing. Olga took his lead and pulled. Sir was rooted and she could not shift him. 'Okay – he wins again.' In resignation, she unpeeled the foil at the top of the bottle and began to push at the cork with both thumbs.

'It's all fun until somebody gains an eye,' said Finch, manoeuvring out of the line of fire before sitting down on the blanket.

'I think that makes you an optimist,' she said, as she passed a glass of sparkling fizz over Sir's head. They sat in a row of three, admiring the scenery.

'So, how long have you been here, Olga? asked Finch. 'How many Leavers like me have you guided from their bygone eras into the present?'

'Two, and many. Years and Leavers. But none quite like you.'

'Do you live here permanently?' asked Finch.

'No. I just come and stay when there's an assignment. There are other locations I also work at – like

SCI-PSY. It's the same job, though. Just, each Leaver is different. The challenges can vary.'

'Do you take them all on picnics with Mrs Danvers here?'

'You have a lot of questions, Mr Henry,' Olga said, apparently to deflect his enquiry. 'Anyway, I'm actually on a picnic with Mrs Danvers. You're just tagging along.' Sir turned and gave Finch a supercilious glare, then turned back and continued his study of the panorama.

Finch laughed. 'Did you actually train him to have comedy timing?'

'No – he does it all by himself. But I do love the little *aristocrat*,' she said, as though the word were a euphemism.

'Have you always had him? I've not seen him before.'

'Yes – but he only comes out to be sociable at weekends and evenings. He's teaching classes the rest of the time.'

'In printing cravats?' Finch suggested.

Olga laughed. 'No. Comedy timing – you don't need to go.'

They ate and chatted, the whole time peering around the obstacle that was Sir, who seemed masterly in his determination to block proceedings at any cost. Finch lay back to admire the expanse of blue sky, hands behind his head. He was enjoying the combination of a blissful, alcoholic haze and warm sunshine. Olga lay back too, causing Sir to follow suit between them.

'Is he extremely possessive of you, by any chance?' asked Finch, through the Sir-shaped blockade.

'I'm not sure that's it. It's possibly more of a power game, or just Sir being literally dogmatic. I've never really figured it out. He's always been this way. Doesn't like anyone else – just me – and he only tolerates me out of necessity as I'm the staff.'

Finch, conscious of Sir's indomitable resolve to create a barrier, changed the subject. 'So you're, what, third generation?'

'Yes – I grew up with the knowledge. My parents did too, but their parents had reservations so their belief was kind of diluted slightly. Third gen, though, we don't have that problem.'

'So when did they introduce the idea? From birth?' asked Finch.

'Pretty much, and we learned about it in class. By the time I was at school the Q-Pho tech had evolved to be far more accessible – we even had our own camera in the science lab, so we studied it first-hand.'

'How? I mean … death? At school?'

'Experiments – the usual scientific route: mice,

frogs. They'd be released on camera.'

'Released? You mean killed? Just so you could see the Q-Pho in action?'

'Yes – when you think about it, it's no different from old-fashioned dissection classes …'

'Seems a bit, well, brutal. But I suppose I understand what you mean – it's just … dying for the sake of that, when it was already so well known …'

'I know – but then so was anatomy, well known, and yet kids still had to dissect creatures. I suppose they wanted to impart actual personal proof to the younger generations, so the whole denial problem didn't arise again. But remember – we didn't kill them in the sense you mean. They were simply released from their physical form. They continued to exist.'

Finch turned his thoughts to the technical side; he was finding this reality difficult to stomach. 'So, Q-Pho cameras were common in schools at that point. Do they still do that?'

'I don't know, actually, but I read that they are developing Q-Pho glass to cut out the camera part completely. The cameras are smaller these days, too. Seb even has an app on his device that does the basics, but that did require serious adaptations to the device. Obviously, not everyone has that. It's a government thing.'

Finch felt the conversation was getting too heavy.

There was much about Olga he wished to understand, and the knowledge that she was part of a class that 'released' creatures just to see the Q-Pho in action was not what he had in mind. A non-apologetic change of subject was called for.

'So, what's your surname, Olga? Where did you grow up? You've been here two years, yes? You can't be much older than me?'

'Oh, wow. Er. Rubens. Scotland … and no, I'm not.'

'Thanks. Just wondered. Miss? Rubens.'

'Outdated – we don't do all that any more. I would, if I were living many decades ago, be a Miss, yes.'

'Let me see your egg.'

Olga waved a hand over Sir's back and Finch caught it, holding it firmly so he could examine the techtoo. He brushed the glowing white egg softly with a finger but could not detect its presence, just like his gull which had begun morphing into an orange tone over recent days. 'Why do you guides have eggs, and we Leavers have seagulls?'

There was a tense pause during which Olga seemed to drag her voice back into action from some distant dream. 'I … think it's so we remember the cycle: gull, egg, gull, egg …' Olga received no response so continued, her voice muffled by a wall of Sir. 'Okay – you'll need an open mind for this, but we come here, to Earth, I mean, repeatedly, to learn from our human experiences, just like attending school, and we sometimes need to remember that our tutors in this life can also be our juniors. Older souls in younger bodies – that kind of thinking.'

Finch leant up on his elbow to look at Olga over Sir's back. He intertwined his fingers with hers and watched her close her eyes.

'You know, I'm not meant to get involved with any Leavers. Ever, Finch,' she said.

'I imagined as such.'

There was a long silence.

***

Sleep was simply out of the question for Finch. Rerunning his conversations with Olga and analysing them from every perspective, remembering her touch and the way she'd closed her eyes, he was beyond restless. He had grown aware of the chemistry between them but this was becoming difficult to handle. He could think of little else. Eventually, when he'd exhausted himself by recalling every detail, his mind would create scenarios, fantasies that Olga would turn up at his door, or he'd visualise the following day's events and his encounters with her. It was not an option – he knew that – so why couldn't his mind find any acceptance or peace? It was immensely exasperating that he was essentially torturing himself, apparently with no power to desist.

At enlightenment class the following day, Finch was

able to meditate and discovered that it offered some relief. Olga didn't attend all of his classes and wasn't present for this fast-tracking session with Jude, or 'focus one-to-one' as Jude had referred to it. Seb's preference to delay the acceleration of Finch's sensitive training must have been dismissed, Olga explained, and the decision had been taken at a higher level. Finch was less concerned now. He trusted Jude and was happy to work on this side of his development, interested to discover the extent of his own ability.

Jude and Finch discussed the various phenomena that had become part of Finch's life on the island, such as his occasional experiences of hearing drifts of disembodied conversation, and his precognitive feelings and dreams. They channelled Reiki again and Finch could see he was improving; the heat energy coming from his hands was clearer and stronger.

Jude guided Finch through some exercises to focus his sensitive ability. They were simple tasks such as attempting to decipher the information around an object just by handling it. He asked questions for Finch to consider, such as whether it was a loved object; whether the person it was attached to had transcended or was still on Earth; what the feelings of this person had been; the overriding themes or issues in their life, and so on. Jude didn't indicate whether Finch's intuitions were correct or not, but made notes and carried on with similar energy reading challenges.

Following that, Finch met Olga at last for his first tech class. There was some awkwardness as they greeted each other and Finch could see her energy was still erratic. She would pulse large ovoid waves at him when they connected, but then seemed to draw them back in, as though trying to control herself. Finch was becoming accustomed to his sensitive ability increasing after the meditation and Reiki practices, which allowed him to be more at ease when noticing its presence. Olga made self-conscious small talk, amongst which was the subject of Koo and Tia's newly printed outfits, and the fact that they had yet to order Finch's. Finch described Jude's focus session approach and the sensitive exercises, in order to fill the occasionally heavy silences.

The tech class was held in the Tech Lab on one of the lower levels, underground. This lesson was to be a broad overview of the main subjects, in a similar vein to the initial film that had explained the Discovery.

The Leavers learned about the prolific use of energy for almost everything on the mainland, even reading a book and flushing a toilet. The tutor, Phil, a middle-aged man who was remarkable only by his normality – a rarity at the AU – explained how, following the Discovery, world leaders had placed a new, increasingly serious emphasis on finding a cleaner energy with which to power the planet. This, according to Phil, was brought on by a sudden development of conscience in the minds of the powerful. Phil suggested it was driven by guilt: a rapid rethink motivated by the idea that their previous actions were actually being observed by a higher power, and that perhaps they should try to make good any of their former, more questionable practices that may have impacted the planet, and therefore their karma, negatively.

The modern world, the greater part of it anyway, was now using a water-based technology that was far less harmful to planet Earth. Finch had only been vaguely aware that this was an issue at all, and was now puzzled that the island was allowed to continue using damaging fossil fuels while the rest of the world had evolved much cleaner alternatives. As if aware of Finch's thoughts, Phil imparted that there were many less developed countries continuing to use fossil fuels because the world had not yet reached a complete state of cohesion in any area, energy included.

The next subject was the online world. Phil gave a brief overview of the internet's development and how it was now the basis for most tech interactions. The Leavers were given devices, not properly connected of course, but with a dummy program designed to present as though actively online. Phil taught them all how to perform basic tasks such as calling, messaging, photography, map routing, online searches and navigating mock websites. He emphasised again that this was a brief overview of the online world and its myriad uses, and further detail would be delivered in later classes. A personal computing device was demonstrated and the Leavers experimented with its basic functions.

Phil moved on to finances and interacting with institutions such as banks, employers and retailers. Money had become an almost abstract concept and this was more difficult for the Leavers to grasp. Cash no longer existed except as an emergency currency, and all transactions were undertaken using tech.

Phil explained how shops on the mainland were not staffed like those on the island and in other less progressive parts of the world. Tech had allowed a walk-out system to develop, whereby your personal device, physical identifiers or techtoo would allow the retailer to note your purchases and the money would then be automatically debited from your account. Employers would pay you automatically and you'd pay for purchases automatically with no need for much action on either party's part. No one ever saw any actual money or physically exchanged it any more.

There were, explained Phil, current debates around future plans to get rid of numbers altogether, so working would give you 'credit', and you'd spend credit on living costs; the actual numbers would be irrelevant as long as the person was contributing. Obviously this would still involve some levels of hierarchy, so high-value workers could access high-value goods and services, and the low-value workers would be restricted to the low-end goods, for example. There, Phil indicated, the problem arose. You'd need to define and police the levels in the hierarchy and their income and outgoing expenditure, so therefore the system may as well continue with numbers. It also entertained Phil that this concept would almost suggest we'd gone full circle, back to bartering – a cart exchanged for a sheep, or a meal for a night's accommodation – a return to the days before currency had even been conceived of.

The tech class finished and the day's schooling was complete, the Leavers' minds struggling to grasp the many elements of this complex new world. It all seemed so unnecessarily complicated to Finch. However, there was comfort in Phil's assurance that the mainlanders' skills had gradually developed alongside this tech, and they had never been in the position of having to learn it all from scratch at any point. The internet had formed and people had gained an understanding of it before it became the central point of all technology, as it was now. They would grasp it in due course and they were advised, convincingly, not to be anxious.

Olga walked Finch to his room as usual. They were

slightly more at ease having had such a monumental distraction in the form of the tech class. Finch invited Olga to dinner and she, to his surprise, accepted.

***

Olga and Finch arranged to meet in the same restaurant Finch usually attended with Seb. Finch had been missing Seb recently. A new assignment had taken priority and Seb had been occupied researching the case. He'd been artfully nebulous with the details he'd relayed, but Finch trusted him. Feeling more able to embrace a new level of independence at the AU, he was less reliant on Seb for support and had begun to value their friendship rather than needing it.

Awaiting Olga's arrival, Finch was aware of his nervousness and used his newly learned Reiki skills to calm his nerves, subtly channelling the healing energy into his stomach below the tabletop. When Olga arrived, she too seemed on edge and had made some effort, looking outstanding in a charcoal-toned dress constructed of a high-tech, neoprene-like fabric. It had blocked areas of what Finch thought must be sequins – clusters of small, dark, reflective elements that reacted to her movement. The dress was minimal, asymmetrical and long line, with a slim silhouette and what Finch assumed to be a contemporary cut, a dress only someone like Olga could carry off. She sat down and placed a device on the table. As she did so, Finch caught a new angle of the sequined panels and realised that they were an illusion. He could see through them at the edges of her silhouette as though they were holographic, almost hovering above the dress. Finch watched as the sequins shifted in a spellbinding deception between seeming to be physically present – convincingly reflecting the surrounding light – to near invisibility, going disconcertingly in and out of focus.

'Hello, Mr Henry.'

'Hey, Olga.' Finch was attempting a relaxed tone, but his voice cracked slightly. He frequently felt intimidated by her and it wasn't helpful that she looked so stunning. 'You look, just, wow – what is that dress *made* of?'

'Oh – previous Leavers,' she said seriously.

Finch's nerves subsided as he laughed. 'I can think of worse fates, actually. Those – sequins? Are they … really there?'

'In a sense. Is anything? Anyway, I couldn't decide – green or grey.' Olga made a few gestures on the screen of her device and a deep emerald green hue spread across the dress in a motion that travelled from her left shoulder downwards diagonally, seeming to rustle the sequins as it recoloured them. It reminded Finch of watching an ink blot spread across damp paper, a quenching kind of saturation, bleeding in, the darker exploring verges feeling their way.

'Green. Definitely,' said Finch, for want of any

starting position from which to grapple with what he'd just witnessed. A change of subject was necessary. 'Where's Sir? Can't he join us?'

'No. He's at his desk, composing his critique of the wine here. He isn't allowed back since, well, *the Incident.*'

'Oh, God. What did he do?' asked Finch with mock intrigue, just as the waiter brought the wine, theatrically displaying the label on the bottle for their approval.

'Later,' said Olga conspiratorially to Finch. She pushed the device towards him. 'So, I brought this so we can get some clothes printed for you at last. Want to choose?'

'Without Sir's sartorial guidance? No. It's unthinkable.'

Olga navigated to an app that presented an overview of styles, clearly modelled professionally and with the polished appearance of swanky magazine photoshoots, moodily lit and beautifully photographed. There were several 'looks' to choose from, Olga explained, and once the preferred look had been established, the actual garments within that range were available and fully customisable; anything could be printed. It was simply a question of finding the right garment bases to convey your 'code', as she put it, and then altering or embellishing them at will.

'Code?' asked Finch. His head was already brimming with new information from the tech lesson so he should, in theory, have been in the right frame of mind for this, but for the fact he'd reached full capacity, mental overload.

'You know, *code* – as in what your clothes convey to the world.' Responding to Finch's blank expression, Olga continued. 'Everything we wear, or don't, come to that, says a lot about who we are, our outlook, background, aspirations, interests – which cultural or religious group we may belong to … no?'

Finch was amused but none the wiser. 'Sorry – it's falling on deaf ears. On the island it was a case of pick the best from a crate of pre-loved menswear. What it said about us, well, I shudder to think. Probably that we were prisoners of our own limitations – trapped in a long-gone era and someone else's choices, or trousers, even. Maybe that's perfect, actually.'

Olga laughed, while perceptibly taken aback. She appeared to be considering how startlingly accurate his decoding of island fashion had been. It had taken Finch by surprise as he'd heard it emerge from his own lips and neither of them quite knew how to follow the statement.

Olga moved to sit alongside Finch so they could share the screen. They swiped through the 'looks', which offered varying degrees of smart to casual fashion styling, and Finch chose one that had a classic smart-casual feel with subtle quirks and a minimal, modern edge. They drank the wine and trawled through the next stage of options, which consisted of outfit combinations rather than the styled fashion-shoot feel of the initial 'looks'. While viewing single garments, Finch noticed you could request 'seamless', 'semi-seam', or 'traditional seam' within the detail of each garment.

'Can we view semi-seam?' he asked. Olga touched the wording, causing a zoomed-in photograph of the cotton shirt to emerge from the screen as though modelled on a tiny invisible man who shifted into new poses at regular intervals. Olga twiddled the hologram around from above with her finger.

'See – some of the seams you'd expect to see are missing, like the side seam and on the sleeves,' she explained. 'They aren't necessary with this technology – it's more of a style thing now. It's traditional to have them – it looks more tailored, defined, but it's contemporary to go without. Look.' Olga showed Finch the seamless option and it looked odd to him – almost featureless, like a face lacking eyebrows.

'It looks like something's missing, though,' said Finch. He turned and admired Olga's dress. 'You have seams, Olga. What were you thinking? How quaint.'

'It's vintage,' she responded. 'Anyway, what you said about the island – we are all the result of someone else's choices in one way or another.'

As Finch laughed, the waiter returned to take their order and refill their glasses. Olga and Finch made hasty decisions based on previous visits in order to minimise the interruption. After some deliberation, Finch had chosen a new wardrobe with Olga's help. The clothes would be printed by the following morning. He was keen to see the machine that could perform such implausible sorcery, but Olga told him it was off-limits, and that the flying monkeys who operated it would not allow just anyone in.

Finch's new wardrobe was largely built around a modern take on classic pieces – seemingly natural fibres and neutral tones. Most of the pieces had the odd streak of irreverence here and there. He was drawn to minimalism – simple contemporary twists on classic styles, and traditional silhouettes but with slightly awkward proportions. He discovered that he was interested in unexpected construction detailing or use of fabric, and soon found himself selecting the seamless options, adapting quickly to the world he now inhabited. This was grown-up attire to fit the man he'd become and he was intrigued to see how well it would collaborate with his occasional make-up habit.

The food arrived and they ate, now sitting opposite each other again, talking entertaining nonsense and appreciating the wine. They enjoyed each other's company to the extent of never having a serious conversation, and during a rare silence, Finch became aware that there was still so much he would like to know. The other Leavers and the lack of interaction between them all puzzled him. Then there was Olga's health, and the fact that he could sometimes detect a faint smoky nicotine smell about her person. *Perhaps*, he thought, *that subject is best left for now.* The other Leavers seemed an easier topic.

'Robert – is he like me? A sensitive?' Finch asked. 'Sorry, I know you're probably not allowed to discuss the others. I was just wondering … he seems more fragile, somehow.'

'It's okay – it's nothing Rob wouldn't tell you himself. He's from your island, Finch. The other side, I'm told. He escaped. They found him out at sea. He'd been drifting in a rowing boat for days, the poor guy. He'd lost his paddles and run out of supplies. He was very ill. In cases like that we are allowed to step in and help without question.'

'My God, I had no idea. So he just set off for the mainland but didn't make it?'

'Suppose so. Ask him – you guys are allowed to talk to each other, you know.'

'I wasn't sure. We always have our guides with us, which doesn't really promote much interaction … I will make more effort, then.'

'I can always leave you to it,' she suggested playfully.

'No. Don't.' Finch was suddenly serious and Olga caught her breath. They looked at each other for a long moment as the mood shifted. Finch was conscious of a mutual frustration hanging in the air between them, that there was little they could do about this situation. It wasn't going away.

'Please don't … say things like that, Finch.' Olga looked vulnerable.

'Sorry … the wine. I think Sir's critique may be right about that. It's just, well, what are the rules? If I left, would we be allowed to – see each other, socially, I mean? What is the time scale with something like that?'

'It's, well, later, when you're not under my care, if there's been a significant length of time, possibly.' She had the air of someone who was trying to convince herself.

'Sounds difficult.' Finch said.

'It is – and frowned upon. I mean, I wouldn't be in trouble, but it might be problematic. There could be implications. I would be seen as highly unprofessional.'

They looked at each other. The seriousness and strength of Finch's feelings, combined with this unbearable position of impossibility, evoked a state of utter exasperation in him, and he sensed it strongly in Olga's energy, too.

'We can be like this. But that's it. For now.' Olga seemed resolute and Finch would never have asked that she risk her career on any basis, so he accepted her words.

'Then we will be like this,' he stated, determined to show strength of character and noticing as Olga's eyes gleamed in response.

When it was time to go, Olga orchestrated their goodbye to take place in an open part of the building where others frequently passed through, as though she did not trust them to maintain their self-control were it to take place anywhere more private.

8 INSULAR DWARFISM

The following day, Finch was preparing to leave for counselling. He was growing accustomed to the one-way nature of conversation during the long sessions, and found it a useful way to introduce some order into his laden mind. He was feeling unusually short tempered and irritable, and thought it convenient subject matter for the session. It had not escaped his notice that this would also help him avoid Olga as a subject.

He was about to shower, considering the oncoming session, when he halted, feeling some external influence abruptly intruding into his world. He stood still, his mind keen to capture this fleeting sensation and examine it before it dissipated. The door drew his attention, and he watched as energy seemed to penetrate through it in waves. There were two knocks.

'Hi, Olga. How long have you been out there?'

'Oh – no, I just arrived.' She was carrying five large fabric bags spread over her person. 'Your new clothes are finished.' She sounded excited, as though eager to see them.

'I have counselling in half an hour, so it may have to wait.' Finch was eyeing the bags, tempted to unpack them where he stood. 'Okay – just a quick look. Come in.'

The clothes were impeccable – tailored by an expert, it would appear, and even folded immaculately. The fabrics were of beautiful quality – soft, natural and tactile, seemingly knitted or woven like traditionally made garments. There were linings and internal bindings – all the expected elements of finely made clothing. The jackets had subtle padding and structure as though lovingly stitched together from multiple materials. The only indicator that they'd been printed was the impossible lack of seams – tubular woven sleeves and torsos, seamless, yet in tailoring cloths. Finch loved them, every trim and buttonhole.

On realising the time, he was compelled to run to counselling, taking the stairs and leaving Olga at the lift. He was almost grateful to avoid the lift; the tension as they stood opposite each other was tangible, and he often inwardly thanked the AU architect for constructing the lifts out of glass. When he arrived at what he'd begun to think of as 'Dr

Lenny's mind aquarium' she was waiting in her chair, reading.

'Finch, hello. Glad you could make it.' She sounded relaxed about Finch's delayed appearance. 'Nice shirt,' she added, surveying his new look over her glasses and smiling broadly, eyes glinting.

'Thanks – it was printed. Sorry – I still can't believe I'm actually saying that. *Printed* last night.'

'A fine choice you've made there … it suits you. So, how are you getting on now?'

'Good, I think. Well – no. Pissed off, sometimes, actually. It's interesting – I've noticed the island seems to creep up on me. Last night, Olga and I were discussing the codes, as she put it, within apparel and I found myself describing the island's second-hand clothing system as being forced to live with someone else's choices, from another, defunct era. I didn't know where that had come from, but although I was having a great time with Olga, I felt really angry about it deep down – the island's *myopic* decision-making and the Founders', well, stupidity. Fucking infuriating *stupidity*. How dare they choose ignorance and captivity for future generations. Why did no one *think* about that? Christ. Even Grandad. What was he *thinking*? I miss the old duffer, but I can't understand the conviction it must have taken. And they just got even *more* obtuse! That's another mind-boggling horror to conceive of – how on earth did they manage to achieve *further* idiocy?'

Dr Lenny was quiet as though waiting until Finch had paused long enough to consider him vented, for now. 'Have you ever heard of Insular Dwarfism, Finch?'

'No.' Finch wondered where this was leading. It seemed such a non sequitur at this point – almost a diversion.

'It's what happens to animals over time if they are living on a small island. They actually grow smaller. Not the original animals of course, but subsequent generations. They evolve to be reduced in size so as to stretch the limited available resources.' Dr Lenny allowed Finch a moment to process this. 'I sometimes think that that's what happens to islanders, mentally, over time. Their minds become somehow reduced, their horizons become limited by habit, and they can cease feeling the necessity to grow, to expand and experience the new. They become fearful of unknown territory and thereby increasingly insular.'

Finch considered it. 'That sounds like you're excusing them,' he eventually stated.

'No, not in any sense. But I am trying to understand them. It can sometimes help if you can extend yourself enough to appreciate the viewpoint of someone who has hurt you. That is the first seed of forgiveness. But I understand you are possibly not ready to hear that.'

'It's interesting. But no – forgiveness is currently low on the list of things I'd like to offer them.'

'I understand, Finch – more than you'd think. Tell me more about how they make you feel.'

Finch delivered another polemic around the Founders' incredible arrogance, then the low-level but consistent propaganda that painted the mainland as such a darkly disturbing place. He continued for some time and even ventured on to how staggeringly inept the Council was at running the island, and that they should not have been allowed to continue, on various grounds. He was angry at the mainland for that. Finch eventually stopped. In his silence he reflected on his mother and the inhumane treatment of her while she was ill – not being allowed visitors. 'If Mum had left, I almost wouldn't blame her,' he said aloud.

Dr Lenny shifted as though waking up and paying attention. '*Almost*? And where did that come from, Finch?' she asked, evidently intrigued.

'It's just something I've thought about a lot since coming here. The circumstances of her death were, well, the more I think about it, bafflingly odd. We didn't see her while she was ill, for months, then we were told she'd died, and still we couldn't see her. Maybe it's just more bizarre island protocol, but I have wondered – did she leave? Like me? I expect they've faked my death to explain my disappearance.

Seb is going to check whether she left, see if there's any information available.'

'Oh – is that wise, Finch? Have you thought about how you'd feel if it emerges that she did leave you and your grandad?' There was a brief but heavy silence.

'I know there's a ... risk,' Finch said cautiously. 'But I'd rather know. And she could still be out there somewhere. I think she had my abilities. She used to complain of migraines that caused her to see things, hear things. Maybe she was, I don't know – recruited? Like me?'

'Is that how you feel, Finch, that you've been *recruited*?' Dr Lenny asked gently.

'Of sorts, yes. I'm not sure I'd be here if my ability hadn't become so obvious. But I'm okay with that. I am glad to be out of there, on whatever basis.'

'Well, I'd advise caution, Finch. You don't know what you might discover and it could be really upsetting,' she warned. 'Our time's up, Finch, but proceed with caution. And I need to make you aware – there are laws. Related Leavers must be given access to information on each other, if they request it from level-five employees. Whatever Seb tells you – it will have to be the truth. He is level five, so you've gone through the right channel. But, Finch, there is an old saying that goes "be careful what you wish for – you might just get it".' Finch was on his way out of the room as Dr Lenny added, 'I wouldn't normally say this to a Leaver, but I feel it might help you. Finch, often I think that Leavers' anger is completely justified, and the correct response, but it's important that you *own* your own anger, and never, never let *it* own *you*.'

'Thanks – I'll think about it. All of it.' He turned back, considering something.

'I'm level four, Finch.'

***

The passing days brought ever-increasing frustration and dissatisfaction for Finch's Olga-obsessed mind. He had become used to the sheer drudgery of going to bed feeling racked with disappointment that no meaningful progress had been, or *could be* made in this area of his life. They would spend time together and inevitably be swept up into their own world where no one and nothing else existed, only to be followed by Olga's manner becoming professional and distant, cold even. Finch was forced to question whether he was alone in his infatuation.

Finch's enlightenment focus classes were immersing him into new depths of experience, and he was gaining more insight into himself and the world he now inhabited. His ability to see energy had become present much of the time and he practised meditation like an explorer seeking new inner frontiers and an ever-deepening comprehension. Olga was inadvertently helpful, her noncommittal approach a catalyst for Finch's frequent meditation practice, which was fast evolving into a new coping strategy, alongside playing his cello.

Having tried and failed to befriend Rob on two occasions, Finch decided to pursue it again today. Now, on his way to culture class, he was free of make-up, hoping it might make the difference; perhaps it was Finch's occasional eyeliner that deterred Rob. He'd asked Olga not to attend, which almost physically hurt him to do, but he suspected that Rob might be more responsive if it were just them. Olga had arranged for Rob's guide to be absent, too. Finch took a seat next to Rob in the lecture theatre and Rob nodded a hello. There was no time for small talk. The lecturer, a middle-aged, formidable woman of African origin, had arrived and was addressing the Leavers. She was dressed like a parade – vivid clashes of colour and blaring pattern from head to toe. Her hair was adorned with a matching fabric turban that finished the glorious look perfectly.

'Hello, time travellers!' she bellowed happily in a strong American accent. 'I'm your introduction to the modern world. My name is Claudine Faroque, but you may call me Claudine Faroque. Welcome!' She grinned, pacing the front of the room like a stand-up comedian. 'I'm going to take any island attitudes you may still be harbouring and toss them into the *trash*! Let us begin. So, I trust you have all reached sublime transcendence during your enlightenment classes? Yes? Who's in the mood for a bit of audience participation?'

'No,' Finch joked loudly, to the amusement of Koo and Tia. Even Rob stifled a reluctant laugh.

'Mr Henry! Touché. I like your sense of irony. I thank you.' She appeared genuinely amused and must have understood that Finch was just being playful, and not actually disruptive. 'Now, let me see those gulls! Hold 'em up – that's right. Higher! Don't be shy, now. Okay. Most of them are either side of green, so you're halfway to liberty.' There was a pause before she asked in a more serious, hushed tone, 'How does that make you *feel*?' There was silence followed by an unenthusiastic murmur. None of the Leavers was ready to consider being set free, and they certainly weren't confident enough to speak up about it. 'Okay, then – I am going to help you all understand just what to expect on *the other side* once you've left here.'

Claudine Faroque listed the main subjects for study. There was language respect, gender politics, racial diversity, tolerance ethos and breakthroughs in orientation limitation. Finch, translating this inwardly, wondered whether orientation limitation would relate to Syrus, the 'tri-mister' he'd encountered on his journey. Then there were world cultures, world politics and social interaction. She would also run a class towards the end of their tenure relating to the practicalities of existing independently on leaving the AU, and this brought a welcome sense of relief to Finch and, no doubt, to the anxious minds of the other Leavers.

'Let's start with gender politics.' A large screen flashed up images of androgynous people from all walks of life. There were octogenarians to young teens, all with aspects of both sexes. There were hundreds – some in uniforms that looked military, others looking like politicians or doctors. 'This could go on for weeks!' she exclaimed. 'You must understand, the world has changed since your forefathers saw fit to lock their children away from progress. Non-defined-gender people account for twenty-eight per cent of the UK population!' She continued by quoting figures for same-sex marriage and was forceful in her message that being non-defined gender did not necessarily mean gay, and being gay did not mean transitional gender. Her no-nonsense delivery was thoroughly direct. She was presenting the information as plain fact that they'd better accept, and there was absolutely no tolerance for intolerance.

While they were on the subject of personal image Claudine Faroque explained that apparel printing was now commonplace, allowing everyone to be their own designer. Fashion trends, as they had been known, were an outmoded concept because there was total freedom of choice. They might encounter some extrovertly dressed people out there, she warned, and it was totally normal and acceptable for men to be as dressed as women, make-up and all, and vice versa.

Finch was enjoying this lecture. The subject matter alone was revitalising his very soul, and Claudine Faroque's bold energy was invigorating to witness. The mainland would suit him just fine. After the lecture, Finch walked alongside Rob to the lift. 'How are you finding it here?' he asked.

'Okay. You?' was Rob's reply. He seemed perpetually fragile, broken. It was something Finch couldn't place, but he knew Rob would become his friend. He could feel it. Finch studied the feeling and found more. It was his own flamboyance that evoked unease in Rob. Finch needed to be more of a 'bloke'.

'Oh, you know – another day, another head fuck,' was Finch's new approach. Rob laughed out loud, which was a first for Finch.

'I'm with you there, mate. I don't know which is crazier – the island or this place.'

'You're from the same island as me, I think – Monk Island?'

'Yeah, I … left, I mean, well … You were from the other side?' Rob was trying to divert the conversation so as to avoid using the word *escaped*, Finch realised.

'Yeah. Beer?' said Finch. Rob looked cornered for a moment. 'No island talk,' Finch added, and the atmosphere shifted slightly.

'Okay,' said Rob, as though he knew it was against his better judgement. Finch sensed an air of the prejudice that Claudine Faroque had just been referring to; it wasn't uncommon on the island. Something told Finch it was okay – Rob would get there. He wasn't adjusting as easily as Finch, but he would, in time.

They sat at the bar together having a pint as the bartender came and went, allowing them intermittent periods of privacy. They discussed the lessons and the characters they had so far encountered, sometimes with an element of comedy. Rob loosened up, revealing a gentler nature than Finch had expected, although he still seemed to be speaking in a minor key. His protective shell had softened and he was more open to discussing the island so Finch made him laugh with his dry take on the eroding horror of the place and they bonded over the cinema and Marilyn Monroe, like good old-fashioned blokes. Rob seemed relieved to learn that Finch liked girls, however, and Finch chose to ignore that side of Rob, sensing that he would learn to be more open. As the evening wore on, Finch noticed that Rob's accent was becoming more relaxed and had developed the bumpkin twang that was prevalent in some areas of the island.

The beer flowed and spirits, of the alcoholic kind, were beckoning. They were, in time, drunk as skunks. Mid-rant about how appallingly the island was managed, Finch mentioned the extraordinary lack of security at the docks when he'd left with Seb, instantly realising he'd waded into risky and insensitive waters.

'Not my problem, Finch. I just went. Saw their videos and none of it added up. So I built me a boat.'

'What – you just sailed off?' Finch feigned surprise to avoid letting Rob feel as though he'd been the subject of discussion.

'Yep. Nothing left on the island. Wife left me for this artsy ponce who taught her pottery class. Pink-trousered, knuckle-shuffling, wank-flute. Ah, prick stew, that place. Anyway, then, when I sees what they'd sent by mistake. Blew my mind.' Rob made a whistling sound while twirling a finger around his temple to illustrate the aforementioned mind-blow.

'Prick stew!' Finch was laughing uncontrollably at that description. Wiping tears from his eyes, he tried to focus on what Rob was actually conveying. 'So, you saw what your wife sent? Or the pink pottery knuckle-shuffle?' he asked, attempting to translate the garble into at least pre-spirits speak.

'No!' Rob said, as though Finch was being obtuse. 'No. Them videos for the big showing. I was working at TV House. I said … I think? No, but they sent the wrong videos to the machine for broadcast. From the mainland – it was all mainland stuff like cars and screens and spacemen. And then stuff like this Q-Pho bollocks … not that it is bollocks, but you know what I mean.'

'Wow – so you knew there was a world out there that wasn't like the one they scared us all with at primary school.'

''Zactly,' confirmed Rob.

'That's severe. The boat thing – desperate. You lunatic!'

'Right. But everything was right turdular and, well, I had bugger-all left. And yeah, I nearly died but then this UFO thing with a lass in it came and picked me up, right? Drone. Yeah, drone. Then I came here and met yous. That's my story. What's yours, make-up man?'

'Don't call me drone,' was Finch's delayed response, and they both collapsed with laughter at the abysmal gag. 'Ah … me? Everyone died. That's it really. Then I was freaking out, seeing stuff … Seb talked me into coming here. Glad I did now. The food is *'mazing.'*

'I'm with you there, Finch. Food so good. We should've 'ad some.'

Finch saw that Rob's head was drooping with

inebriation and his eyes were working hard to find Finch from their low position.

'Come on. Time to go.'

With that, they zigzagged their way back to their rooms, trying in vain not to look utterly ratted to the many quietly entertained people they passed.

9 A NEW PERSPECTIVE

Having lost a day to a marathon hangover, Finch stood in the bathroom, shaving and preparing for his enlightenment focus class. His thoughts turned to his mother and the possibilities surrounding her. She could be out there, or was he in denial, chasing ghosts? He was considering this deeply, while another part of his mind was busy concentrating on the job at hand, when he became aware of a slowing sensation within his perception. He had the notion that he was being overtaken by the stationary objects that surrounded him, that time was sucking him backwards. He saw a horizontal blur in his peripheral vision and his ears told him there had been a pressure change – a kind of turbulence, drawing the sound and light from his immediate vicinity.

Finch held on to the edge of the sink cabinet and focused on his breathing. This was just another vision, he told himself. He was back in the restaurant. Seb was there in front of him with his fork of coiled pasta being lowered back on to his plate. A random memory but now in full 3D reality for Finch. Things moved again. The sensations that had occurred around him reversed and he was back, breathing heavily, half shaven, both hands gripping the edge of the sink. 'Holy mother. Some hangover,' he muttered.

Finch became aware of a knocking that seemed to travel from a distant land to his room in an instant. It was the door. Someone was knocking. He opened it, still dazed. 'This came for you, Finch. Enjoy,' said Clydie, handing him a parcel. 'You all right, Finch?' she asked, his condition apparently evident.

'Yeah – thanks,' he managed, absent-mindedly swinging the door shut in her face as he wandered off with the parcel.

Once he had recovered physically, he opened up the parcel to find a stack of antique sheet music: Elgar, Hofmann, Dvorak, Bach – some pieces he didn't even recognise. There was a handwritten note that read:

Dearest Finch,

I hope this finds you well – I am sorry I've had to go but hope to see *you before too long. In the meantime, I thought you'd appreciate the enclosed – I found them in an antiques place. I do miss our dinners together and hope you're continuing to progress as well as you had done up until my departure.*

Your friend, always.

Seb

Finch made his way to enlightenment focus class in a daze, unsure how to decipher his out-of-bathroom experience. What was the significance of seeing Seb return a fork full of food to his plate over dinner that night? Finch couldn't recall the exact context during which he'd noticed it. Surely it must have been a precognitive experience – the sheet music had arrived directly afterwards. It was all Seb-related. It must have been the arrival of the music that had triggered the sensation.

As he relayed his bathroom phenomenon to Jude, it was clear that Jude was impressed by the depth and detail of Finch's experience. He mentioned that some high-level sensitives were able to relive experiences as though actually present a second time, and he asked Finch many questions to establish whether this was what had happened. It seemed the only explanation, aside from Finch suddenly time travelling, and even Jude would have found that inconceivable. Jude made some notes and moved on, seeming eager to find out what else Finch was capable of.

Jude explained that he'd decided to accelerate Finch's development more rapidly than he'd initially planned, given this latest experience; Finch was astonishingly capable and perhaps ready to try the more complex exercises such as remote viewing, interfacing and channelling. Remote viewing, Jude explained, was a technique some sensitives were able to employ that allowed them to view people and places at a distance. Any distance. Finch was given a map with nothing but an X drawn on it, and he was to attempt a remote viewing of this place, reporting his experiences back to Jude afterwards.

Jude started the experiment with meditation as usual – allowing Finch to clear his mind and become connected with his higher self. Jude then guided him through an introduction during which Finch mentally placed himself amid the clouds, over the landscape to which the map pertained. He could be in the clouds – that was no problem, and in his mind it felt wonderful: ice-cold, crisp oxygen and crystal-clear blue sky. Following Jude's prompts, the clouds were to part, revealing the land below that would be of interest. Finch saw a green landscape beneath him, similar to the expanse of green on the map he'd been shown. Now Finch was to focus more on the X in order to zoom in. He saw a building below him with a spattering of smaller buildings behind it that were screened off by a wall of trees. His attention was drawn there. One small building in particular. It looked like a chalet; they all did. He went inside, his viewpoint still from above, and he was with Olga.

She lay fully dressed on her bed, smoking an actual old-fashioned cigarette and talking on her device. Finch could hear Clydie's voice saying, 'Yeah, he was half shaven and something was up. He was pretty aloof and distracted.'

Olga blew smoke into the air above her, temporarily distorting Finch's view of her. 'Okay. I'll check. How was he when you left?'

'He wandered off and let the door close on me – God, that boy. Even half covered in shaving cream and wearing a towel, he still looks like a god,' said Clydie.

Olga laughed, saying, 'I know. It doesn't help.'

'How are you feeling physically now, Olga? Do you want me to send someone else?'

'It's improving. The treatment worked. I'm okay, just tired now, I think. I haven't seen Finch for a few days. He wanted to get to know Rob, then he stayed room-bound for a bit, presumed hung-over, by all accounts. I should go myself – check on him. He's with Jude now.'

163

Finch was stunned to find himself remote viewing Olga's chalet, of all places, which must have been situated just a few hundred metres from his own physical position. He had never been there in person. It was a modern building, in keeping with the main body of the AU: floor-to-ceiling glass and an open, spacious feel. He looked around and noted that there were 'Get Well' cards placed here and there. The interior looked like her character – a combination of what Finch assumed to be contemporary design along with interesting period pieces. A beaten-up old black leather chair with darkened wood, that would have looked shabby in any another setting, gloried here in its modern surroundings as though placed in one of the art galleries Seb had described – adopting a new connotation or significance. There were photos of what must have been Olga's family, siblings, parents and, of course, Sir.

More captivating though, was Finch's acute awareness that he could *feel* Olga – sense her emotions, almost as though they were his. He examined the sensation and became aware of a magnetic force – an intuition that she was resisting a gravitational pull towards him for both their sakes. He could sense the exasperation on her side, the relentless aching she felt. She was employing every possible strategy to manage her own feelings in an attempt to protect them both. He felt the fear she harboured. Fear both of the scale of her own feelings for Finch, and of the possible consequences, should she lose control. Then there was her fragile state, the guilt she felt about smoking. Finch noticed Sir. He was sitting upright on the sofa and he seemed to be looking directly at Finch's viewpoint, alert and apparently aware of his presence.

Abruptly, Finch was back, now conscious of Jude's soft voice repeating, 'Finch, time to return. Come back to the clouds. Gently come back, Finch. Open your eyes when you're ready.' Finch opened his eyes. 'How was that?' asked Jude. 'Did you see anything?'

Finch was gathering himself. The experience had left him feeling momentarily fractured, dispersed. He had no idea how he'd been drawn unintentionally to Olga's chalet. He knew the experience had been real, however. 'I … it was just fields – nothing, really,' said Finch, determined not to find himself involved in an Olga-based conversation with any of her colleagues.

'Wow – you did well to see fields, Finch. We'll try again next time. Let's move on to something less demanding and give you a break.'

Jude's device buzzed and he typed something quickly before returning it to the table. 'Olga, just checking you're good,' he said.

***

The day had been exhausting, what with Finch's extraordinary bathroom experience, whatever that had been, and then the remote viewing, which had left him emotionally shattered. He could only think of Olga – her valiant struggle to refrain from becoming involved, and her worrying health. His feelings for her had grown increasingly profound as he began to understand the strength of character she was deploying in her resolve to resist. He was, on one level, ecstatically happy that clearly she felt exactly as he did, but on another, desperate and hopeless that she seemed so determined to avoid any possibility of a relationship.

It was evening and Finch's mind was pacing the room, head in hands with unreserved frustration. Seb's new cello music called. It was Saturday tomorrow and Finch was dreading two long days of nothing but his own unsettled thoughts for company. He sat down to play and worked his way through several of the new pieces. Even they could not drag his thoughts into line. He took a shower, but still, Olga. He decided to go for a brisk walk in the gardens. Perhaps a change of scenery would help.

Finch strode the grounds like a man on a mission. He'd good knowledge of the entire area now and had half planned a rough circuit to follow. It was a light evening with a bright moon and Finch was vaguely aware of the summer air feeling slightly enchanted, but his mind was so heavy with answerless questions that he barely noticed. He found himself at the scenic spot where Olga and Sir had picnicked, Finch just tagging along. *That wasn't helpful*, he thought. He should have had enough sense to circumvent it. Surrendering and weary, he sat down. The view was even more bewitching under the still blue sky and its few bright stars.

'Finch.' It was Olga's voice. Finch stood up. She was there behind him, with Sir, and seemed shocked to see him.

'Olga,' Finch found himself saying, with a kind of urgency he'd rather have disguised.

They approached each other. Olga looked emotional, maybe upset. Finch wasn't sure. He stood face to face with her, studying her beautiful eyes for what was wrong. He placed a hand on the side of her face as she tried to turn her head and avoid his scrutiny. 'Are you …' Mid-sentence, Olga stepped forward, kissing him and flinging her arms around his neck. They dropped to the ground. They were both clumsy, desperate, covering the other in adoring kisses and consumed by the release of sheer emotion they were finally able to express.

Sir sat admiring the view, determined in his denial. *Nothing* was happening behind him. Even he had no power over this. He knew that much.

***

Some hours later, Finch and Olga lay clinging on to each

other as though for dear life. Finch was, at last, supremely happy, not wanting ever to let go of Olga. They wondered at the night sky and laughed about the inevitable search for far-flung garments. Eventually, as the sky lightened, they conceded that perhaps it was time to dress and return to their usual existence.

Sir was deeply grateful.

Finch and Olga walked back together, making plans to freshen up and catch a few hours' sleep before meeting for lunch. Neither of them mentioned the boundary they'd crossed. They were both conscious that they'd taken a risk but there was a sense of complete inevitability. They couldn't go back, so they may as well stop agonising over their feelings and bask in the bliss of being together at last. Of course, they'd have to be careful not to allow their relationship to show, but that would be easier than abstaining altogether.

They met for lunch at the garden café part of the canteen. Sir was allowed to join them if they sat outside, so Finch had chosen a table under some vigorous grapevine that had commandeered a modern wooden trellis structure. As he watched her approach, she flashed a look at him and their faces relaxed into beaming grins of a knowing kind.

'Sir.' Finch stood and made a hat-doffing gesture at the dog, then cast his gaze to Olga. 'Olga,' he said, using a very different tone of voice and an earnest expression.

'You may be seated,' she said. They ordered food and talked about everything but what had occurred between them. Finch wasn't sure whether it was caused by the sleep deprivation or Olga's presence, but the food had never tasted so good.

'New chef?' he asked. 'This is exceptional.'

'No. I don't think so – it's maybe a different sub?' was Olga's considered response.

'Sub?' asked Finch.

'Substitute … meat substitute.' Finch was no wiser. 'You know the meat here isn't real meat, right?' Olga seemed entertained that Finch had somehow missed this fact.

'Seriously? This isn't meat?' Finch opened his sandwich to examine what was obviously steak.

'No – it's really *not*. You haven't had *any* meat here, Finch – none.' This was followed by a silence.

'How is it so … real?'

'It was developed in labs, decades ago – it's been mainstream for a while. Surprised you didn't know. Maybe it's one of those things that gets through the net – I thought Seb had told you. He must have thought I did …'

'Wow – it's, very real. I mean, it's *rare*.'

'Yep. If I remember my history correctly, it was made mainstream by an American tech company after the

Discovery. As with everything, people's attitudes to food were affected. They became more concerned when the Q-Pho showed chickens and cows have soul energy, too. There was also the opposite reaction, of course, where people felt less guilty knowing the animals would also be released, so it was less, well, final, I suppose, but the majority rejected meat on the whole. Maybe it was more of a karma thing.'

'God – I'll have to have words with Seb. He's gone to research a new case. I haven't seen him for ages. He sent me some new music.'

'Ah, yes. He said he was droning you something he'd found. I'd love to hear you play.' Olga's eyes glinted at Finch. It was distracting.

'That can be arranged.' There was a pause as they looked across the table at one another. 'As long as Sir permits, that is. So, where *is* Seb?'

'At the SCI-PSY facility, I think. No idea when he'll be back. You'll probably see him there first. They have plans for you.'

'At SCI-PSY? You work there sometimes, don't you?'

'Yes – settling in new employees,' confirmed Olga.

'So, their plans? If I were an employee there, does that mean you would still be my guide?'

'Possibly, but employment there is highly sought

after, my Finch. People with your talent go far and live well, so we'd have to be sensible about it. Take the long view.'

'When you call me *my Finch*, the long view looks bearable.'

After a lengthy lunch, they went back to Finch's room so he could play for Olga. She and Sir sat on the sofa waiting while Finch prepared. He emerged from the bathroom wearing just his pyjama bottoms and plenty of black eyeliner. Seated on the wooden chair, he started to bow Elgar's cello concerto from memory. As he progressed through the movement he began to feel strangely physically displaced, as though his arms were raised and floating above his head and his torso twisted sideways in his seat. Part of his mind was quietly studying this peculiar sensation while another part was absorbed in his playing, which flowed from him almost unconsciously. He sensed a connection with Sir, and then with Olga, as though his music was binding them or perhaps somehow connecting with their energies.

Olga watched with an expression of wonder as Sir approached Finch and lay down in front of him, resting his chin on his paws as though moved, or experiencing a new-found respect for him. Finch sensed that Olga was similarly mesmerised. He focused in on her energy and found multiple layers, like a strata formation of thought. At a conscious level he found her analytical mind studying her own reaction – that she had never *felt* music like this before. Perhaps it was being in such close vicinity to the cello, or maybe it was that she was so in love with Finch. At a deeper level he found a gut reaction – that the deep tones and reverberations seemed to saturate her being and she was barely able to breathe as she watched him play, aware of his soul on display – ironically, she thought consciously – more so for the eyeliner.

Olga got up and switched the glass in the windows to one-way view, an electrical voice confirming 'glass view: out only'. She gently removed Finch's bow from his hand and they soon found themselves in a tangle of limbs on the rug, out of control and desperate for each other.

As the weekend progressed, they existed in their own private hedonistic reverie, able at last to show the other how intensely they felt. Even Sir's characteristic glares that he directed so frequently at Finch seemed downgraded from outright contempt to merely withering. If he wasn't careful, Finch commented, he'd end up at ambivalent. Then what? No. Finch would try harder to make the odd social faux pas, use the wrong cutlery and drop his Ts, until full hostility was restored.

***

The blue gull on Finch's palm was conveying alarming notions of time limitation, and in no uncertain terms. Many days had passed since Olga and Finch had become inseparable and they met most nights for dinner, discussing Finch's development and any fresh understanding he had acquired during class.

Today, Finch was Olga-less at culture class. She had an appointment to attend for her health so had left the AU for a few days. Finch had the honour of serving Sir in her absence and because Leavers were not physically allowed in guides' chalets, Sir was camping out in Finch's room.

The subject of the culture class was gender equality and the language of respect. The students were to decode the gender of various people whose description was read aloud by Claudine Faroque, including profession, domestic arrangements, family situation, personal concerns and ambition. The exercise had highlighted their subconscious bias, as she called it; the islanders naturally superimposed elements of their patriarchal societies on to the characters in question. Lawyers and firefighters would be assumed men, while care professionals and stay-at-home parents expected to be women, and so on. Claudine Faroque corrected their assumptions with her usual heartiness, thoroughly enjoying her position of being able to influence things for the better. Right the wrongs.

They discussed the correct language to use when referring to fellow mainlanders of all races and genders, in order to appear native to the mainland and not from another time. Terms not to be used were also discussed, and it was explained to them in Claudine Faroque's uncompromising style that they would appear ignorant, offensive and purveyors of bad taste, should they voice any of the outmoded island terms in public, the workplace or even among friends. These were generally casual terms used to describe different races or sexual orientation, and Claudine Faroque had the students repeating sentences involving these terms, but replacing them with the language of respect instead.

Sitting with Rob, Finch noticed an upturn in his general demeanour. He seemed softer, more open and better informed. The feeling that Rob was humouring it all cynically had passed. They ate lunch together and Finch asked how Rob was doing.

'Good, cheers, Finch,' was Rob's upbeat reply. 'Out of the dark place, generally. You?'

'Yeah, similar. I feel more like I get it now – the mainland – how it works. Still not entirely sure I'm ready to leave at any point soon, though.' Finch withheld the main reason for his reluctance to leave, and changed the subject. 'Not missing the prick stew, then?' which caused an outburst of laughter from Rob.

'You know, I do miss the island sometimes. Not the bog roll, mind. Those dispensers that only let you pull out one bit at a time – like pulling handkerchiefs out of a magician's arsehole. Not like the *vanishing* bog roll here that disappears the moment it touches the water. That's even *weirder*.'

'Rob, you've given it all *far* too much thought,' said Finch through his laughter.

'Seriously though,' continued Rob, 'I do miss odd things, like riding my bike around. I was talking about it with Dr Lenny. I sometimes miss my wife – well, the *idea* of her, anyway. I'm clearer now, about it all. Why she left.'

'For the pink-trousered idiot?'

Rob laughed. 'Er – I think you'll find the respectful term is *wank-flute*. And yes. Think it was me. I was just being the bloke, sorry, *person*, I thought my father wanted me to be.'

'How so?' asked Finch.

'He was, like, a strong character – you know? Big personality, filled the room. Expected me to be the same, but I never was. I wasn't a bully like him either, but that's another story. Now I wonder why he needed to be like that. Insecurity, I suppose. I think I'd grown up trying to emulate him on some level, even adopt his bigoted views, but that wasn't why she was with me. It drove her away. We'd grown apart anyway. Maybe it was just, well, over.'

'You've been working hard, Rob.'

'Yeah – I know. But the therapy is really helpful, isn't it? When else do you sit talking to yourself for hours, trying to understand everything?' Rob was only half joking and Finch laughed at the idea that Dr Lenny was not actually necessary to the process, while aware that she was crucial to it.

'The old arsehole, sorry, *sphinctral specimen*, is dead now anyway. But then I can always pick a fight with him later, I suppose. He wouldn't have liked me talking to you, though, Finch. He'd have said you were hell-bent ...'

'Hell-bent on what?'

'Nah, just hell-bent, mate.'

'Dead, though, you say?'

'Yeah, a while back. Died in hospital after a car crash. Lately I've wondered if he was actually droned here for treatment, though. I heard that can happen because the island's hospital is so defunct and outdated. Not that I'm desperate to see him again. But you wonder who else that you thought had died actually just left. Bet they think *I* died.'

'I've had exactly the same thought about my mum. She died in hospital and we didn't even see her.'

'Can't you use your *ooga-booga* to contact her, psychic boy?' Rob made mocking spell-casting gestures with his hands that made Finch laugh.

'Apparently not, yet – maybe one day. Anyway. How are your tech focus classes going with Phil?'

'Interesting. I'm learning coding – like programming computers. Turns out it was a computer I was using on the island to broadcast the entertainment.'

'Wow. It must have been pretty well disguised?' Finch was bemused.

'It was – and old, compared to what they have here. They called it the Machine. Obviously I had no idea, so I didn't question it.' Rob saw Koo and Tia looking for a table and whistled for their attention. 'Oy! We're here.'

'Whistling? No, no, Rob. You'll be considered ignorant,' joked Koo as they approached with trays of food and sat down.

Over the course of the meal it emerged that Koo and Rob got on very well, and seemed to like each other. Tia was horrendously sarcastic and blunt to them about it, causing much embarrassed coyness.

10 GRANDAD'S FRUIT BOWL

Finch was slightly late for enlightenment class but Jude seemed not to notice. He was preoccupied with an envelope that he waved at Finch. 'Here, brother – for you,' he said jovially, smiling at Finch as he handed it over, one hand on Finch's arm. As Finch took the letter he observed a kind of parental joy on Jude's face.

'SCI-PSY. They're offering me a job. Good grief.' Jude was brimming with pride at his prodigy. 'I can take it immediately on leaving here and live at SCI-PSY. It's a level-three sensitive position. God – is that really the salary?'

Jude looked at the letter. 'Yes – they look after their sensitives. I used to work there myself. You'll love it, Finch. Will you take it?' The excitement in Jude's voice was infectious.

Finch realised he had no idea how being a sensitive

could actually be a paid job, so asked, 'What's it actually doing?'

'Everything you do here, developing your skills, channelling, remote viewing, general precognitive and energy reading. Nothing you can't handle by the time you leave. We will make sure you're fully prepared.'

Jude allowed Finch some time for the offer to sink in before suggesting they move on to some exercises.

***

That night, Finch dreamt of his mother. They were sitting together on the ground by the koi carp pond, watching the fish in the early light of dawn.

'You know, there's a counsellor down there,' Finch said, pointing into the water.

'Grandad's fruit bowl?' asked his mother, who had just released a large teal dragonfly from her cupped hands.

'Go on, then,' said Finch, but he was becoming aware that his face was being pawed at, and began to rouse towards consciousness. Sir had been sleeping on Finch's bed and had woken him up with an absent-minded paw, dream-running frantically on Finch's chin.

He got up for some water, sat on the sofa and watched the pre-sunrise sky through the glass wall. His room was dark and the world felt quiet as he considered the dream he'd just experienced. Finch often dreamt they were together again, just hanging out. It always hurt to wake up to the reality that she was gone. No matter how hard Finch tried, he couldn't completely accept that she was just somewhere else now; the grief was too entrenched, too established. Somewhere in his mind, the question of why she wasn't with him if she still existed hovered in the background. She could still be alive; it was likely if she'd had similar abilities to Finch. He thought about Grandad's fruit bowl. He missed his grandfather's company so much. Finch felt heavy, as though suddenly bearing the full impact of the grief he'd been happy to shelve while distracted by his passion for Olga. He broke down. He knew it was illogical. They were both still out there, in one form or another, but it was their day-to-day absence that hurt. They weren't in his life any more, and he still needed them.

He felt a paw on his knee. Sir had come to investigate and was attempting to comfort him. The dog climbed up on to the sofa and lay across his lap, allowing Finch to lean over and hug him as he wept.

Some time later Finch awoke, feeling the sun on his torso. He and Sir had slept curled up together on the sofa. It was time for tech class, so Finch got himself together and left. En route, he was warmed by thoughts of Sir's compassion and emotional intelligence. He would miss the dog when Sir was returned to Olga's chalet later. They'd become friends.

***

After tech class, Finch met Olga in the restaurant for dinner. She was back at last. The world became a brighter and far more thrilling place as she took a seat opposite him and they said their hellos.

'How is my lord and master?' asked Olga.

'I'm fine, thanks,' responded Finch, dryly.

'Not you. Sir! I trust you saw to his every need?'

'I did. And he mine.' Olga looked confused as to what Finch could possibly have meant. 'He actually did – he's really quite a lovely little guy behind all that aloof pretension.'

'You'll need to explain,' Olga said, appearing genuinely mystified.

Finch took a breath, considering how he should word the onslaught of night-time grief he'd weathered. 'Well, I had this dream, about my mum. We were hanging out together. She'd just suggested a game of Grandad's fruit bowl – we play that sometimes, in my dreams. Suppose we used to play it a lot before she died, too. Anyway, when I awoke I felt pretty desolate – you know, missing her. Then I began thinking about Grandad too, and it got to me, badly. I don't know – it all seemed quite lonely and dark at the time. Sir, though, he put a paw on my leg, jumped up and basically hugged me. He was really compassionate. We woke up hours later still curled up together – he's adorable.'

Olga looked dumbfounded. 'He actually did *all* that?'

'Yeah. Seriously – he was really empathetic.'

'Never. *Never* has he done *anything* like that before. In his whole life.'

'Oh, right. Well – maybe he's going soft?'

'Wow. That'll take a while to process in my head. God … I need to think about something else before my brain crashes. You mentioned Grandad's fruit bowl – what's that?'

'Oh, well, my grandad, he had this comedy fruit bowl – I mean it was a regular bowl, but it never had any fruit in it, well rarely anyway. It would be full of all this other, random stuff. It became a running joke – the things you'd find in there… A bronze-age axe head, some pegs. Maybe a few springs. Mum and I used to laugh at it. Anyway, it ended up as a game.'

'Fishing for random stuff?'

'No, it was like a memory game. So she would say, "I made the fundamental error of looking into Grandad's fruit bowl and I found … a wizened tangerine that on eating was discovered to be actually fizzy." Then I'd have to repeat it, and add another arbitrary object, but using totally different words. So, I'd say, "I peered naively into Grandad's fruit bowl and I found a zombie citrus that, on being consumed, was found to be sparkling, and I found a ball of elastic bands with a small doll's leg sticking out of it" – true story, by the way – and so on.'

'I like it.' Olga was laughing at the image of the doll's leg elastic band ball. 'And you won by …?'

'By the other person saying a pre-used word, or allowing themselves to be corpsed – making them laugh, that is. Or forgetting something, of course. We worked out a complex points system but never stuck to it.'

'Your mum sounds loads of fun. You must have got on well.'

'We did. I could talk to her about anything. She was quite young in her outlook – open-minded. Kind of wise, really. I miss having her around.' Finch felt a surge of emotion that was not convenient right now and which he'd rather quell, if possible.

'Well. Don't be sad. You'll see her again.' Olga said, as though puzzled at Finch's emotion. There was a silence as she studied Finch, who was not meeting her gaze. 'Are you okay?' she asked.

'Erm, give me a minute. Sorry – it gets to me sometimes.' Finch was pinching the bridge of his nose, looking down.

'But Finch, you know she's not *actually* gone, right?' There was an air of shock in Olga's voice, as though Finch was being obtuse, or laughably childlike in his thinking.

'Yes, well, it still—' he began, but Olga interrupted.

'My Finch, think of the Q-Pho.'

'You're right, of course,' Finch conceded, after taking a deep breath. 'So, how was your appointment? Let's talk about something else.'

'Oh, okay … My lung has nearly recovered. No more treatment, hopefully.' Olga said this as though Finch were fully aware of her health situation, which he wasn't. They'd never discussed it because he was wary of intruding, so had never asked.

'Your lung? What was wrong with it? But you smoke,' said Finch, regretting it immediately as Olga shot him a fiery, irritated look.

'Yeah, sometimes – how do you know that, Finch? And have you discussed *personal boundaries* with Dr Lenny or Claudine yet?'

'I-I can smell faint smoke sometimes – figured it was coming from you,' he said, attempting the most casual tone he could muster, and avoiding the truth. *Oh, I inadvertently spied on you while trying remote viewing – boundary thoroughly stampeded upon …* 'Anyway, that's great news.

How are you feeling?'

'Fine, but Finch, haven't you got news of your own?' she asked, clearly aware of his job offer. The mood lifted as he handed her the letter.

'Oh, my Finch – that's just great. Are you going to accept?'

'Yes – I think so.'

'Wine! Let's celebrate.'

They drank a toast to post-AU freedom. There was an unspoken understanding that this independence could mean the possibility of being more openly together, something for which Finch would have been deeply grateful as they admired each other across the table, unable to touch or hold hands. Instead, they intertwined their ankles and made plans to collect Sir from Finch's room after dinner.

***

'How much do you know about the cycle structure of the non-corporeal life?' asked Jude at the beginning of Finch's enlightenment focus session.

Finch thought about his many other classes and the knowledge he'd so far accumulated. 'The recent film we were shown explained it a little – that Earth is almost a secondary school level learning environment for the evolution of soul energy. So, we come here, take physical form in order to learn from experience, and we come back repeatedly until we get it right?'

'Yes, that is a very matter-of-fact explanation. It's much more beautiful than that though, Finch. It is understood that Source, God, Spirit, the universe, whatever you want to call the higher intelligence, well, it split itself into tiny fractions in order to have life experience and learn, to better itself, and we are those fractions, Finch – every living thing here. The point of these many lives is to become progressively then supremely enlightened, so that we may join with the Source once again. We all return with our learning and it helps the Source evolve. Some of us have volunteered to return, even though we have finished our learning, just to help raise Earth's vibration. I suspect you're one of those, Finch.'

'From what I understand, much of this is not yet scientifically proven though, so mostly circumstantial – secondary information. It's just the existence of soul energy that's actually proven – is that right?' asked Finch.

'Yes. That's the challenge. It's the non-corporeal evolution that we are trying to establish. Your job at SCI-PSY will be to try and help decipher some of this using your skills. The Q-Pho tech has evolved into different tools to measure sensitive experience in new ways, so it will all become scientific fact soon enough. Much of this has been known about through hypnotists, mediums, energy workers, for decades. It's just that we need the next piece of the puzzle now.'

'Okay. So we're all students here. Is that why Earth is such a mess? Claudine Faroque gave us a rough impression of world politics earlier – it was quite perturbing. There seem to be such gaping chasms between the modern world and less developed areas. And some of the characters in power simply shouldn't be allowed near a banana, let alone given authority to run a country.'

'Brother, you are right, of course, but you need to see the bigger picture here. You see, we may reincarnate with the same soul group repeatedly – maybe playing different roles each time. Perhaps we are learning about a particular subject, let's say abuse of power, for example. So in one life we may be the abuser, in another, the abused and powerless, in another, the close family of one or the other, and so on, until we have understood it from all perspectives. That is why we need to be open and forgiving to those who may do things we find unthinkable – they are learning, as are we, and so are those they affect. When people are medically brought back from death – apart from not wanting to return because it is so full of indescribable, unconditional love there, and so miserable here by comparison – they all describe experiencing a life review, a panoramic and instantaneous rerun of every minute of their lives, experienced in one single moment. They also actually *feel* the emotions of those around them – so if they hurt someone, they then feel the hurt that person felt. If they helped someone, they feel the gratitude, the positivity it brought. It makes for good learning. The point is, though, to become so enlightened that we can become part of the Source again, and no longer need to keep returning. Buddhism has proven to be right about a lot of this.'

'So we may be on our thirtieth life? Why don't we remember them, and our purpose for coming back, come to that?' asked Finch.

'Ah,' Jude continued, 'during interfacing – channelling, with higher entities – that question is often met with the response that it wouldn't be a test if we knew why we were here. We all make a plan before coming: what our challenges will be, who our friends and partners will be, how we all affect each other, the main themes of our lives – failures and successes – how we live and die. Lessons, all of it. And thirtieth? More like thousands. We've been everything before becoming human. We start as the more basic life forms just to gain an understanding of living as a physical being. Then we move on to the more complex creatures, animals, humans. Have you had any memories bubble up during meditation – of being someone else before, or anything along those lines?'

'No, not really – but I have had some weird experiences. I wasn't meditating but I felt like I went back in time, as I told you. It was like a memory, but I felt I was actually there again. Nothing important. Just odd.'

'Remind me – what was the memory?' asked Jude.

'It was just of Seb. We were having dinner. He'd just reacted to somethi—' Finch stopped. Now it was clear. Momentarily he was back there and saw it plainly. As Finch looked into Seb's eyes from his current perspective, he knew undoubtedly that his own request for information on his mother was the reason Seb had disappeared 'researching' and had swiftly become unavailable. There could be only one reason for that. Next, as though switching channels, Finch was in the mind aquarium for the first time, observing Dr Lenny's many files that read 'Henry' on the side. Surely these could not all have held information on Finch. There were so many files, yet he'd only just arrived at the AU.

'… something? Where've you gone, Finch?' Jude asked, obviously wondering why Finch had just stopped, mid-word.

'Something I asked. I asked about my mother.' Finch was saying this almost to himself, astonished that he'd overlooked the obvious all this time. 'He knows. He knows what happened to her. That's why he's been unavailable.'

'Finch, my friend – you'll see her again. It's

dragging you down, I can feel it. You have to move on. This was her plan, and yours. Let her go, brother! And your grandad, too. Release them, Finch. Live *your* life now.'

'Do *you* know?' As he asked, Finch sensed a wall of solid energy rising up like a drawbridge in front of Jude.

'I'm level four, Finch. You're asking the wrong person. But it's not good for you, my friend. You must try to release it. She's *not* dead. There's no such thing. You know that – no matter what. This was the plan. Acceptance will free you!'

Finch knew that although Jude seemed to be withholding something, he clearly wasn't able to share it. Jude and Finch had formed a bond of understanding between fellow sensitives that Finch was loath to jeopardise. He searched inside for a connection with his higher self, the Finch that would be able to note the development and move on with dignity, rational and composed. There it was. He breathed deeply. It would all become clear. He felt the reassurance as knowledge, a certainty transported straight into his mind from a wiser place.

Jude was watching him closely, and Finch knew he had detected the shift in his energy.

'You're doing amazing work, Finch,' he said, with complete empathy for Finch's situation. 'Amazing work.'

***

Recent tech classes had covered much about computers and the internet, even social media and various forms of online dating. The students had, under close supervision, set up their own online bank accounts using a working internet connection. The initial danger of accessing the internet had diminished as their time at the AU progressed – they now knew much of what to expect on leaving the AU and had been given the facts in a carefully organised sequence so as to avoid mental melt-down due to information overload. They had recently been asked not to interact too much with any newcomers who sported red or orange gulls, so as not to influence their learning pattern. Finch now understood why the established Leavers hadn't appeared to notice the new Leavers' presence when he'd first arrived at the AU.

The remaining subjects to cover in tech class related more to the practicalities of living on the tech-centric mainland: how to operate self-driving cars, to use public services, catch a drone cab, synchronise all personal tech and security with domestic systems in the home.

On returning to his room, Finch discovered Sir wearing a note that read, 'Excuse me. Yes, you. You may wish to walk me, or regret it. My usual help has a holo-conference meeting with SCI-PSY. God speed.'

'It'll be my honour.' Finch responded directly to Sir, as though the dog absolutely understood. They walked the grounds together, Sir trotting in his usual noble, elegant way, Finch strutting alongside, enjoying the company of his aristocratic friend.

Finch's mind was occupied with the many questions raised by Seb's avoidance of him since they had discussed the subject of Finch's mum. His gut feeling was to trust Seb, although he wasn't sure whether this was some form of denial – a concept relatively new to Finch. However, Seb was undoubtedly in possession of some information that he intended to keep from Finch. Maybe the information was unpleasant. Perhaps that was the reason for Seb's absence. Again, Finch's higher self found a fracture in his troubled thoughts through which to drip feed the reassuring message 'It's okay – trust Seb.' Finch, aware of this feeling and its apparent origin, from a more enlightened level of existence, resisted further paranoia relating to who else might possibly be holding information from him – Dr Lenny, Jude? Even Olga? No, he thought. Seb is a decent person and so are the others. He could feel their good intentions within their energy and chose to trust them all, whatever they were holding back.

Finch took a new route for variety but was starting to feel the presence of the perimeter as though the place had reduced in size, or perhaps he'd grown. He considered whether Sir felt the same. Perhaps not. Sir had stopped a few paces back and wasn't moving.

'Sir, come on. Sir … Sir?' Nothing. Sir simply looked at Finch. 'What's wrong, Sir?' Finch knelt down to inspect Sir for answers but could see nothing that would cause the dog to stall like this. He tried pulling Sir's lead, but Sir refused to move. 'Come on. Let's go back, then. Yes? I'll have the butler draw you a bath.' With that, Sir stood and started walking back, limping slightly. Finch watched, concerned. It seemed to be Sir's hind left leg that was causing the problem. Finch stopped him and checked his paw for thorns, but he could detect no obvious reason for the limp.

When they reached Finch's room, Sir lay down on the rug and was asleep within minutes. Finch connected to Reiki and placed his hands on the dog, hoping to ease whatever was causing the pain, and feeling drowsy himself. He was sound asleep when Olga's presence became a feature of his dreamy haze.

'Finch,' she whispered. 'Finch.' He started to laugh to himself. His mother had just offered up the most amusing yet of random fruit bowl occupants.

'You can't have that. It's abstract,' he said, laughing with his mum by the pond.

'It's a dream, darling boy. I can do anything,' she said through a playful, poppy-red smile.

'So this is *your* lucid dream, then? I didn't know that was possible.'

'It isn't. Your turn, Finchiebobs.'

'Okay – I stumbled unwittingly across Grandad's fruit bowl of nonsensical gibberish and I found a disembodied toy dog's nose; a sizeable Edam, inside which a family of clog-wearing rodents had set up home; a miniscule glass vial containing an undetermined and ominous blue liquid; and a low-level sense of impending doom wearing a leotard, which is thoroughly against the rules.' Finch was laughing. The image of the leotard-wearing-doom-demon was still with him as Olga's presence transported him gently from one world to another.

'What's so funny?' asked Olga, sounding entertained by Finch's sleep laughter.

'Oh – fruit bowl – doom, I think. What was it? Hello.' He kissed Olga with his still smiling lips. She was far more interesting than the dream he could hardly recall. 'There's something up with Sir's leg – he was limping,' he said with kindness. Olga inspected Sir but could find nothing to explain it. She said she'd keep an eye on him and have him checked.

***

Dr Lenny met Finch's comments with a look of concern. He'd just explained his reasons for suspecting that Seb was holding something back from him. Finch examined his gull, deep in thought. It now glowed light purple. Just white to go, he understood, then his world would change again.

'What I'm hearing is that you do, deep down, trust Seb,' she concluded.

'Yes, I think so, but I just can't seem to be able to let it go like everyone thinks I should. She was my mum. She could still be out there somewhere. I miss her.'

'I understand, Finch. We wouldn't have a term for closure if it wasn't a necessity for us all, no matter what our background.'

'Yes – it's as though the knowledge of a definite afterlife is rendering life's day-to-day issues irrelevant. I have trouble with that. Someone disappears, supposedly deceased but probably not, it seems, and I'm meant to just accept that. It makes me think of something Grandad used to say. It was that in life, if you're lucky, you get to play all the parts – the baby, the infant, the teenager, the professional, the parent, the grandparent, the old person. There are many roles, many lives, when you think about it. I suppose his philosophy was based on actually engaging with life *here*, rather than having your mind half in the clouds, in another existence and many other incarnations. I get that.'

'It's good to have balance, Finch. It sounds like you're grappling with assimilating the Discovery into your existing framework. I'm actually glad to see you making that progress, although I appreciate you may not see it in positive terms right now.' After a long pause, during which Finch didn't respond, she added, 'I noticed you studying your gull. How do you feel about its progression to purple?'

'That – oh, I'm not sure. On the one hand I'd like to go. See the world. I feel more … ready. And I could find out what happened to her. On the other, it's … trepidation. Being thrown into another deep end, I suppose. I don't relish the idea of that.' What Finch was avoiding was the Olga question – what would happen? Would they see each other as much, or would they still have to remain a secret if she were to be his guide at SCI-PSY? A negative frame of mind could be tempted to view it as a lose-lose situation, but for the wonderful fact that they were together at last. This unknown factor troubled Finch daily. Their relationship had grown into something more serious; they were desperately in love, and the thought of long stints apart probably explained the sense of impending doom that his mother had referred to, albeit without the leotard. There was a silence while Finch considered his own feelings about the situation. He wanted so much to give them air, but knew this was absolutely not an option.

'I feel as though you may be holding something back, Finch,' said Dr Lenny, slightly unnerving him.

'There are people here, well, I'll miss,' he said, honestly.

'You've grown attached – that's natural. You've been through a lot, and fast. You know there are many ways to keep in touch. You must have learned about holo-calling in tech class by now?'

'Yes – maybe it's just fear of leaving. So much new upheaval after leaving the island, too.'

'That is natural, Finch. A common experience.'

***

Olga's gaze was fixed on Finch's gull. 'I've never disliked that ultraviolet colour as much as I do right now,' she said. They were having dinner together. Olga was looking at Finch with apprehension. He was accustomed to her taking control and being strong. To see her so concerned about his inevitable departure felt at once reassuring yet heartbreaking. She was usually the one with the answers, but appeared to be in need of reassurance herself, which did not bode well in Finch's mind.

'Whatever happens, it's up to us to make it work,' Finch said, hoping to convince himself, too. 'Jude says existence doesn't happen *to* us, it happens *with* us – we can steer it, decide how things work out. It's the law of attraction, apparently.'

'I like your positivity, Finch. Let's talk about something else. How are the other Leavers doing?'

'Rob and Koo seem to be together. I'm not sure, but

it looks that way. He is a changed man. I was talking to him about his development; his energy is totally different now. He credits it to Dr Lenny.'

'I've noticed. He seems more open, somehow. That is quite common with Leavers after some time here. They shake off old attitudes that they realise they'd actually inherited. The mindset of their parents and grandparents is usually a strong influence, powerful enough to desire island life to start with.'

'Yes – I still can't understand how my grandad thought it a good idea back then. He must have been a different person.'

'Well, the world was a different place – scarier, what with the extreme reactions people were having.'

'Yeah, I know – the historical facts make sense. It's just Grandad making that choice that I can't understand.' Olga's response was silence so Finch shifted to a different subject. 'Rob was saying his dad was a character – the life and soul, but too demanding on Rob and a bigoted bully. Sounded pretty dire … at least Grandad was a decent person. Rob thinks his dad could still be alive. He apparently died in a car crash so could have been droned to the mainland for treatment. He said he'd heard that can happen sometimes. Made me think about Mum. Maybe she was brought here for treatment – if she *was* actually ill?'

'Finch – you're not still pursuing this thing with your mother?' Olga had an impatient tone that threw him.

'Yes. Absolutely – wouldn't you?'

'No. If she's transcended then you'll see her again. You will anyway – whatever happened. If she's here somewhere, then she *left* you.' Olga quickly softened her tone as though she'd heard her words sounding harsh. 'I'm sorry, Finch, but you know how it all works now, so I don't understand why you can't let go a little. Searching endlessly for answers is not going to help you. I want you to be happy and this obsession is absolutely not having that effect. It's holding you back.'

'I can't *just let go a little* – she was my mum. Why can't you understand that? It's something I *need* answers to.' Finch recognised how perplexed he was by Olga's lack of empathy. He looked for a better perspective and thought for a moment. This always seemed an inflammatory subject, one where their natural philosophical frameworks appeared to clash in a frustrating stalemate. The last thing Finch wanted was to argue with Olga, especially now, with their probable parting imminent. In a moment, he found a deeper understanding that she'd grown up in a very different world. 'Why don't we decide not to discuss this any more? I will go about my search for her somehow, and we won't talk about it. I don't want to argue with you, Olga. I, well, you know –

I love you.'

Olga's expression melted into one of love. 'I'm sorry, Finch. I forget sometimes that your programming is so different to mine. And I love you so much. I just want you to be happy.'

***

The days seemed to flash by, accelerated by Finch and Olga's acute awareness of their limited time together. Olga hadn't yet received confirmation of whether or not she would join Finch at SCI-PSY as his guide, and suspected that therefore she wasn't being allocated the assignment. Guides were not always assigned to new employees and it was possible he didn't warrant that level of support, given his progress at the AU. They discussed the many variables and how they would approach each potential situation, which allowed some comforting veneer of control.

Finch awoke to find that his gull had finally morphed into white light. He spent a while looking deeply into its soft glow, saddened that his time at the AU was nearly over. It was up to him now. He would decide when to leave. His job offer was open and he could start any time. He'd accepted the position and simply had to give SCI-PSY a week's notice. His classes had all finished with the exception of counselling and his focus sessions with Jude. Those would continue for as long as he remained at the AU.

Finch had relied increasingly on meditation to help him through the darker moments of uncertainty. He found that just fifteen minutes of transcendental meditation could vastly improve his outlook, casting a lighter perspective, throwing any concerns into proportion. He usually emerged from his inner world with new insight on the relevance of any issues he'd been wrestling with. Often, when considering Olga's views on his curiosity about his mother, Finch would find himself seeing it as genuinely unimportant; he and Olga had a deep connection and this issue was simply a result of their fundamentally different backgrounds.

Jude had taught Finch some 'manifestation' techniques relating to what he referred to as 'the law of attraction'. Finch had come to understand that this was a way of thinking geared towards achieving the desired outcome in any situation by positive visualisation techniques and actively *feeling* the emotion of the preferred end result, be it relief, joy, gratitude, all prior to the outcome of the situation in question. Jude explained that everything, *everything*, in our world is governed by laws of one kind or another, and we were no different; we could create our own reality with our fundamental expectations about how things would pan out.

Jude explained in detail how, according to the law of attraction, our thoughts were energy vibrations – they were *things*, and not completely passive as previously believed.

Finch learned that we were like satellites, broadcasting our expectations and general mood out into the world, and what we receive back is a reflection of our state of mind – often of our own self-imposed restrictions. It was an impersonal system, like electricity, and simply responded to thought and emotion. Jude described how we usually limit ourselves unconsciously based on our past experiences, or our 'paradigm', a term used to describe our own patterns of self-inflicted restriction. These assumed limitations had usually been learned during our upbringing – sometimes from parents living in survival mode, and not in the mindset of abundance, so we may grow up expecting struggle, which the universe would then reflect back to us by presenting the people, events or situations that created struggle, for example. Jude emphasised that the aim was for Finch to rid himself of his paradigm and begin to expect abundance – full spectrum success in all areas of his life.

Finch learned that, fundamentally, the law of attraction opened up the mind to new possibilities allowing progress to be made, achieving results beyond those of previous expectations. By employing these techniques, he could have more control, harness his own thoughts to attract any required outcome, magnetising the right elements for the desired result to him quickly and easily. Jude cited many accounts from people who'd experienced near death, who had returned from discussions with their spirit guides, bringing a new understanding that this was indeed a reality, and not just goal setting or confirmation bias, as had been the assumption prior to the Discovery.

Finch steered his thoughts towards positivity in line with his new understanding of the law of attraction; he actively felt the relief and delight at the oncoming news that he and Olga could remain together at SCI-PSY, as though it had already happened. He spent time in total gratitude that they were able to continue their relationship and that, in fact, their situation was improved there. He felt it as though it was done, as though he was looking back at it and there were no other possibilities. It was inevitable. He felt positive as a result of this visualisation, and could almost feel its self-fulfilling cycle at work.

During focus class with Jude, they meditated together for increasingly extended periods, sometimes undergoing a shared experience – as though they were together in their inner worlds. Finch would frequently feel himself to be in a calm and loving place of infinite consciousness, and he often felt Jude to be there with him.

Finch had cultivated, at an enhanced pace, a sophisticated comprehension of the non-corporeal world. During meditation he'd held what he felt were conversations with familiar-seeming enlightened entities who transferred knowledge into his mind before he'd even finished forming the question. The communication seemed telepathic and their wisdom immeasurable. He could feel how it was possible to exist in several places at once, how the future could be shaped by thought alone, and how the restrictions of time and space were not as mandatory to the human existence as he'd previously thought – they were almost constructs, and not universal law when it came to the world of energy. Time did not really exist and space was a complex, multi-dimensional network.

11 THE ISLAND

Finch would drift from his focus classes with Jude to counselling, his approach less confined, more uplifted, his perspective on his past coming from a higher place, a place where actually, none of it mattered in the slightest. It was more about curiosity than feeling the need for help, now. On this occasion Dr Lenny was wearing a casual white suit that almost glowed against the deep tones of the room.

'Hi,' said Finch, smiling. 'Looks like we're coordinated.' He held up his palm, displaying the soft light of his newly white gull.

'So we are,' she responded with a knowing smile. 'So, how does that make you feel, Finch?' was the inevitable question that followed.

'I feel, well – balanced.' He almost surprised himself. He thought back over his long meditation and the thoughts that had presented themselves. 'I have a better view of things now – even odd things from my past that pop up when I'm in meditation. I understand them better afterwards.'

'Tell me more about that.'

'Okay. Today, I found myself back in my church lodgings on the island for a split second. I was alone in my room, playing my cello. He wasn't visible, but I felt the presence of Akton. I'm not sure if you remember – he used to have a go at me every now and then. And I used to let him, sort of. But, well, when I was back there, I could feel the *reality* of the situation – the real truth of it. I was doing it for *him*. I know that sounds like an excuse, almost, but I could feel the bigger picture during meditation and the truth of it emerged. Akton needed that experience, his soul, I mean, and I let him have it at my expense because I could easily handle it. I felt this epiphany that I was actually teaching *him* something. At the time, I wasn't aware of this. I was so wrapped up in my own problems, I couldn't think straight, and part of me just found it easier to put up with him – to suffer it. But, the thing is, I was always aware that I could have easily stopped him at any point. I did, eventually.'

'Wow. That's, well, very enlightened, Finch. You've made *such* progress.'

'I know it sounds, from an earthly perspective, like I

am trying to superimpose the notion that I had some control over an unpleasant situation, but that's not it. I always felt *above* him – I genuinely pitied his low-minded existence – and I always knew I was so much more advanced than him somehow. He was to be casually endured in the same way you might, say, bat away a persistent fruit fly, or a nagging child. I mean, it was a kind of *knowing* that surfaced about this, not a theory.'

Dr Lenny took a moment, allowing Finch to reflect before commenting. 'It sounds like a realisation to me, rather than a coping mechanism, Finch. I don't see that you'd need to find a coping mechanism at this point. His treatment of you has only come up once, to my recollection, and you have never seemed traumatised by it, so my feeling is that you are making progress spiritually, and not making excuses, as you put it. Did you feel any forgiveness towards him?'

'I felt compassion for him – a relaxed kind of understanding that he needed to experience that behaviour in order to learn. I suppose we've all been through it during our various lives, in order to grow wiser. I felt less judgemental of him – in the same way you wouldn't judge a child, who maybe deliberately trod on an ant as a toddler, to be a bad child.'

'You certainly have grown, Finch. How are you feeling about everything else?'

'The convoy has ended. I mean, when I first came to you, I always felt that there was a queue, like a convoy of issues that were all awaiting my attention. I'd deal with one and the next would immediately be there, demanding attention at the front of the queue. That's gone. Sometimes I find myself focusing on detail – thinking about some tiny issue that I could turn into a mountain. Then I realise I'm finding things to bring here, to you. I suppose I'm delaying facing it – that I'm okay, I could go.' The realisation occurred as he said it. A silence followed as he took in his own words.

'You look surprised, Finch,' Dr Lenny commented.

'I-I am … I just heard myself say I'm ready to go, and I hadn't wanted to admit it before.' Finch thought for a moment about the AU in general, and his daily existence there. 'I suppose I'm aware of how small this place is now. It felt huge when I arrived, but now it's, well, restricting. I've eaten all the food on the menus over and over again. I know the grounds like the back of my hand. I suppose I would have been ready to go a while ago if it hadn't been for … friends I've made here. Even so, I started to feel frustrated during my last classes, as though I'd like to stop talking about the mainland, and actually experience it for myself – to get off *this* island.' He stopped abruptly, recognising what he'd just said, and the force with which he felt the sentiment.

'Finch, when this place has started to feel like an

island, it's time to go,' Dr Lenny said, gently.

Finch was privately astonished that his own feelings had made themselves known to him at such a time and in such a way. He looked at Dr Lenny, experiencing a combination of poignancy and trepidation at the prospect of his suddenly very real departure. 'There will be mixed feelings about leaving, Finch,' she said, as though reading his mind. 'After three months it is normal to feel frustrated, almost contained here, wanting to experience more. Those feelings can come into conflict with the need for ongoing security, for an end to upheaval, the desire to stay with the known rather than risk the unknown. You've built relationships, made friends, become a whole new person, gained so much knowledge. You are ready, though, Finch. Your feelings of anxiety around leaving are to be expected, but don't let them control you. The tail should not be wagging the dog.'

Finch left, knowing exactly what he had to do.

***

Finch returned to his room having informed Clydie that he was ready to leave the AU. She was to notify SCI-PSY and let them have the official week's notice on his behalf, as instructed in his offer letter. He thought about Olga and how she'd react but he knew that, had he awaited her response, he might have lacked the courage to make the move. Now, it was done. When Olga came to his door he could see the energy pulsing through it in waves. Anger, he suspected. He opened the door. She looked hurt.

'You've given notice without discussing it with me.'

'I had to. I'm sorry. I knew I wouldn't be able to do it if I thought about it for even a minute longer.' Finch closed the door behind her. They sat side by side on the sofa. 'I was in counselling and it emerged that I was ready – *very* ready to leave. And yes, it's painful and uncertain and alarming and I didn't want to do it, but I had to. I can't stay here forever, living in fear of how we will survive if we're separated – we must survive. We must deal with this and make it work.'

'I have had confirmation from my superiors that I won't be your guide there. I had requested not to be, on the basis that you're sufficiently independent now. You no longer need a guide. I did that because I thought, well, that we could be more open about all this if I weren't your guide. I don't know which is worse – the idea of a long-distance relationship or being together but having to conceal it constantly because of the risk it could destroy my career. But now, you're going so soon. They're collecting you and Rob in two days, Finch.'

'Two … I thought I'd have a week?'

'Rob had already requested the transfer and they want to take you together. He's going there also, to work in the tech team.'

'Oh. I didn't know. Two days,' said Finch, attempting to absorb the unexpected hastening of the situation.

'Yes,' Olga said as her tear-filled eyes met his.

'I'm sorry, I should have talked to you. I just thought I wouldn't have the strength to go through with it if—'

Olga interrupted him, taking his hand. 'No – I should've told you I'd requested not to be your guide. Then you would have known. We wouldn't be in this mess.'

They sat and hugged for a while, breathing each other in while they still could. Finch felt the Reiki energy flowing through his hands into her back. He hadn't meant to channel the energy; it seemed to happen of its own accord sometimes, when he was feeling loving and compassionate, or someone was in need of it.

'There's lots to do,' Olga said, as though her mood had shifted. 'We must look at your accommodation options. Did you tell Clydie you'd live at SCI-PSY?'

'Yes.'

'Okay – let me message her. That's not the best option. There are some apartments nearby which are far superior – and more private. Let's go for some food and we can use my device to figure it all out.'

They headed down to the canteen and sat outside together in the most secluded spot available. Olga showed

Finch images of apartments that were available near SCI-PSY. They were subsidised and not free like the on-site rooms, but by London prices, not expensive. They trawled through the specs and chose the best option: a modern apartment within a beautiful old converted mews house, one of several in a cobbled courtyard perpendicular to the narrow street. The apartment was fully furnished and the 'mom-tech' – a slang term for the dom-tech due to its butler-esque role, Olga explained – would be prepared and answerable only to Finch's identity. He'd set up voice ID along with retinal and fingerprint scans during the tech class when they'd opened their bank accounts, and those identifiers were all he'd need to access any product or service, because they were automatically linked to his bank account. SCI-PSY would be transferring a lump sum into Finch's account imminently for relocation costs, so it would all work out. They put down the deposit on the apartment using Finch's identifiers and it was as simple as that.

Next came printing some new clothes, attire more appropriate to the corporate ethos at SCI-PSY. Olga persuaded Finch to go for darker tones with pale neutrals, and smarter, cleaner lines conveying a formal look. Everyone wore dark tones there, and sometimes super pale shades, she explained, describing the look as almost monochrome, but with darkest navy and tinted blacks paired with neutral pale tones, rather than simply black and white. It wasn't a uniform, but everyone seemed to understand that it suited the organisation.

They decided on several outfits consisting of smarter slim-leg trousers and tops whose closest surviving relative may have been a shirt, but Finch could see they had little in common now – these were made of shirting fabrics, but lacked the button placket, the cuffs and seams, all the visual code that conventionally equalled a shirt to Finch's mind. The openings were either angled, like a raglan seam, or maybe an invisible zip at the back. The collars, if there were any, were small and neat, standing up like a grandad shirt, or asymmetrical and nothing like the traditional collar shape Finch would have expected to find on a shirt. They appeared highly tailored, and there was little other detail, which balanced the contemporary edge of their existing features well. It was a new level of smart for Finch. Then there were jackets, shoes, accessories. Finch insisted on some flashes of colour within the accessories and kept the jackets simple, some lacking collars and lapels completely. He liked the look of a range of fine-knit polo-neck jumpers, so added them to his new wardrobe and considered it complete. Next, Olga contacted the AU porters who brought various containers to Finch's room so he could pack up his belongings.

***

It was Finch and Rob's final full day at the AU. Their rooms were cleared and the containers ready to be collected early the following morning. They were to attend a last Leavers' class followed by drinks, to see them off in good spirits.

Koo and Tia were also due to leave, but weren't headed to the SCI-PSY headquarters. Instead, Tia was to study medicine and Koo had enrolled on a course to train as a drone pilot, inspired by Rob's tale of ocean rescue.

Finch sat through the final class with mixed feelings. The purpose of the class seemed largely to say goodbye and offer some closure. It was also a chance for the AU to reinforce the values they'd taught and for the Leavers to ask any last questions, so quite informal. Jude was present, along with Dr Lenny, Claudine Faroque, Phil, and all of the Guides.

Afterwards, Jude popped open some champagne and Clydie, along with some of the friendlier waiting staff, dropped by to toast the Leavers and wish them well in their new lives. Jude held up a glass to the Leavers. 'Remember, there is only *one* life, but it is *eternal*, so live it well!' he joked, to the amusement of the Leavers and dismal groans of the staff members, who had no doubt suffered the joke on a thousand other occasions. 'We have a gift for each of you, for your onward journeys. Finch? Where is my prodigy, my soul brother?'

'Here, Jude. I'm standing right in front of you. Third

eye need testing?'

'I will miss your sarcasm, my friend. Here. A gift from us.' Jude, smiling warmly, handed Finch a box then continued to hand others out as Finch opened his. It was a device. As he handled it, holo-text grew out from the screen and pulsed in mid-air, reading, 'Hello, Finch,' in large transparent bubble lettering as delicate as freshly blown bubbles and complete with a swirling surface film of rainbow liquid.

Jude continued, 'You'll find you have some contact details pre-programmed in – ours, of course. So please stay in touch and keep us updated on all your adventures. I want to hear from you all on a regular basis. If not, I'll see you on the other side, and we'll have words.'

It was an emotional few hours. Finch did not like goodbyes and this seemed to elongate his suffering, but he understood its necessity. They had all been through so much at the AU. The Leavers had evolved into improved versions of themselves and they needed the chance to thank those who had so carefully guided them through the process.

Afterwards, the four Leavers and their guides continued the party at the bar, enjoying each other's company. It was an optimistic attempt to evade the tinge of sadness that was always present at the end of an era, but this avoidance wasn't remotely effective. Rob seemed particularly distressed to be leaving Koo, having got together so recently and now being forced to take different directions in order to progress their lives on the mainland. They would still see each other, Rob said, but it wasn't going to be as easy, and they'd miss this special time they'd had at the AU. Finch and Olga connected with a look of private knowing, an understanding they were both trying desperately to avoid for fear of becoming beset by uncontainable emotion. They made separate excuses and left, meeting at Finch's room and making good use of the switch that altered the glass to one-way view.

12 THE NEW REALITY

Waking alone as usual, Finch wished Olga could have stayed but she was too aware of the risk it carried and would never do so. His room felt barren, everything all packed up. It made him want to leave quickly, to get it over with. He showered, dressed and answered the door to Sir and Olga. They fell into each other's arms. Even Sir seemed troubled by the parting of ways. They reminded themselves this was not an ending, just a practicality to overcome. Finch tried hard to maintain his visualisation of them enjoying an easier existence once he'd left, and he asked her to envisage the same.

Finch and Olga attended the canteen one final time for breakfast while the porters packed Finch's few boxes and cello into the shipping drone, along with Rob's meagre belongings. He and Rob were to catch a helidrone to London, which would take two hours, and their possessions would follow later.

When the time came, Finch hugged Olga amid the gale and buzzing din of the helidrone, and told her how much he loved her. He ran to the door and climbed inside to join Rob, glancing back to see a distraught Olga standing alone, waves of subdued energy revealing her determination – that she was desperate not to show the devastation she felt at watching Finch fly willingly out of her world. On connecting with this truth, Finch's own anguish plummeted to new depths of its own.

Once the AU had swung low behind them, Finch sought a diversion from his own hurt while sensing a necessity to make small talk with Rob, who was openly distressed at leaving Koo, oblivious to Finch's identical turmoil. Rob's response was at best monosyllabic, forcing Finch to seek an alternative distraction. He found himself studying the palm of his hand, thoughts turning inward. There was no sign of the gull that was once so novel. Clydie had removed it as easily as it had been applied. Although the process had been quick and painless, Finch felt the sting of the gull's absence nonetheless.

Rob and Finch watched through their own personal fogs of emotional suffering as vast swathes of green passed below them, a spattering of stone houses here and there breaking up the expanse of rugged land. They retreated into their own worlds as they observed the glare of bright sunlight bouncing off a stony stream that wound its way through the land, somehow appearing solid and static at this distance, as though switched off, fluidity stalled. Finch searched for something comforting to say to Rob, but he could find only platitudes, nothing meaningful. He knew himself that there was little anyone could say right now that would lift his own spirit, and Rob would be no different.

Eventually the land became more populated, the buildings more densely packed together. The balance shifted and the green areas became fewer, the built-up areas now sprawling, connecting with others as though making contact. London had become evident when clusters of high-rise buildings in implausible forms pierced the distant skyline – rounded, spiked, even leaning, impossible – and, as with so much of the mainland, seemingly constructed entirely from glass. This new vista demanded their attention and they sat fascinated, pointing out one astounding piece of architecture after another.

The helidrone seemed to be entering the heart of the city and touched down on the roof of a mid-level building amid many high-tech skyscrapers and some older, more classical architecture. Their pilot, Francesca, told them that this was SCI-PSY. They'd arrived.

***

The Leavers emerged from the helidrone, stretched their legs and were met by a middle-aged man with bright blue, friendly eyes and white hair, who introduced himself as Clive Vincent.

'I'll be taking you to your accommodation so you can relax, move in and enjoy the weekend before we see you on Monday for your inductions to SCI-PSY. Welcome, Robert, Finch,' he said as he shook their hands with far more force than was necessary.

Clive led the new recruits down through the SCI-PSY headquarters. It appeared that they were in a grand old building that had been refitted with a tech-centric modern interior of a security-conscious kind. They passed glass meeting rooms housing serious-looking, stylish people in discussion over holo-screens that doubled as tabletops. There were multiple security doors that Clive opened just by approaching. Finch could occasionally see the flash of a techtoo on Clive's forehead but it faded when not in use, becoming completely invisible. He couldn't ever catch the particular form of the glow, but it was an almost fluorescent royal blue tone. Clive walked fast, making observation difficult for Finch, who would have liked longer to absorb the environment. Finch was pleased to note that Olga had advised him well in relation to his sartorial choices. There was indeed a monochrome feel to the overall impression of the environment.

When they emerged from a lift they found themselves on a mezzanine level above a foyer. Finch could now appreciate the nature of the original building. There was a gravitas, a solemnity enforced by an immense marble floor, great stone pillars and a series of beautiful and almighty arched windows framing muted stained glass with a stylised, art deco aesthetic.

Clive was leading them towards a magnificent, sweeping, white marble staircase that descended to the ground floor, all old-fashioned grandeur with its curved lines and wide, shallow steps. As they approached it began to move, the steps themselves descending gracefully before flattening, sliding silently underground as they met with the identical marble floor.

Finch had heard talk of escalators but the island's few examples had long ago ceased to operate, suffering from the same lack of investment and diminishing expertise that had permeated much of the island infrastructure. He had seen an escalator in an old precinct once, motionless and lethal looking with its sharp metal ridges and brutal angles. This, however, was a world away. It somehow grew in width as the steps widened towards the base, able to navigate curves and seemingly clad in marble. Its motion was smooth and completely silent. The balustrade alongside the escalator was static but for the top surface, which rolled gently down at the same pace as the steps, curving into a spiral where it met the impressive newel posts that flanked the bull-nose step at the base.

Finch stood on a moving marble step looking backwards, admiring how the top steps emerged before gaining depth and descending. It was hypnotic and Clive had to remind Finch and Rob that they were nearing ground level and that they needed to be ready to step off. Now Finch noticed another curved escalator sweeping in the opposite direction, carrying people up to the mezzanine level. This one was black stone, highly polished and reflective. They curved gently around each other as though trapped in a perpetual dance move from one of the older Hollywood offerings Finch had enjoyed on the island.

Finch and Rob exchanged a look of mutual astonishment as they stepped back on to solid ground, both glancing behind them occasionally in disbelief. Clive had said very little as they'd traversed the interior. He seemed aware that they were absorbing so much new information. Small talk would have been extraneous and very possibly poor quality, given the level of surrounding distraction.

They were delivered to the back of the foyer by the escalator, its black counterpart taking people up from the front entrance. The foyer was busy with smart people coming and going. As they walked towards the multiple sets of doors that led out on to the street, Finch noticed that each person seemed to develop a double image of themselves, a vertical reflection in mid-air, just for a few seconds as they approached a certain invisible threshold which seemed to span the width of the entrance. As they continued walking – without losing pace, Finch noticed – they all passed casually through their own reflections, which instantly vanished on contact.

'What's that?' asked Rob, observing the energy mirror making its presence felt with each new entry and exit. He sounded uneasy.

'Just security. It's a … shield, if you like. It reads the identity of everyone, so no unauthorised people can wander in,' was Clive's explanation. Rob stopped short of the general area and held out a pointed finger, as if to test the safety of it. A small periphery of crackling energy became visible as his finger approached, and he moved it from side to side, apparently mesmerised by the shallow reflection that showed only his hand and forearm, transparent and spectral.

'Ah, Robert and Finch, I take it,' stated a woman who had just entered the building and could not have missed Rob's trepidatious stance and dumbfounded expression, which had drawn some quietly amused attention from passers-by.

'Yes. Morning, Edith,' replied Clive. Edith held out a dainty and beautifully aged hand to greet the new recruits. Her skin was a mass of fine wrinkles, white and delicate. She wore several large rings displaying heavy cut stones of various hues and her long nails were painted darkest navy blue. She was, Finch considered, at least eighty, but had the sharp energy and presence of someone several decades younger. Her outfit was a cinched-in navy suit comprising a shaped jacket and long pencil skirt, with a diaphanous white blouse tucked into the skirt waistband. Her long, dark grey hair was pinned up into a bouffant style – the old-fashioned kind adopted by the island girls whose influences were born of the silver screen, and she wore bold black eye make-up in a style also reminiscent of that era. Edith's demeanour was one of authority and control. Her eyes were piercing and noticeably active, darting over the new recruits, assessing every detail. 'Finch, Robert, this is Edith. She heads up the Defence Division,' said Clive.

'Pleasure to finally meet you, boys. I've heard good things from Seb about you both. Great to have you on board. Clive – look after them. I must go. Meeting with the minister in ten. Ciao.' She was still speaking in her cut-glass British accent as she marched away, the click of her heels resonating around the lobby as percussive accompaniment.

'This way. To your accommodation first, Rob,' said Clive, turning towards a side door rather than guiding them through the energy force field. Once through the security door, they took a glass tunnel to another block which was situated behind the main building. The journey took some time, even though they walked on a travellator that snaked inaudibly through the passageway. They entered the reception of the SCI-PSY accommodation unit and were asked to look into a panel by a door for a retinal scan. This was all the security they'd need until their inductions, at which point they'd have a new techtoo applied, Clive informed them.

When they reached Rob's room on the twelfth floor, they found it to be fairly basic. A bedsit of sorts consisting of a sleeping area, some lounge seating, a tiny bathroom and some essential kitchen equipment, all furnished and equipped in a space-saving, economical style. Once Clive had shown Rob how to sync his device with the domestic tech, they made arrangements to meet up later and left Rob alone to settle in.

Finch approached his newly materialised reflection at the security force field and leaned forward, putting his face through first. The closer he got, the more transparent it became, which reduced his natural instinct to back off. He walked through the image of himself in the manner of an apparition moving through a solid wall for the first time, aware of a psychosomatic tingle on his skin as he did so.

Clive led Finch out on to the street, still walking at an accelerated pace. Finch was keen to see the building from which they had just emerged. They'd passed between colossal stone columns outside the main doors, and there were shallow stone steps leading down to pavement level. Finch could now see that the exterior of the building had the look of an old Roman temple. On leaving it, he noted a change in atmosphere and realised that the ambience of the interior had emanated a slightly self-important character. This wasn't being emitted by its present occupants, but was more of a historical tone, an echo of the past. It felt as though everyone there had, at one time, taken themselves very seriously.

'The building used to be a bank,' stated Clive, as though aware of Finch's interest, 'but we've made a lot of changes since taking it on. Updated it, adapted it. It's more a façade that remains. We are in the City. Your apartment is a few minutes' walk away. Watch out.' Clive held an arm out in front of Finch as a completely silent vehicle passed in front of them at the junction. It was a low car, similar to Seb's in shape, but it was barely visible, its surface coated in some reflective material that allowed it to blend into the background, bending the light, appearing almost transparent. 'Security vehicle. Look out for those. Soundless and camouflaged. It should *not* be in cloaked mode *here*. Must be the minister. The chauffeur tech is designed to adjust for their stealthy nature, but still.' Finch watched it pull into a side street next to SCI-PSY. It was like trying to grasp an optical illusion that the brain couldn't quite understand, switching between possibilities – seeing first the object, then the negative space surrounding it, unsure to which it should adhere.

'Are they common around here?' asked Finch.

'No. But I'm not sure whether that's a help or a hindrance. If they were, we might be more aware of them,' responded Clive, whose annoyance at the danger they posed was evident from his sharp tone.

'So, will we be working together? What do you do at SCI-PSY?' Finch asked as they continued towards his accommodation.

'I'm involved in the personnel side of things. Ensuring you're all progressing as well as can be. From what I hear, you won't have a problem with that. Your apartment is down here.'

Clive took a right turn into the courtyard that, on some level, Finch recognised from the images of the apartment, although without conscious acknowledgement;

his mind was engaged in processing the virtually invisible car and how it was such an amazingly irresponsible use of tech.

On arrival Finch spoke his name into the security box that was mounted next to his new front door, which they'd accessed via an external wooden staircase that led up to first-floor level. An unnerving white light flashed over Finch's face, scanning his eyes and confirming its acknowledgement with a deep clunk as the mechanism repositioned itself, unlocking the door.

Inside, Finch was pleasantly surprised. Rob's room had set the bar reasonably low so Finch had expected a similar level of accommodation, but this was going to be just fine. There was a large and spacious living area, open plan and furnished in a modern style but with a slightly rustic, possibly Japanese feel. Finch wasn't sure.

Within the open-plan space was also a high-tech kitchen with dark reflective cupboards against pale, exposed brick walls. There were long expanses of slim worktop in a dark tone, and flashes of metal that looked white, but in a highly reflective manner as though the metal itself was actually white, and not just coated in a white finish. The dining area next to the kitchen featured a large table in a heavy dark wood with long benches either side, positioned underneath a low-hung, elaborate white light.

As Finch approached the table, he found that it

wasn't completely solid wood – it had been constructed out of repeated wooden elements that left a pattern of gaps in the surface. The identical blocks that formed the tabletop were deep, resulting in a weighty looking table, and they were shaped, even below the surface. It looked as though the designer had taken a complex angular shape, turned it on its side and joined it to other identical forms, leaving space between them at regular intervals. The effect was beautiful – it reminded Finch of some art his mother had shown him years before, featuring tessellating shapes – perhaps birds – that morphed into altered forms as they progressed across the artwork. The lamp that hovered above the tabletop was as air-light as the table looked substantial. It appeared to be paper, folded into origami shapes that clustered together to create a large modern chandelier formation. The lights had all activated automatically as Finch had entered, and this paper chandelier seemed to glow throughout. There was no light bulb at the centre. It glowed everywhere, the folded edges of the paper material shining more brightly, highlighted as though smouldering, like tiny veins of lava or actual embers of burnt paper.

Clive spent some time talking Finch through the various electrical appliances and demonstrating how they all synced with his device. Failing that, he could use his identifiers as an ad hoc connection and his previous programming for direction. The coffee table sprang to life at Clive's request, the glass top lighting up as a screen, holo-elements protruding from it in three dimensions. Clive explained that it was holo-hybrid, meaning it was an interactive hologram at times, and a regular touch screen at others, depending on the particular use.

Finch's apartment was positioned at the end of the terrace and benefitted from an arched end wall, his bedroom situated within what was now a converted loft. The double bed spread out beneath an old circular window at the end of the beamed room. They'd climbed a handful of turning wooden steps up to the bedroom, which had low ceilings and deep carpet, evoking a cosy, cocooning sensation. The side windows had excessively long, lustrous, heavy curtains in a dull-coloured matt silk, with floating sheer white fabric covering the windows for privacy, casually pooling on the carpet below.

Off the bedroom was a modern bathroom where Clive demonstrated the voice activation tech, unaware that Finch had already exchanged Monty Python quotes with a similar piece of tech back in the hotel when he'd first arrived. Eventually, when Clive seemed satisfied that he'd educated Finch to an adequate degree, he left, citing an urgent meeting at SCI-PSY. Finch spent some time gleefully examining each room, marvelling at his new home, aware of its stark contrast to his dilapidated church lodgings back on the island.

He made himself a cup of tea and sank deep into the grey-blue suede pillows that formed the sofa, studying his device for any new communication. Just as he did so the coffee table flashed a white light and produced a low knocking sound. Like his device, it was unfathomable quite how the glass top of his coffee table acted as a holo-computer. It simply appeared to be a regular sheet of thick-cut glass rested over crudely cut hunks of ancient wood, though stylish nonetheless. On activating the screen, he discovered a message and requested 'open'. Olga sprang up out of the table – not the real Olga, but a smaller, radiant, three-dimensional image of her. She was looking directly at Finch and smiling. 'My Finch! How are you finding it? This is just a video message so I can't hear your responses, but I just wanted to send you all my love, and hope that SCI-PSY wasn't too intimidating – I know it can be, sometimes. How do you like your apartment? Good, isn't it!' Olga was grinning happily at him. 'Anyway, I hope to be able to visit soon. And look – I have stubble.' Olga showed her scalp with an even covering of dark hair, just a few millimetres long. 'So, you and Rob look after each other and I'll catch you soon, Mister Henry.' And she was gone. Finch played the message again, then again, eventually deciding to stop obsessing and do something else. He sent Rob a message asking if he were free to meet yet. Their possessions would arrive in a few hours and Rob didn't have to be present; the porters would take care of it for him. They arranged to meet outside SCI-PSY and go exploring from there, find some lunch and see the city.

***

Attempting to don the ease of relaxed natives, Finch and Rob wandered the streets of central London, taking in the sights. The place was manic with bustling tourists, street performers and busy professionals taking lunch as every imaginable form of transport swished by. The population was diverse, with people of innumerable ethnic origins. Vociferous snatches of foreign language seized Finch's attention as passers-by held heated debates or chattered into their devices. On coming across a little pizzeria down a less frenzied side street, Finch and Rob entered, relieved to find a haven of calm, and settled in for a beer and some food. Rob seemed in brighter spirits having spoken to Koo at length on his device and the city seemed so upbeat it was difficult to remain in one's own personal bubble of gloom. There was excitement in the air, Finch noted, a vibration of new discovery and potential fun to be had, and he looked forward to Olga's presence, the adventures they might enjoy together. When, eventually, Rob was messaged that his possessions had arrived, they each returned to their accommodation to unpack, the very act instantly transforming Finch's new apartment into a friendlier and more familiar environment.

The weekend progressed; Finch and Rob hung out together, visiting tourist attractions and enjoying the city. They found a charming little eatery where they could while away a few hours in the evening. It was unlike any restaurant either of them could have dreamed up. The ambience was designed to enhance the taste experience of each customer, and everything was considered: lighting, the ambient sound, the fragrance in the air, the décor and furniture. All these aspects shifted like magic, once orders had been placed, to more appropriate stimulation for the senses in order to enhance the taste of the chosen food. They had ordered some prawns, fries and a couple of blonde beers. Without obvious perceivable change, the walls in their booth began to show nostalgic seaside images in filtered, polaroid tones. The soundtrack adapted so that the faint squawking of gulls and the crashing of ocean waves could be detected behind the modern, rhythmic, low-bass music. There was the occasional jazz flourish of a fluid golden trumpet, as though Louis Armstrong were performing at a distant party, a few notes escaping on the ocean breeze here and there. The air adopted a slightly salty, ozone suggestion and intermittent gusts of wind came their way as warm lighting flooded their table with a deep, sunny hue.

At first the theatre of it amused Rob and Finch. It crept in slowly, subtly, as if they were being transported gently to an old-fashioned seaside resort, the eatery completely ignorant of the connotations this brought to the rapidly flattening moods of Finch and Rob.

'Wish I'd gone for the Thai noodles, now,' commented Rob.

'Yeah, weird, feeling the presence of the place again. The more distant it becomes, the more unbelievable I find it,' Finch said, increasingly aware of his mind conjuring island memories into perceptible sensation.

'I know. Now we're here, have you looked for your mum at all?' asked Rob.

'No. You? Your dad?'

'Yeah. I did a search for his name on my device. Turns out there are loads of Max Peter Duffys in the world. I need to trawl through them all. Find a way to narrow the options. At the AU I put in a request for a level fiver to let me have any available info, but nothing so far. I'm surprised you haven't searched yet, Finch. Thought you were keen to find answers.'

Finch thought for a moment. He had considered it a couple of times but had become distracted. The feeling that it was potentially an enormous mistake – that he might be opening up a can of worms, was stopping him. It wasn't something he could just do while he waited for the kettle to boil – it needed space. 'You're right. Think I'm possibly delaying – in case I find that she chose to leave us, I suppose.'

'You don't have to do it,' said Rob, in a reasonable tone. 'You have a choice, you know. Anyway – isn't it the case that we all chose the paths of our lives before we came to live them? So you *chose* this, mate. Maybe you like a mystery? Maybe you needed to experience loss? Suppose you've got to have some faith in your previous pre-life choices, if you're going to buy into all that.'

'Yeah. Point well made, Rob. I'm … I'm going to have to make some room for it,' he said, as he considered the light Rob had just cast on the situation. Rob was right. This wasn't it – there had been a plan, and he would, regardless, see his mother again. He could remain passive and never know, or he could try to find answers. Either way, he should stay philosophical about it, slightly more detached so as to keep his emotional footing.

***

On Monday morning, Rob and Finch met at the reception desk of SCI-PSY. They were greeted by Vhas, a rotund young man of Chinese origin, bald, wearing heavy white-rimmed spectacles and a smart dark suit. He took them through the introductory procedure and applied new techtoos to their foreheads, which were invisible when not in use, exactly like Clive's. Finch's was shaped like an eye: a golden third eye for the psychic recruit. Rob's was a cloud form in sky blue. They were shown around the premises, taken to the food hall, the roof garden, the gym. They ate lunch with Vhas, making polite conversation about the institution and its structure.

After lunch, Vhas delivered Rob to the IT department and took Finch up to the Psych Lab, which was at the top of the building. The vast, circular room they entered was flooded with natural light from an elaborate domed window set into the ceiling. There were several people wearing what looked like fine white dressing gowns – Vhas explained that this was more to do with philosophy than practicality – and there was a series of glassed-off rooms around the edge of the open-plan area. The main space held a spattering of glass desks on one side and a maze of unfathomable tech hardware on the other.

Vhas guided Finch into one of the side rooms to meet Boff, the head of Psych. Boff was not what Finch had expected, but he felt an instant warmth for Boff's character. Finch sensed that he somehow managed to emanate enormous charisma by doing absolutely nothing, but by doing it with charm. He was an overly relaxed man in his late sixties who had receding grey hair, long at the back, and wore wire-framed glasses with tiny circular lenses. He was lounging at his desk in a white robe, bare feet resting on a chair opposite, and a sizeable bag of crunchy potato snacks in his hand.

'Ah, do we have Finch?' he asked, idly throwing the bag of crisps on to a chaotic desk top and removing his spectacles.

'Yes, we do, Boff,' replied Vhas, who obviously liked Boff, judging by his cordial tone. 'I shall leave him in your hands now. Be nice, old man.'

'Be gone, young thing,' was Boff's retort, delivered with a straight face and lazy ease of wit as he waved Vhas out of the room. 'So, Finch, sit,' Boff said, kicking a chair that wheeled roughly in Finch's direction. 'I'm Boff. I run this ... department? Yes, department. And I'll be looking after you. Any questions?'

'Er, ye—'

'So, I'll be training you up personally. I don't usually do that but Jude tells me you've quite the talent. You're from the Isle of Wight, yes?'

'Yes, from St James's,' confirmed Finch.

'Oh, interesting – I'm from there myself. There was this guy – Vine, in charge. Must be long gone by now, I imagine.'

'No. He's still in charge,' said Finch.

Boff sat up, looking stunned. 'No – he can't be – the

old bastard was rickety when I was there.' He paused then laughed hard at the idea. 'How has he *done that*? Well, that's some serious determination to deny the afterlife – resist dying so you never have to admit it's there. Impressive. You have to hand it to him. Ha!'

Finch, slightly nervous about his new position in this daunting organisation, felt his coping strategy kick in, responding, 'He is, ancient, I mean I don't know if it's possible to anthropomorphise a corpse, or perhaps haunt a body from within, but I think he's as close as you'll find.'

Boff paused before dissolving into laughter. 'I like that, Finch,' he said. 'But Vine, I mean, he was, what, *eighty*? when *I* left, forty years ago. To think he's still there! He must be immortal. Ah, unbelievable. Anyway, to work. *Vine – God*. Wow. Okay. So, let's concentrate here. What do you know about us and what we do here?'

'I know the general aim is to, well – define? – the architecture of the afterlife, to develop our skills in all areas of psychic ability so we can be tested under Q-Pho and gather reliable information … evidence. Is that right?'

'That's it, pretty much. Edith, our overall director, is pushing for info. So we are under some pressure to come up with solid answers, but as a newcomer you won't be subject to much of that.'

'Edith? We met her when we arrived, in the lobby.

She's in defence, though, isn't she?'

'Yes. As are we, as are we, dear youth. It's all defence. Otherwise the government would not be ploughing money into recruiting talented islanders and establishing the science behind psychic ability. They are all in a race – a mad scramble for the info, of course. They all want to get there before other countries do – for control. It's frankly tedious. But as least we can do what we're good at, and are no longer stuck in fairgrounds giving tarot card readings to punters for a pittance.'

'You said for *control*?' asked Finch, slightly concerned at what he'd become involved in.

'Absolutely. What would some governments do with the knowledge of how to get into heaven, or *stay out of hell*? Not that there *is* one – unless you want to experience it, that is. Anyway, then there's the sheer competition of it – to go down in history as the person in charge when the details were uncovered. It's all ego, Finch, but we are at least making progress in our own worlds. There is an upside; we're being allowed to bring our light to the world – to enlighten the planet. That's not a bad thing.'

Finch thought for a moment – he needed to consider the defence aspect over time, so changed the subject. There was something he'd never asked Jude because they'd always concentrated on progress, but maybe Boff was the person to ask. 'I've always wondered, how is it we have a light to bring, but others don't appear to? I suppose what I'm asking is, why am I able to do things that others can't?'

'Well, what is reality?'

'It's – well. Is it …?'

'Quite.'

'I'm … not sure how my, well, sadly lacking definition of reality answers that.'

'Think about it: as humans, we all construct reality in our minds. Our brains themselves can't see or hear. They rely on the information sent to them and they construct their best simulation, which is what we experience as reality. Our primary reality is already a *virtual* one. So, we find that other people have a similar experience, and we agree on that experience, leading us to believe that we have found *reality*, but it's actually just a shared hallucination. In a sense, we are actually *projecting* our world, not absorbing it. Sensitives like us, Finch, are not restricted to other people's notions of reality. Our brains detect more. That's all. Maybe some people see blue a hundred times brighter than others. We would never know. But with sensitive ability, the difference is easily recognised.'

'It's just a difference in what our brains are able to perceive?'

'Perceive, predict, interpret – the experience is

240

idiosyncratic to each of us, anyway. You might very well ask, *is* there a reality, but that's a longer conversation. And we are just talking earthbound reality here, viewed through the physical eyes of a human body, which as we know, is not everything. Come on – let's start you now. To the lab.' Boff stood and tied his robe casually, causing Finch to drive his eyes in the opposite direction as he consciously computed the eyeful of reality he'd just been subjected to. Boff didn't seem to mind the exposure. He took another white lab robe from a hook and passed it to Finch. They left the circular room and entered a dark booth. Inside it was warm and comfortable. To one side it featured a glass wall, behind which were various pieces of technical-looking equipment – cameras possibly – many screens and other ambiguous boxes of tech, along with what appeared to be stage lighting. A single chair was placed at the centre of the clear space on the other side of the glass. Boff told Finch to sit and he disappeared among the equipment. 'Now, meditate, dear Finch. And do whatever comes naturally – Reiki, channelling, OBE, RV, whatever you're good at. I'll set the Q-Pho to record you and we can start assessing your capabilities. Ah. Put this on.' He handed Finch a helmet of sorts.

Finch sat in the comfortable chair and introduced his mantra, at first, quite self-consciously. Before long he was lost to his own world, a drifting succession of daily thoughts that plateaued out into a vast expanse of tranquil peace. This state of mind was rich with a certain hyper-conscious feeling that he had grown to associate with being connected to a higher intelligence.

Finch spent some time in appreciation of the blissful sensation before becoming aware of other, familiar beings within his surroundings. They were enjoying his presence and sending him support. There was no conversation between them, just a sense of joyous harmony and complete connection. Finch felt as though one of them was handing him something. It wasn't a physical object, more the concept of one. It felt like a pair of binoculars. Finch had never seen such things before as they were contraband on the island. Anything that had the capability of exposing the vast chasm between island life and the mainland was illegal. As Finch considered the gift, the description of binoculars fitted. He took in the offering, feeling that it came with a message of trust, or an instruction to trust, he wasn't sure. Then he was gone, and he was with Olga at the AU.

From his visual position in mid-air, he could see that she was with fresh new Leavers, watching the first film in the series that Finch had been shown, and she was thinking of him. He could feel her exasperation at being stuck there, her desire for him and her logical mind searching for a solution to the problem. There was worry, too, about something. He wasn't sure what; it was a backdrop, not at the forefront. It was possibly related to their parting; he couldn't quite catch it. Soon, he felt himself returning to his usual perspective, and he opened his eyes to find Boff studying a device closely.

'Finch, Finch, Finch,' Boff muttered, as though talking to himself. 'They may have a point when they tell me you're talented. Where have you just *been*?' he said, looking up with an expression of new-found respect.

***

At the end of the working day, Finch returned to his apartment and slept deeply. The tech had prepared his dinner and there was a hot bath awaiting his company once he'd eaten. He spoke to Olga every night, never mentioning his inadvertent and recurrent remote viewing of her, but keeping to lighter subjects and making plans instead. As the weeks progressed, he grew accustomed to Boff's engaging yet blasé manner, and started to understand that although he didn't feel it overtly, he was indeed being carefully managed by Boff, who seemed privately to have a more serious side he preferred not to show, or even acknowledge.

At times, Clive would visit, talk to Boff behind a closed door, and then chat informally with the psychic team. There were several other sensitives working under Boff. Most were older than Finch and didn't seem interested in connecting with him. He'd suggested they have lunch together but the response had been a group murmuring about pre-existing plans and they'd all scattered in separate directions. It didn't make sense to Finch; he had expected an eccentric bunch but, of course, they were just people with particular abilities, like him. A few of them seemed to display colourful personalities at times, but only to each other, and not when they became aware of his presence. Finch suspected that it was his position as Boff's personal project that was affecting his image within the team – that it may have created some tension.

Finch was on the sofa nearing sleep. He'd only just returned home and was feeling frazzled from the many hours of testing he'd undergone to ascertain his level of ability in remote viewing. The female mom-tech voice broke through his silent thought, stating that he had a visitor. Finch got up to open the door, unable to fathom whom it might be through his sleepy haze.

'Seb.'

'Finch!' said Seb, grinning, his arms filled with groceries, wine and a bunch of flowers. 'I hope you don't mind? I have been trying to find time to catch you since you arr—'

'No – please, come in.' Finch felt his previous mistrust of Seb melt away. It was good to see his friend at last and he naturally ushered Seb into the apartment.

'I brought dinner – hope I'm not too late. I can go if you've plans?'

'No – please – it's great to see you.' Seb came inside, took off his jacket and put the bag of food on the table.

'Great choice of accommodation, Finch. Here – open this.' Seb handed him a bottle of red wine. 'Grab some plates. I brought fusion. It should still be hot.'

'Wow – thanks. Smells incredible,' Finch said happily.

'So, how are you getting on? I heard about the job offer you'd received – good going, Finch! Jude was really pleased with your progress. How are you finding SCI-PSY?'

Finch was busy spooning fragrant food on to plates. 'I really like the work. It's challenging and it takes a lot out of me sometimes, but it's pushing me further.'

'And Boff?' Seb asked, with an air of mischief in his eyes.

'Boff's, well, is Boff *real*? He's like some kind of legend. He's amazing – I'm starting to understand how he operates. I like his lackadaisical style, but it would be good if he'd remember to do up his robe.'

'Yes – he is misleadingly easy going, and you'll always get an unwanted *vision*, but he's a seriously good guy. So, how've you been? I'm sorry I vanished for a while there. I've been stuck here on an assignment – couldn't make it back up to the AU, but I knew you were in good hands.'

They sat down at the table with their plates. Finch poured the wine and they toasted new beginnings. He watched as Seb raised a fork of noodles to his mouth, completely unaware of the significance this held for Finch, who was actively resisting the urge to immediately open his line of questioning. Something told him to be patient and he listened to this inner wisdom.

Seb asked, 'Did you receive the music I droned over? I didn't know whether you knew it already but the pages themselves were so beautiful. Oh, that reminds me – I picked these up for you a while ago but I didn't get time to drone them out – here. For your new horizons. Congratulations on everything, Finch.' Seb pulled an antique pair of binoculars from his bag and handed them to Finch. 'They're twentieth century. They still work.'

Finch was trying to conceal how dumbfounded he suddenly was. He thought about trust, the message he'd received, and feigned a reaction of delighted curiosity while internally pondering the 'synchron-dipity' of the situation, as Boff would have put it, using his most ironic tone.

They ate, discussing the AU, Rob, their progress, and Finch's experience of London so far. 'You haven't mentioned Olga, Finch,' Seb stated in a knowing tone. 'How are you two getting along together now you're here? Are you finding it hard being apart?'

'Oh, thank God. You know. Yeah, it's not easy. But, Seb, we'll figure it out. I still can't believe we managed to get together despite all the potential trouble it could have caused. We both tried with all our strength to resist, but it happened.'

Seb was silent. 'I *didn't* know. You and Olga are having a relationship?'

Finch, horrified at his own ineptitude, replied, 'Yes,' hoping Seb would not make too much of it. A silence followed as Seb gathered his thoughts.

'Well, she's not your guide any more, I suppose. It's not the done thing, on her part. And Finch, relationships between islanders and third gen never, well, they're notoriously difficult. I hope you know what you're doing.'

'We do, Seb. It's serious. Otherwise we wouldn't have let it happen. She was desperate not to get involved. She tried so hard not to … But anyway – you asked? As though you knew?'

'I suppose I suspected. I've noticed Olga, the way she talks. She's started sounding like you and I've seen her deal with Leavers for quite some time without ever adopting their speech patterns, so I wondered … Well, it's nothing to do with me, now. Just, be careful – be discreet for a while. I won't mention it to anyone and I suggest you do the same.'

'We will. So, tell me about what you've been up to – any Death Wishers trying to crash your car lately?' It took some time for Seb to warm up, having heard the news, but after another glass of wine he was back to his old self again. They had ambled blindly on to the subject of Rob's father and the possibility that he could be on the mainland, and an enormous elephant materialised in the room between them.

'Now, Finch, you asked me something when we last met. You asked me to look into whether your mum came here, and I do have news for you.'

'Yes?' Finch wasn't sure he wanted to know now and he felt the anticipation of the news in his legs, as though they were frozen.

'She did. I'm so sorry, Finch.'

'She did?'

'Yes. She came here a few months before they told you she'd passed on.'

'For treatment?'

'No. I'm sorry Finch, but she wasn't ill. She came because she was recruited by my predecessor. She was gifted, like you.'

'Oh.'

'I really am so sorry, Finch. I've had the approval to inform you for a while, but I didn't want to destroy your progress at the AU, so I gave you some time to settle in.

Leavers are known to undergo serious personal turmoil in the first few months and it isn't taken lightly. I didn't want to disrupt it – you'd been through so much. It might have pushed you, well, too far.'

'Where is she now? Do you know?'

'I don't know. She was working at SCI-PSY for a while but she left.'

'With Boff, and the other sensitives?'

'Yes.'

Finch was silent, trying to gather his thoughts through a veil of descending desolation. 'Okay. Thanks, Seb. I appreciate your reasons for holding back,' he managed.

'Listen, Dr Lenny told me that she's happy to video chat with you if you need some support.'

'So she *left* us. Willingly.' Finch said, as the news began to take hold.

'It was my predecessor who recruited her so I don't have the details and the files are unavailable. There was a system error a year ago and some were lost, so that's all the info I have. Boff may be able to tell you more. Or some of the other sensitives who were around at the time?'

'Ah, well, they don't talk to me much. Maybe that's why. If they remember her or something.'

'Listen, if you can find it in yourself, try not to judge her for leaving. Remember the state you were in? She had the same ability. People think they're actually mad when they experience phenomena they can't explain. I've known many that attempted suicide, so destined to leave their loved ones one way or another, despite the love they felt for their families and friends. It's unique – and difficult – for everyone I've met who has the gift, and none take leaving lightly.'

'I do understand that, but is she still here? She left SCI-PSY – to go where? Who were her friends? Did she have another job to go to?'

'Okay – let's find out. I'll do all I can to help you find the answers, Finch. I'm not going anywhere this time.' Seb's earnest expression reassured him that he was genuine and that Finch wasn't alone.

Finch spent the rest of the evening putting on a brave face and avoiding the subject until Seb eventually left him to his own thoughts, while assuring Finch that he would gladly help with the search for his mother if he so wished. Finch, relieved to have space to reflect after the realisation, lay curled up on his bed, his mind buzzing with shock. After several hours of failing to sleep, he decided to meditate. He sat, eyes closed, mantra playing on a loop in his mind. He hadn't expected to feel this way – she was *alive*. This was *good* news, wasn't it? The image of his mother's funeral kept presenting itself. It stood prominent in his mind demanding attention no matter what evasive tactics he employed. He considered the trauma of losing her and the wrecked state that he and Grandad had been in for months, no – *years* afterwards. She wasn't there. She had simply left them both. Forgotten them. Started a new life. Gone.

13 THE LUXURY OF NOW

The following morning, having spent many fruitless hours searching online for Mia Henry, Finch entered Boff's room and closed the door behind him. Boff was at his desk with one eye closed, muttering to himself. 'No, not great. Back to the drawing board. Finch, something troubles you.' Boff looked down and appeared to be taking something out of his eye. 'Augmented reality lenses – not working yet. Excellent. It seems we still have a way to go. Good, good.'

'Mia Henry,' said Finch. Boff stopped fiddling with the lens case. There was a silence as Boff shot a serious look at Finch.

'You've been officially informed?

'Yes – Seb told me last night. He said she'd worked here?'

'Please sit. At last. Yes, your mother was here. She

left us around eighteen months ago. She said she had other employment to go to but didn't say where or what it was. I got the impression it wasn't finalised because she was reluctant to discuss it. I don't know where she went, Finch, but I can tell you she was here for about a year before that. Have you tried remote viewing her?'

'No. Well, yes, but with no success.' Finch was feeling the hurt of the abandonment profoundly and hadn't attempted in any serious way to use his abilities to find her – possibly because he wasn't at all sure he would like the results. He did, however, feel a need for all available information from those who'd known her; perhaps it would shed some light on her reasons for leaving. Boff was studying Finch as if allowing himself to empathise with Finch's energy and seemed to become momentarily immersed in the upset, his expression rapidly sinking into grim despair as he connected with Finch's condition.

'Oh, God. Finch. What can I do to help? Do you need to take some time off? See if you can locate her?'

'Maybe. I …' Finch wasn't sure whether this was a terrible idea. He knew keeping busy and not dwelling was a good strategy for dealing with internal distress, but could use the time to adjust, maybe even to find his mother – or at least figure out if he actually wanted to.

'Okay – take two weeks, as of now. I tried to get in

touch with her when I heard you'd taken the job here but there was no response to any method of contact. I'll give you her details because you may have better luck. I couldn't find anything online either. But that's not surprising – she was a private soul. What else can I do? Hold on. I'll get the team in. Let's ask them now.' Boff stood up and headed towards the door, white gown open, billowing behind him as he walked. 'In here, everyone. That's right, all of you, into my space.' The psych team filed in and lingered around the edge of the room in awkward anticipation. 'Those of you who have been here less than eighteen months, please leave.' About half the people left, bemusement on their faces. 'Those of you remaining all worked with Mia Henry. I want you all to tell Finch here, who, as I'm sure you're all aware, is Mia's son, everything you can about her so that he can attempt to locate her. Finch – have my room and see everyone one by one. You lot – be generous. Finch here needs you. Start with Oscar. Everyone else wait outside for Finch to call you in.' Boff and the others left, subdued discussions beginning between them.

Finch sat looking at Oscar who was in his fifties and alarmingly thin. Oscar had honest eyes and looked emotionally back at Finch, awaiting the questioning.

'Do you remember Mia?' he asked, aware that his question lacked imagination or forethought.

'Yes, Finch. I'm sorry that we couldn't tell you

before. We were told we couldn't discuss her with you until you'd been officially informed. You know how it is, protocol …'

'Can you tell me everything you remember?'

'Sure – although we weren't close. She always seemed a bit of a loner. Didn't really mix in with us, so there's not that much to tell. She was a good sensitive – could actually see energy sometimes. She could interface, but not on demand. She had trouble with RV, too. She seemed, maybe, a bit in her own world – distracted, I always thought. That's all I remember, really. I wasn't all that surprised when she resigned.'

'Did she have any close friends?'

'She was probably closest to Nancy, but even then, not what you'd call close. No … she really did keep herself to herself. Sorry I can't be more help.'

'And you've no idea what job she went to or where it was?'

'No – I'll send you the contact details I had for her but I don't know if they're still in use.'

'Okay, thanks. If you remember anything else, and I mean *anything*, please let me know. Thanks, Oscar. Can you send Nancy in?'

Nancy was one of the more extrovert members of the psych team. She sported a mane of metallic gold; it looked natural to a point, but with the contrast turned up, intensely saturated – especially under the light of the domed window. Finch had thought it a wig until he'd seen the range of hair dyes available in a chemist's, some in pill form, and realised that all sorts of iridescent and metallic shades were on offer, although he hadn't seen many people exhibiting them at SCI-PSY. Nancy was somewhere in her mid-thirties so would have been closest to Mia in age. She was more outspoken than other members of the team and her personality seemed to intimidate some of the men. Sitting opposite her, Finch saw that she was also relieved that the information had finally been revealed to Finch.

'I'm going to tell you everything I know, Finch. And we all wanted to – but we couldn't. Mia was great. She had a really fun side, but I think I was the only one who saw it. She was slightly, inward – reserved – with most of the psychs here. I think she was troubled. She mentioned you and Hope sometimes, but whenever I tried to ask about you, she would shut down, change the subject. She got angry with me once for asking about her life on the island, saying she couldn't go back there mentally. So I stopped asking.'

'I'm sorry it was so hard for her to remember us.' Finch had a sudden violent anger bubbling below the surface. An anger that she'd allowed them to believe her dead, that she'd left him, let them grieve for her so torturously. Anger that she'd left Grandad.

'Oh, come on, Finch. We, well most of us know it's never that simple. But anyway, she went to Leavers' group every week – not sure which one.'

'Sorry – Leavers' group?'

'Yeah, you know – support group for Leavers. Everyone talks about their experience and they meet others in a similar position.'

'Around here?'

'Yes, but there are a few. I don't know which one it was.'

'Okay – so what about when she left? Did she say anything?'

'I think she'd met someone, a man. I don't know if she actually went to another job, though. I got the impression it was more to do with him. She sometimes expressed some disagreement with this department, how the info was being used – the Russian and Korean threats and the UK's need for clarity on the eternal aspect of life. She may have annoyed her superiors a little, I think.'

'So she didn't agree with the work we do here?'

'I think it was more the government's motives … She liked the work itself.'

'So, who was this man?'

'I couldn't tell you. I can barely remember if I'm

right about that. Although I was probably her main friend here, she was really cagey at times – very concerned with something. She seemed fragile. None of us wanted to push her on it – we just accepted it as her nature. We didn't know you'd be here later, needing answers. Ironic, I know – a team of psychic people being oblivious to the significance of something at the time. It happens.'

'Anything else you can think of?'

'Just … she lived in the SCI-PSY block. You could ask there? They may have records of who she allowed in.' There was a pause while Finch searched for further angles of questioning. 'Shall I get Chikra to come in?'

'Thanks.'

Chikra was a Native American with an Irish edge to his accent. He was somewhere in his fifties and known for his affable manner and colourful language.

'I can't tell you anything you probably haven't already heard, Finch. I didn't know her well. Sure, I was here. Oftentimes I saw her hanging with Nancy, but we'd never gotten to know one another. She just wasn't into us, I'm guessing.'

'So, nothing about where she went or who she was close to?'

'Sorry, Finch – I didn't pay her too much attention. I was new here, just after her, and concerned with my own path at the time. All I remember is that she'd go AWOL for a day or two, then return looking sick – tired. I wondered what was going on with her.' Finch took a moment to consider the image he was forming of his mainland mum but his thoughts were interrupted by Chikra.

'Finch – you have to remember everything you've learned. Whatever your path, well, you *chose* it – don't let it eat at your soul. Think what shit you can learn from it – this must've been the plan, no?'

'Yeah – I know, but it's hard to see it like that, sometimes. Knowing she's out there somewhere.'

Chikra got up to leave. He put a hand on Finch's shoulder. 'If there's anything else, I will come to you.'

'Thanks,' said Finch hopelessly, his tired eyes locked on a vacant point in mid-air.

After talking to everyone available, Finch had developed a new image of his mother as a loner – even a shy, introverted person. This wasn't something Finch had ever expected to uncover. His mum had been so much fun – she was always the one initiating the party, gathering people together. Finch began to ask himself whether he'd really known her at all. *His* Mia could not have left her family willingly, so was the very basis of his opinion built on unstable ground to begin with? He was having to rethink all that he'd previously assumed to be solid knowledge. He returned home, dazed, not knowing how, or even whether to continue his investigations.

A few days passed. Finch found himself swinging continually between hopeful faith and desperate misery. He could, at times, convince himself that of course there *must* have been more to it – his mother would never have just left them like that. Then came lengthier periods of doubt that he ever knew her properly at all. After that, enormous rage, taking the initiative where hurt truly resided. Either way, finding his mum seemed the only option. He could find out the truth. He could shout at her. He could maybe, eventually, move on. What he absolutely could not do was just let it go.

Having spent some time considering whether to use the contact details he'd been given for his mother, Finch eventually placed the call. He had no idea how he would respond should she answer, but it didn't come to that. The only response was an automated 'number not recognised' recording. His message to her online address bounced back, leaving him with no clear avenues to pursue other than accessing the SCI-PSY accommodation records, as suggested by Nancy. He sent a request for information and received an automated acknowledgement stating that someone would be in touch within the next thirty working days.

Finch spent long hours playing his cello, part of his

mind endeavouring to connect with this new idea of his mum, only to find himself wrecked and exhausted. She had become a construct in his mind since she'd apparently died. He'd tried to keep everything about her alive by purposely remembering the detail, even embellishing, imagining new conversations with her, hearing her views on his current situation, on Olga, on SCI-PSY. Sometimes he would be reminded of her like it or not, by his own inherited expressions or mannerisms. He could only find those established aspects of his mother, along with the profound hurt she'd inflicted by putting him through terrible, avoidable sorrow. Searching within, he couldn't find this Mia that everyone described. He really *hadn't* known her, he concluded, and she'd left, proving his point.

Utterly lost and disorientated, Finch stared at the knives in the drawer. The sensation of being cornered by hurt and rejection was too much. Alarmed at his own thinking, he decided to meditate and try remote viewing instead, but he couldn't stay focused. The thoughts of his mother and her abandonment simply stood like a looming edifice in front of his consciousness and made it clear that 'none may pass'.

Finch hadn't spoken to Olga since all this had occurred. He had missed some calls from her, and was so distracted that his replies were badly timed for when she'd become unavailable herself. Deep down he was conscious that the conversation may not be beneficial, so was circumventing it. He knew that Olga was sometimes impatient with the subject, as though she thought Finch's need for answers was perhaps childish, or worse, indulgent.

Some supportive messages from Seb had appeared on Finch's device, and he'd replied in a sufficiently upbeat tone so as not to warrant concern. Rob had gone off grid. He'd mentioned something about Koo being cold with him and that he'd vague plans to confront her. Ensnared within his own, all-engulfing turmoil, Finch hadn't enquired as to how that had gone. It had slipped his troubled mind completely.

It was late evening and Finch was at his coffee table device, researching Leavers' groups. He was having a slight emotional upturn and was consciously putting it to good use. He'd found several long-standing Leavers' groups that were still active within the city. Finch knew it was highly unlikely that he'd find his mother at one, but he had to do something. A voice entered his world. 'Finch. Finch, are you there?' It was Olga calling at last. Finch swiped the city maps away and connected to the call.

'Olga?' Then she appeared, the miniature hologram version of her head and shoulders emerging from his coffee table like the ghost of a doll.

'Finch! I've finally got you!'

'Hi, how's it going up there?' he asked, attempting a cheery tone.

'I'm great thanks. How is my Finch? Seb called and told me you've been informed about your mum. He *knew* about us, Finch.'

'Yeah. I thought he knew – he kind of asked and I replied assuming he already knew. He suspected, though. How was he about it?'

'Okay – level-headed. Was keen to stress that gen-three and Leaver relationship stats are predominantly depressing … Can't believe you told him! If I didn't miss you so much I'd be so angry with you!'

'Sorry, I …'

'Seriously, Finch, please, be careful. Does anyone else know? Rob?'

'No. No. Of course not. I …'

'Listen – it's crucial that you don't tell him. Okay?'

'Olga, I wouldn't. I didn't. Seb let me think he knew already.'

'Okay. Listen, Rob is having a hard time. Koo has ended their relationship and he's been holed up in his room, drinking. He missed work three days in a row. Can you keep an eye on him? Maybe go over there?'

'Oh, no. Poor Rob. That's awful. He was so heartbroken to leave her. He must be distraught. Sure. I'll go—'

'Not now – Seb is on his way there.'

'Ah, okay. So …'

'So – how's work?' she asked.

'Work? It's … I've been given some leave, to deal with …'

Olga was looking behind her at something. 'Oh, hang on. Sorry – what were you saying? Sir was whining again. I need to get that dog checked out. I walked him tonight and he was lagging behind, limping slightly. The dark red dahlias are looking stunning here. And they've cleaned up the pathways at the periphery. It's less rocky now. Think they're making another rockery or something near the pond. Sorry – what were you saying?'

'*My mother*, Olga. I have been given leave to deal with the situation. I have just discovered that my mum didn't die. *She left us*. She's out there somewhere. It's a lot to take in.'

Olga was silent for a moment. 'Please don't be like that, Finch. I'm sorry – I just thought you must have known … I mean, on some level. And you did ask. You *wanted* to know about her.'

'And that alleviates the hurt how, exactly?'

'I know it hurts, Finch. I'm sorry. But you're not seeing it in its true light. You need to remember everything you've learned! You'll see her again, regardless. Have it out with her then. She's trying to teach you something, or you her. This is all just a bit of theatre. We shouldn't take it so seriously. You know?'

'What? No. Sorry. I *don't* know. I can't believe you're being like this. You seem to have no idea about all this – the implications to me … my world, my reality.'

'Your reality, Finch, is exactly that – yours. And only yours. You can make this life whatever you want, but you are choosing to chase your mother's ghost around instead of *living*.'

'Olga. I'm not sure you heard me. She left us. She *left*.' At that, Finch felt the sudden release of hot tears streaming down his face. He was on the edge and finding this situation testing enough without Olga seeming to trivialise it.

'Finch, I'm sorry. I just, I can never understand this obsession and I probably deal with it very badly. Please. Finch? Are you okay?'

'Yeah,' said Finch, wiping his eyes on his sleeve, embarrassed to have melted down so spectacularly with no self-control whatsoever. 'I just … I wish you could understand how it feels to have grieved – actually grieved.

The loss – it's unbearable. And then I find it wasn't even *real*. She was alive the whole time.'

'Either way she's still alive, Finch. Anyway, what do you think all those who knew you on the island have been going through since you *disappeared*? Sorry – I don't mean to make it harder, but you did the same thing. Do you see that, my Finch?' She sounded calmer and more gentle as she at last acknowledged the depth of Finch's distress.

'It's not the same. I wasn't a parent. I had no family. God – I wouldn't have been able to leave if Grandad hadn't committed suicide.'

'We don't use that term any more, Finch. He *freed* himself. Can you see that? I hate to see you like this. I suppose I do understand it – I maybe can't feel it like you do. I love you, my Finch. Please – are you okay? I'm so sorry.'

'Okay. I probably need some time to deal with all this. I'll call you tomorrow.' Finch swiped the call away abruptly, dissolving into sobs as soon as the connection was cut.

***

The Leavers' groups met most nights of the week in various locations. Tonight was one of the better known groups and Finch felt an impulse to attend. He was emotionally broken and any kind of action was a positive distraction – misdirection for his traumatised state.

Olga had caused Finch to question their relationship for the first time. His love for her was intense, but the ease with which she could belittle such sensitive aspects of his world was challenging. However, the search for answers to that particular situation was something Finch simply couldn't accommodate right now. He wished he could just press 'pause' on the relationship and deal with it later, when his emotional resources had been replenished. So, avoidance would be the best strategy, he'd loosely decided.

The journey to the old library where the support group was taking place took longer than Finch had anticipated and he'd missed the start. The library housed a number of small cafés alongside public use device tables, but no books except those that appeared to be antiques, displayed behind glass. The atmosphere was exactly like the heavily edited island library, the quiet respect for other people's experience and a weighty esteem for learning concentrated in the air of the place. Finch could see a group of people sitting in a circle of sorts, being talked to quietly by a man who looked as though he'd come straight from his day job in an office.

After ordering a pot of Earl Grey from the nearest café, Finch took a seat close enough to hear the group conversation and observe the members. The man who appeared to be leading the conversation was asking another man to tell his story of 'leaving' as he was a newcomer so should introduce himself. Looking carefully at each woman within the group, there were none that could have been his mother, Finch quickly observed. He would finish his tea and leave. The man about to tell his story shifted in his seat and began to speak in a hushed tone.

'Hi, I'm Mitch. I left my island, the smallest in Scotland, eleven months ago now. It wasn't by choice – I had a boating accident. Was in over my head and the swell was unremitting – couldn't get back. All for a good catch. A drone thing pulled me out and took me to this AU wing of a hospital on the mainland – then they said I couldn't go home. I miss my life there. I mean – it's better here – everything's way better than I could have known, but I had my job, my cat, pals. I don't know what they did with my cat when I didn't come home. They offered me hypnosis to return but it would have wiped my mind. They say it's the choice of the island, not the mainland, that you can't return, but to me, it seems farcical. How can a world like *this* not have some strategy to return people if they want to go back, without wiping their memories completely? So I'm here. For good. Anyway. I hope that wasn't too miserable for you all.'

One or two people forced out a subdued chuckle at his final comment to help him feel welcome, and the leader thanked him for his story. 'How many of you would have liked to return if the memory cleanse hadn't been part of the scenario?' he asked. A few hands went up, three in total out of fourteen people, Finch noted. 'So, Gregor, Lucia and Amanda. All of you left due to poor health, am I right? Yes, okay. We see that a lot – more with accidents than general medical treatment. Did any of you think about returning of your own accord?' Mitch raised a hand. 'Go on, Mitch.'

'Well, for a while I thought about just sailing back myself. "Surprise! I'm not dead!" Freak out me pals! But they told me there are drones that watch for you, to stop anyone *breaking the silence*. Why can't we just open up all the islands? That's what I want to know.'

'Well, that's a debate we're all familiar with.' The leader sighed. 'It's a constant issue for government. They talk about holding a referendum to decide. They talk about the rights of founding islanders as opposed to the rights of second and third-gen *captives*. There are rights and legal issues that weren't foreseen at separation. It seems we are passive-aggressively letting the islands rot in the hope that their inevitable decline will somehow force discussion or resolution. It's clear that the eventual removal of borders is the mainland's preferred outcome, but this really isn't the most humane way to go about it. I think sometimes we are just going around in circles. It's almost as though we're stuck in a stalemate situation. But we, at least, can move on. Gene

– this is your second week at group. Did you feel differently about the vegetarian food after our discussion last week?'

Finch tuned out. A dragonfly was hovering over someone's device top in hologram form and it took his mind away from the subject for a moment. He finished the tea and headed home.

'Welcome back, Finch,' said the voice of the mom-tech. 'You have received a message. Would you like to play it?'

'Yes.'

Finch's tabletop device produced a hologram of an old-fashioned scroll, turning gently in mid-air. It wasn't opening by itself so Finch reached out and touched the red wax seal that featured the relief image of a hound. On Finch's contact, the scroll unravelled, holding its open position so that Finch could read the calligraphic text it displayed. It read:

Dear Finch Henry, esquire,

Your presence is cordially demanded for dinner tomorrow evening at 7 p.m, your abode. Food will be delivered. Bring your best conversation and an empty stomach. Dress code – formal, of course.

Disorderliness will absolutely not be tolerated.

Yours condescendingly,

Sir

So, Olga was coming, Finch thought, filled with a sudden sense of relief that he could see her at last, that they could return to their previous modus operandi and repair the fracture that had developed between them.

***

Finch found that focusing on Olga's visit, along with Rob's situation, was sufficient distraction from the search for his mother. Having tidied his apartment and had some premium dog food droned in, Finch's thoughts turned to Rob and how he could help. The apartment was ready for Olga's arrival so Finch headed over to Rob's, having messaged him ahead to check he was in the mood for company.

The state of Rob's accommodation was alarming. For a person who owned few belongings, the place looked chaotic in the extreme. There were clothes and rubbish strewn on every surface, empty food and drink containers, and Finch was horribly aware of the all too familiar stench of rejection in the atmosphere. He set about tidying the kitchen, talking to Rob about what had happened with Koo, and attempting in vain to reassure Rob that there was another future out there for him, that this wasn't *it*.

It emerged that SCI-PSY had allocated Rob a guide, having acknowledged his state, and that the guide would logically be Olga because they'd already developed a relationship. Rob asked how Finch had found Olga as a guide, seemingly nervous about having a new pair of eyes watching him, and Finch assured Rob that Olga had been great – not too involved, yet supportive. As he spoke, intimate imagery of their relationship flashed through his mind.

Having vastly improved the state of Rob's room, Finch suggested they get a change of scene, perhaps go out for lunch or maybe a walk. Rob reluctantly agreed so they headed for their favourite haunt, which was hidden down a narrow street. It was, paradoxically, non-pretentious yet exclusive to those who knew where to find it. Concealed behind a regular panelled wooden door, any passer-by would have assumed it was just the front entrance of a house. There was nothing to indicate that the establishment existed. No sign, no noise pollution.

They'd initially discovered the bar when they'd been wandering down the road and seen a group of inebriated people stagger out, allowing a peek inside at the interior. The space was long and narrow, with low lighting and touches of original Victorian period grandeur.

Rob and Finch had become regulars and knew some of the staff by name. Perry, the owner, showed them to a dark corner with comfortable armchair seating and several disembodied candle flames hovering in the air above the low table as though from lit candles set within an old-fashioned candelabra. Finch always found the incorporeal flames enchanting, especially as they gave off the same dancing, golden light that real candles radiated. They were, of course, holographic, but the effect was stylishly beautiful in this setting. Finch enjoyed their realistic reaction as he passed his finger through them. On first encountering the charming formation of single flames, Finch had shown some interest in how they worked and Perry, who was passionate about his establishment, referred to them as his 'phantom candelabras'.

Aside from the floating flames, the place was solid, authentic. Any effects employed to enhance the food were not explicitly noticeable. Massimo, a waiter who was never without a full face of immaculate make-up, approached them with a tray of tiny drinks.

'With Perry's compliments, boys. Enjoy!' he said as he offloaded two of the drinks on to their table. Finch was wary of Rob's reliance on alcohol, but before he'd had time to consider the suggestion that they remain sober-ish, Rob had downed his miniature drink.

'Woah, that was good. Wonky Bob would not have

approved of that down the Dog and Codger – tiny drinks. Unless they were shots of foul, gullet-melting spirits, that is,' Rob commented. 'These would *not* have worked with their dirty cottage pie.' Rob sometimes mentioned infamous islander and inexplicably alive Wonky Bob, so called because of his permanent drunken stagger.

'Wonky Bob. Still going strong when we left. How?' asked Finch.

'Vampire,' said Rob, with absolutely no humour.

'Of course,' conceded Finch, 'that would explain the eyes, the teeth. Those *nails*! Like brown talons. I can see it now, in slow motion – the way he wrapped those claws around a pint glass. Clink, clink, clink. Had me doubled up every time. I think I developed a Wonky-Bob-shaped blind spot in an attempt not to notice his ghoulish presence.'

'He hissed at me once. Terrifying. I accidentally kicked his spittoon. Oh, the island,' said Rob through a sigh. 'I sometimes wonder if I did the right thing, escaping.'

'You *serious*?'

'Yeah – sort of. I mean, here, everyone's glued to their device like a fucking moron. Everyone's young and perfect. God. Since when was it *normal* to be perfect? Where are all the meat-faced, turkey-bearded, swively-eyed uglies with rancid gobs full of tombstone teeth? It's like they're all *obsessed* with their own image or something. And all this tech everywhere – don't you think it's all gone a bit far? It all seems a bit, I don't know – soulless?'

'If there's one thing everyone here is sure about, Rob, it's the presence of soul. But I know what you mean. And no. I don't miss it. I don't miss the archaic, repressive, ignorant shit hole. No. And neither should you. You can't have loved it, Rob, or there's no way you'd have taken the risk you did.'

'I know, I know. I wouldn't *actually* go back. I just miss … parts of it, I suppose.'

'Not the Wonky Bob parts, I hope.'

'Shuddering at the thought, Finch.'

Rob took himself off to the bathroom, leaving Finch to consider his views on tech. Finch had formed a mixed view of the mainland and its ubiquitous tech-fetish that he wouldn't discuss with Rob. Not now, anyway; he didn't want to reinforce Rob's negativity. Internally, while he found the many forms of tech incredibly useful, consistently mystifying and sometimes even enlightening, he did find everyone's omnipresent device-hunch supremely tedious. He had started thinking of the word 'device' as 'the-vice', as though the constant interaction with tech were an accepted pervasive addiction.

It seemed to Finch that tech, although bringing much convenience into people's lives, had also removed some of the richness. It was normal to *know* everything in detail, from fitness statistics – how many paces were taken in a day, calories burned – to the actual existence of an afterlife. There was certainty in all areas. He sometimes wondered if there was any benefit in *not* knowing all this – in the slower pondering of life, death and everything in between. Where were the spaces that might allow for reflection or consideration during the day? Those times were now filled with tech-based activity, rendering its users less open to chance encounters or genuinely new influences.

Everything online seemed geared to appeal based on the users' existing interests, therefore limiting the chances of any new development in their choice of activity. There seemed to be a risk of existing in an ever reinforcing bubble of one's own ideals, shut off from all else. Finch found himself questioning whether people were better off for being served so well – for all this information and such control. Could they be missing the value that came with exploration of the unknown, of uncertainty, of space for reflection?

Then there were people's heavily curated online existences. Finch had observed the difference between people he'd met and their online personas, avatars even, and how their online reality seemed more important to them than their real day-to-day life. They seemed to be living as multi-faceted creatures, presenting themselves through many lenses, reality diluted as a result of being stretched so far. Although these aspects of tech had prompted questions in Finch's mind, he would never have chosen to reject tech in full. It was more a question of redressing the balance.

Rob returned, breaking Finch's train of thought as he slumped into his chair and leaned close to Finch, as though conspiring. 'This bloke at work – Grobert, yes, his name is *actually* Grobert, like Robert but with an extra 'G', he was a hacker, you know? Someone clever enough to break into computer systems. Well, he told me that Leavers *can't* return – not even if they *want* to. Have you heard that, Finch?'

'*Grobert*? That's the best name I've come across, yet,' said Finch once he'd stopped laughing. 'Yeah – I went to this Leavers' support group thing to see if my mum was there, and they were discussing it. I can't believe they didn't explain that at the AU. I suppose none of us even thought to question them about returning. From what I understand, you *can* return, but only if you have some memory-wipe procedure. Sounds pretty awful.'

'God – so if my dad had come back, he wouldn't have remembered me?'

'Think that's how it would work. And imagine – going back and being considered insane on the island. That would not be a good position to be in. Rob, whatever you're thinking, don't go back. You'll find your feet here – you just

277

need time. Shall we eat?'

'What, after remembering Wonky Bob's curly brown nails – fuck no. I'll never eat again.'

***

Rob was in better spirits after a few hours in Finch's company and seemed slightly more optimistic, or perhaps slightly less pessimistic. He appeared interested in the Leavers' groups so Finch passed him all the relevant details in order that he could attend, should he feel the need.

Olga was on Finch's mind. He was busy freshening up when the mom-tech announced her arrival. He flung the door open and cast his eyes on her at last. Wrapping his arms around her with no consideration for who might witness their affection, he lifted her inside, kissing her and taking Sir's lead from her hand as he did so. He eventually placed her feet back on the ground in his hallway before holding her face with both hands, admiring her beauty and the look of adoration she was beaming back up at him.

'You're here,' he said quietly, close to her face.

'I am,' Olga whispered back.

'And you have *hair*! Let me look at you.'

Finch stood back to admire her. She had somehow grown thick, dark, shiny hair that had been cut into a cool, blunt shape – almost nineteen sixties in style. It was short, and suited her enormously.

'How? How did you grow so much hair so quickly?' he asked.

'Magic hair pills, then hair extensions earlier today. Do you like it?'

'I do. You look stunning, Olga,' Finch said, gazing at her in wonder. After a few moments he acknowledged Sir pawing at his leg, bent down and made a fuss of the dog. 'Come on – I believe Sir needs feeding.'

Olga handed Finch a bag of hot food, but as she did so he pulled her towards him and kissed her again, unable to resist. They soon found themselves collapsing on Finch's bed together, caught up in an uncontrollable expression of their love for one another.

Some time later, as sunlight shone in through Finch's circular window, he entered the bedroom holding two glasses of orange juice. He stopped and looked at Olga; a surge of disbelieving joy swept over him as he watched her lounging on his bed in person – in *his* reality, there in his room at long last. They lay together, chatting, talking the usual fantastical nonsense they typically defaulted to in the absence of anything more demanding that required deliberation. Finch realised they hadn't even discussed how long she would be in London.

'So, you're here as Rob's guide now?' he asked.

'I am. For as long as he needs me, according to my

superiors.'

'Wonderful,' Finch said, grinning unashamedly. 'Not that I wish Rob any discomfort, of course, but I'm glad you are here, obviously.'

'So am I. And I'm sure Sir is pleased to see you, too, my Finch. He seems to really love you – I've never seen anything like it from him. He has clearly missed you. He actually became all excited whenever you called.'

'Well, we're good friends now. Did you ever find out what the problem was with his leg?'

'Yeah – the vet said it's not good. I-I didn't want to tell you yet. He has hip dysplasia, Finch. It's bad news.'

'Okay, so, what *is* that, exactly? What can they do about it?'

'Oh, nothing really. I don't want to put him through the surgery. It's his hip joint – the bone has become eroded. It's probably time I let him go, Finch. I'm sorry. He is old, now.'

'You're thinking about having him *put down*?' Finch asked, alarmed. 'How bad is it?'

'He needs a new hip, Finch. They could do it, but I think it's cruel on him.'

'How old *is* he?' asked Finch, hearing his own fear and frustration uncontrolled in his voice.

'Twelve – in human years.'

'How long do they live, generally?'

'Ah – maybe until they're fifteen, possibly seventeen?'

'So he could have several more good years if you let him have the surgery?'

'Yes, but, he is *old*. I know it's hard for you to understand, but I've been thinking perhaps it's time I released him – let him move on. He's been with me for a while – he probably *wants* to go.'

'But he could be fine, given the surgery?'

'Yes, but …'

'So you're going to put your beloved friend to sleep, no – *kill* your loyal friend, when he could have three, maybe five more perfectly good years with us?' Finch was finding it difficult to conceal his anger at the blasé manner with which Olga seemed to be considering the decision.

'Don't be like that, Finch. He is really old – those years may not be so good. And there's no such thing as killing. Look – imagine if I had to go away for years, decades even, but you knew I'd come back – fact. You wouldn't grieve for me, would you? And you'd let me go. That's what it is – a temporary goodbye. Just some time apart, not the end. Please try to remember that.'

'But, you could just let him go, that *easily*?' Finch was almost panicking; the thought that he was the only obstacle standing between Sir being put to sleep or continuing to live a happy life was all too much.

'Not easily – but I think it's best.' Olga looked stressed, as though she had reached her limit with the subject.

'So *yes*, then.' Finch was outwardly furious now.

Olga put the heels of her hands to her forehead as though despairing. 'I can't believe I'm having to say this again, Finch – it *isn't* goodbye! *There's no such thing*. Please. Try and understand.'

'No – I can't believe you'd do that when he could just have an operation and be fine! What's *wrong* with you?' Finch had lost control of his voice and realised he was shouting, but Olga was now furious too, and responded in full sarcasm.

'Oh – says the man from an island that isn't allowed any more live animal shipments because of the inhumanity with which you treat them. Did you know that, Finch? You're the expert, right?'

'Know what? There were loads of dogs and cats on the island.'

'All inbred. No new ones, right? The government made the decision to turn down requests for new pet breeds based on animal rights laws. You islanders let them go on, in pain, when they're ready to leave. It's cruel. We don't treat them that way here. When they show signs of age, we release them. They can't talk, Finch – we have to be totally fair to them. Err on the side of caution, because they can't *say* how they're feeling.'

'No – erring on the side of caution would be letting them live until their quality of life is so substandard that they clearly want to go, and they make it obvious.'

'No – you islanders, you're wrong! You don't euthanise them soon enough and you *prolong* their suffering.'

'Oh, like you're so wise and stable – you smoke, Olga. I can see your energy now. It's so weak on that side. You've clearly had some horrific lung problem and yet you continue smoking – that's *denial*, isn't it? It's not exactly enlightened, is it? It's having no respect for your own life. It's just fucking stupid.' Finch was exasperated. He noticed Olga's glowing white egg techtoo in her palm. He took her hand and held it up so she could see the egg. 'Look – *look* at your egg. You once told me that the meaning of this was so that you could be mindful that your juniors, your inferiors, could actually be your teachers. Well, maybe Sir is trying to teach *you* something – or maybe *I'm* even right. Maybe you need to start valuing your earthly life.'

Olga whipped her hand away angrily and started dressing. 'I'm going. This is not working. What was I thinking? Of course this was always going to fuck us both up.

Oh, it's booked by the way. Sir's being released because it's the kindest way to deal with him. You're going to have to accept that.'

'Please. *Please* don't go through with it, Olga. Just, *think* about it for a while – please! I know you love him! I know you'd miss him.'

Olga subjected Finch to a hard glare as she continued picking up her clothes. 'You *still* don't get it,' was her coldly delivered response.

'Wow – the arrogance. You really think you know it all, don't you?' Finch sat down on the bed, exhausted, realising the severity of the dispute they'd found themselves involved in. He lifted his head from his hands and spoke in a calmer way. 'Grandad – he used to talk about fishing a lot.'

'What?' Olga looked perplexed. She sat down by Finch's side but leaving a gap, half-dressed and holding her jacket as though hugging it for comfort.

'Fishing, Olga. I used to think it was cryptic nonsense, but I get it now. It was maybe about rejecting some of this – about the importance of contemplation. *Not* having the answers. Waiting hopefully for a fish to bite, and not knowing if they ever would, but in the meantime, thinking – thinking about *everything*. Without knowing – just *considering* everything.'

'You think ignorance is better?' she asked.

'No – but there's a happy medium.'

'There is, and it's not you,' joked Olga, frowning as though aware it was a thoroughly inappropriate, cringe-worthy gag. Seemingly conscious of her own new lunacy, she burst out laughing through her tears, causing Finch to do the same. However, they were both grimly aware that it didn't solve the serious problem they repeatedly found themselves caught up in, and the laughter soon subsided.

'That was truly appalling, Olga. I'm actually proud of you. I think that was possibly better out than in,' Finch said flatly, now staring at the floor in a state of hopeless resignation. 'Listen to me, though. I mean – you all *know* everything … it leaves no space for … for appreciation. You take it all for granted. Life. Life is amazing, to be savoured, wondered at. Every minute. It's like the luxury of now. The luxury of this minute. Maybe it takes uncertainty to appreciate the little things, to see the wonder of it all, amid the daily grind. To find a moment of real joy in just *being* here – no promises. It could all end at any moment. To recognise that brings an awakening – that electric excitement of the present moment. But here, on the mainland, it's just another stage in some long-winded process and it's fine because you have so many lives – none of them really *matter*. But they do. Every day does! Sir matters, and Sir's time here matters. Rethink it, Olga, please. Give him more time.' Finch took her hand and looked into her eyes, searching for some hint that she might reconsider.

'Finch,' she said, weakly, 'it's booked – for in four days' time. I'm sorry. I have to go. I think … I think this was all a mistake.' She took her hand away, bundled up her remaining belongings, attached Sir's lead to his collar and left the apartment, tears streaming down her face.

14 THE MERMAN

Following Olga's unceremonious exit, the day progressed at an excruciatingly slow pace. Finch spent it repeatedly checking for messages, hoping for some contact from Olga – anything, but nothing came. By the evening, Finch had become desperate and morose. He needed to take a walk for the sake of his sanity. He still felt angry at Olga's decision but was distraught at the way they'd left things and desperately worried for Sir, whom he did not wish to say goodbye to either. As the night drew in, the absence of any contact became a heavy certainty in the atmosphere: it was actually over. Above all else, he could not deal with losing both Olga and Sir.

Finch walked for an hour or two. On his return to the apartment, he continued, spending the night pacing his room. He couldn't help but envisage his options, the various scenarios that could possibly reunite him with Olga, but then the question of Sir would bubble to the surface leaving Finch all the more devastated for his uncertainty. Did he even want her back? How could she possibly consider letting Sir die when there were reasonable alternatives available? Then there was Olga's attitude about his mother, and her own fragile state. He wondered if their problems had been obvious for some time, and that perhaps they'd simply been in denial. It was all too painful to face.

Finch went to bed but sleep eluded his churning mind, his thoughts growing blacker as the night wore on. He wondered if wine might help him switch off.

He eventually awoke at midday, hung-over, his left arm sticking to the sheets. Bleary eyed, he peeled the sheet away to discover blood – he'd cut himself in an alcoholic stupor. He was no longer bleeding, and the blood he could see wasn't worrying in quantity, but he'd reached a new low and still felt engulfed by the hollow ache that Olga and his mother had left behind. In the morning light he knew that no amount of wine or self-harm could ever shift this pain.

Seb showed up, aware of the break-up, and tried to help Finch out of his personal hell, but nothing anyone could say was going to alter the situation. Seb implied that Olga was equally shattered because she felt their relationship was genuinely unsalvageable. Finch sat on the sofa amid the mess and gloom of the apartment, paralysed by the loss, Seb at his side offering support.

'Third-gen islanders and mainlanders may as well come from different planets,' Seb said. 'That's why relationships between them are particularly difficult. Both worlds have had decades to grow so far apart that meeting in the middle is still an almighty compromise. Each partner is convinced their way is the correct one – the issues that arise need to be managed in such a way so as to require a permanent, on-site, couple's therapist.'

'That's depressing,' Finch commented darkly.

'Yes – sorry. I know. But there are ways to meet fellow Leavers, maybe second-gen mainlanders, if you don't mind the age gap …'

'I can't even think about that,' said Finch, feeling thoroughly bleak. 'I don't want anyone else.'

'Give yourself time. Get back into your meditation, your own growth. You'll eventually start to feel better, bit by bit. I know it's unthinkable now, but I promise, you will come through this. Maybe try to imagine yourself in a happier relationship with someone new – dream up your ideal and try to focus on that, instead of the loss. You know the law of attraction – use it, Finch.'

'My ideal would be Olga.'

'I know, but in time, you'll see past her.'

Seb had a new level of concern in his eyes as he noticed Finch's arm dressings. 'Oh Finch, you didn't …'

'What? Oh. Yeah. I wasn't all there, Seb … wine – lots.'

'Please, don— Shall I request a new guide to help you through this?'

'God, no. Please, I'm fine. I was drunk. I'm not going to do it again. Seriously.'

Seb's expression became grave and he promptly suggested they get a change of scene. They went out for a late lunch, then walked by the river, sometimes in silence as Finch's mind turned inward at every opportunity.

Apologetically removing the remaining alcohol and anything bearing a blade from Finch's apartment, Seb advised him to get some sleep, saying he'd return tomorrow. Finch was incapable of decision or comment – aware only that he had descended into the full zombie state of paralysing heartbreak: an exhausted, inward realisation that nothing and no one could fix this. Ever.

***

Beautiful fish swam in the air around Finch's head. They were small fish, a multitude of varied hues and shapes, and their presence was magical. Finch had experienced this dream many times before. While absorbed in it he usually recognised it as a dream and, as always, relished the enchanting sight of these exquisite air fish, his mysterious visitors. He'd been shopping in the dream before the fish had arrived, buying wonderful new clothes from a rail of couture, something he'd never done in real life. He was in the changing room when the fish began to appear. Finch had no idea what, if anything, these fish symbolised, and it didn't matter. The way they swam silently around him was hypnotic and delightful, reflecting the light with colourful flashes, darting so gracefully through the air. Then he remembered. Olga.

'Fuck!' he shouted, waking himself up with the shock of his own yell. The full horror of the previous few days flooded back in an instant. Finch sat on the edge of the bed, his head in his hands, catching up with his ruthlessly abrupt journey from mesmerising dream fish to harsh reality. Yet another day to face amid this relentless fog of dreadful heartache.

As the week progressed, Finch found himself with more space away from Seb, presumably because Seb had begun trusting that he would not try to harm himself again. Wrecked and preoccupied, Finch would walk the streets in the evenings as though that could distract in any way from his gaping loss that was so impossible to ignore. He noticed now more than ever how manic the city seemed, raucous with the gaudy verve of mass merrymaking. Now it looked laughably like a caricature to Finch; he numbly remembered some ancient cartoons his mother had shown him that depicted comically sketched debauchery on the streets of London in olden times. The basic nature of people was unchanged though so much time had passed. The world was vastly different, but people were just as driven by their vices, Finch thought, in his desolate state.

He had been walking without any particular plan, simply going where his legs decided to take him, when he recognised his surroundings. Above his head was an incredible structure like a cylindrical tunnel of glass between two buildings that was in fact a suspended, tubular swimming pool. Finch had noticed a few of these in the city, but they were usually rectangular. Now it was lit up and complete with swimmers as seen from below through the glass – and there was the library he'd attended in an attempt to locate his mother. He stood outside for a moment. The possibility occurred to him that he could attend the Leavers' group in person, for the right reasons this time. Perhaps it would help. The larger part of him was reluctant, but he knew the time was right to catch the group and something in him suggested that perhaps it was more of Boff's 'synchron-dipity', and that maybe he should just go with it.

He could see the group sitting quietly. There were fewer attendees this time and Finch loitered nervously on the outskirts, indecisive and self-conscious, hoping that he wasn't thoroughly conspicuous as an anxious newcomer.

'Are you with us?' asked the leader, who had obviously noticed Finch's hovering position and air of apprehension.

'Can I?'

'Of course, please sit. I'm Marko. We are a Leavers' group – you are a Leaver, yes?'

'Yes.'

'Then welcome, we're glad to have you …?'

'F-f-Richard,' lied Finch, transparently.

'Okay, *Frichard*. My predecessor as group leader was a Frichard, too. Anyway, welcome. We were just discussing the omnipresence of tech here – feel free to contribute whenever you like. In a moment I'll ask you to tell us your story, in brief.'

Finch tuned out the tech discussion in order to prepare his story, but had barely started thinking when Marko prompted him to begin, so *Frichard* began. 'I came here from Monk Island … I mean, the Isle of Wight. I was recruited. I, well, I started a relationship with my … with a gen-three mainlander, and it was disastrous. That's it, really. Now I'm here.'

'Ah, thank you, Frichard. Relationships with mainlanders are notoriously complex. I'm sure we've all discovered that the hard way, haven't we?' asked Marko, to a murmur of shy agreement from the group. 'It's not all bad though,' he continued. 'With work, they can flourish. It just takes a lot of managing, that's all, so no one despair – and there are always other Leavers, too.'

'I met my ex-husband at a Leavers' group,' stated an elderly gentleman in a mild tone.

'Well, presumably you had *some* good years, though, Archie?' suggested the leader in a clear attempt to offer a positive angle on what was swiftly becoming a dismal travesty of a subject.

'Oh, yes. But that's my point, Marko. Relationships end *anyway*. Sometimes it's just because they do, and not because you're incompatible due to your upbringing. So you may as well have a good crack at it, regardless. There's no correct formula – just trial and error, as with all relationships – it just takes work.'

'Exactly! Point well made, Archie. Frichard, feel free to tell me it's private, but it may help others here to understand. Was there any particular catalyst that caused the problems in the relationship?'

'It's fine – yes. She was going to have her dog put to sleep when he could have had an operation and would have been fine. I just couldn't get through to her about it. She had decided, and that was that. She didn't even seem upset about it. We – well, we clashed. I begged her not to go ahead with it … She left.'

'Oh. So, a typical scenario that highlighted your differing views, then. I'm sorry to hear it, Frich. It's never easy.'

'I can't help thinking it should be, though. It's just … where's the balance? I mean, I am a sensitive so I'm lucky to completely *know* there's more to this world – I've encountered it on many occasions – so why can't I just let the dog go, too?'

'Well, generally speaking, it seems to go against the core values of a Leaver. Leavers have been brought up to survive, and to value life, whether or not there's anything afterwards. When you consider it from a young mainlander's perspective, say, imagine you were a teacher. There's this kid in your class that you know would be better off if you moved them along to another class, but you also know, even though you'd built a good relationship with this kid, you wouldn't see them again until the big party at the end of the year. Well, that's how casual born-and-bred mainlanders can be about death decisions. Death isn't real to them. It's not their fault – and they're right, really. It's just that we are programmed with the opposite attitude, with basic survival instinct: to preserve life at all costs.'

Feeling slightly bombarded, Finch was grateful

when the leader moved the subject on to the sometimes antisocial use of augmented reality lenses. He tuned out, lost in an impenetrable confusion of concerns over Olga, his mother, and Sir, that he had no idea how to navigate. Once the group had dispersed, Finch began walking again, feeling more confounded and thwarted than ever. He couldn't turn a corner for confirmation that no, his relationship with Olga was not workable, so neither was it retrievable.

The dark water of the Thames looked cold. From his position on the bridge, Finch could see that he would be a lost cause should he slip from the high railings he held on to. But then, did it even matter? He wasn't going to stop existing completely. It was just his human form that would be gone, this life. The one with Olga in it. He remembered the Death Wishers tearing past on their kamikaze mission to the beyond. Perhaps they were right. But then, what if you *wanted* to be switched off forever? There was no such possibility as far as Finch understood. Eternal heartbreak – no release. Perhaps that was his future, he thought. If he did die, he would still be Finch after death, and he imagined that Olga would still be his primary concern. Nothing would change, so perhaps he should just climb down and walk home. There really was no escape.

Over the following days Finch attended several different Leavers' groups. He found it helpful to talk about

Olga with people of his own mindset, and was starting to see the benefit of attending. He had begun to make a mission out of finding the lesser-known groups, the ones held in more remote locations. He would turn up, to the surprise of a few long-standing members who had rarely been treated to a new story from a fresh face. Tonight, Finch was headed towards Shepherd's Bush for a meeting with a group who called themselves 'the Vers.'

Eventually Finch located the group at the far end of an old theatre that was having a night off, so had opened its doors to various other activities. The theatre was miniscule yet ornate, like an inside out, old-fashioned wedding cake. The ceiling and walls were adorned in beautiful white plasterwork. The stage was hidden behind heavy velvet curtains, complete with antique golden fringing and appliqued brocade tape. Finch walked towards the group, eyes up, admiring the ceiling and the colossal chandeliers. As he approached, a few middle-aged faces looked up at him as though they were about to redirect him to the correct place. So far there were just seven people in this group.

'Are you the Vers?' asked Finch, aware of the group's enquiring eyes on him.

'Yes,' replied a woman from inside a cloud of curly yellow hair. 'Would you like to join us?' she asked in an astonished tone.

'I'd love to, thanks. Shall I grab one of these chairs?'

'Will you look at those cheekbones? Handsome boy,' she said quietly to one of the other women in the group. 'Please do. Come and sit. I'll introduce you to everyone. Now, where to start … This here is Otto – he's been with us for six years. Next to him are Freya and Isabella who are twins. Then we have Caleb, Tyler and Rex. I'm Gracie. We've all been doing this for a while. Rex, you're newest, aren't you – a year and a half? Am I right?'

'Yeah, Gracie,' confirmed Rex.

Finch sat down and was inspected by seven pairs of eyes. 'I'm Frichard,' he lied, having become accustomed to the name and mildly entertained that people always accepted it unquestioningly.

'Welcome, Frichard,' Gracie said. 'So, do you want to tell us how you ended up on the mainland?'

'Okay. I was, well, pretty much alone in the end, and my friend – a priest and ex-tutor – saw that I could, well, that I *have* some sensitive ability, and talked me into leaving. I had nothing left to lose so I agreed. I came here just a few months ago. I'm still finding my feet, I suppose. I don't regret my move like some do, though. That's not why I'm here. I started coming to Leavers' groups because, well, I was in a relationship that ended – with a gen-three girl – and, I suppose, I didn't know where to turn. Other Leavers feel more like family than anyone else.'

'Well, you found us, so you're doing okay,' stated Gracie as she patted Finch on the knee.

'Poor Frichard! Breakups are just the *worst*,' said Freya. 'Was it recent, lovely?'

'A few days ago. We fell out over her dog. She's having it put to sleep when it would have been fine with surgery. Seemed nonsensical to me. But I suppose I should have seen it coming. I really miss her, though.' Humiliatingly for Finch, their kindness was causing him to connect with the sadness of his situation and he felt himself becoming emotional as he sensed their compassion. Gracie must have noticed his discomfort, and changed the subject.

'So, who's managed to turn their devices off at night like we discussed?' she asked, and a couple of hands went up. Finch found the conversation distracting enough to pass through his lachrymose reaction and back to normality without dissolving. This group, he thought, felt like home for some reason. Perhaps it was the ancient building, or maybe the slight air of eccentricity he picked up from its members, but he liked it, and feeling anything other than profound grief was a welcome relief.

He looked at the members. Most looked around fifty and they were an eclectic bunch. Rex, appearing to be of maybe Pakistani origin, wore a thick moustache and what looked like a Chinese housecoat – padded silk brocade in pale yellow, complete with frog fastenings and matching tassels. He seemed to be in possession of a sense of humour, as they all did.

Otto seemed intelligent, but Finch detected some serious disturbance in his energy, something had happened that had changed him in recent years – a trauma or distress; Finch couldn't pin it down. He was in good shape and wore smartish attire. Otto seemed to take the conversation more seriously than everyone else. His white hair looked too old for his skin, and his eyes were surrounded by deep laughter lines which had seen more active days. The twin sisters were not identical. Freya was feminine and soft in every way, and the other, Isabella, seemed far more modern and dynamic, maybe businesslike in her appearance and demeanour. Caleb was younger than the others and looked bored to the point of nodding off, but would then contribute some witty remark that implied he was nowhere near asleep after all. Tyler seemed slightly down on his luck, dressed in grubby casual wear and appearing a little unkempt, with long strands of greying hair curling around the hood of his soft jacket.

Finch didn't get too involved in the conversation. It emerged that Tyler had been experiencing some health issues, and that became the main subject of conversation – unrelated to leaving, and more the kind of conversation old friends or family would hold around the dinner table.

On his way home, Finch decided to return to the group at their next meeting in a couple of days, and felt marginally less wretched for an hour or two, before the cold reality of losing Olga returned at full pelt as he climbed into bed alone.

15 BEAMED

The mom-tech had drawn Finch a hot bath and he was sinking below the surface when a call from Rob came through. Finch wanted to tell Rob everything, to compare feelings of loss and rejection, to help each other through it, but he knew he couldn't. Not a word.

As he listened to Rob's chit-chat, he noticed a new resentful or bitter tone in his friend's voice. He asked if Rob was okay, gently explaining that he sensed he was dealing with an undercurrent of anger, and Rob had replied that too right, he was angry. He'd spent his life as a prisoner on the island, escaped, found happiness, then had it taken away again. Finch questioned the term *prisoner* as being a little extreme, but Rob defended his choice of words as not being strong enough, mate. Apparently, Rob had been spending time with Grobert, an Irish Leaver as a result of bad health, who hadn't dealt with the transition as well as Rob and Finch. It seemed to Finch that Grob, as Rob now called him, had stoked the flames of Rob's upset and Finch detected that he was a thoroughly negative, possibly even dangerous influence.

Olga, now of course Rob's guide, would need to be made aware of this development if she wasn't already, Finch thought. He didn't want the contact with her and wondered if Seb would be a better conduit for the information he'd perceived. He decided to mention it to Seb rather than deal with it directly. Olga was playing on his mind even more than usual. It was about the time that Sir would be going through his 'release' and Finch was still in turmoil about Olga's determination to let Sir go, whether they were a couple or not. Finch was tormented by thoughts of Sir, his dear friend, knowing he would soon be gone – if he wasn't already.

The afternoon arrived and Finch made his way back to see the Vers again. Tonight's meeting was to be held in the function room of a restaurant that had been transformed into a virtual diner – one of a chain. Finch had heard about the brand of diners known as 'Beamed' but had never before visited one. Beamed was based around a gimmick that allowed friends in different locations to enjoy dinner together, regardless of the distances between them. Each party would attend their local branch, be seated, and eat opposite the live holographic streaming of their partner, who would, in reality, be doing exactly the same thing in another branch of the restaurant. The arrival of the food, along with all reasonably predictable encounters with the waiting staff, were synchronised to perfection so that all interruptions were a joint experience. The menus, music and ambience were identical in every branch, enabling each patron to feel their partner was having the same experience as they would, were they physically together. The concept had been successful and Beamed eateries had proliferated quickly over recent years, spreading far and wide.

Finch was led through the restaurant by one of the waiting staff to a back room. Fascinated, he noted each table had one solid customer and one ghost-like presence, and everything else was as he'd expect. The sound was surprisingly good and he could hear the holographic customers as though they were present in the room. The corporeal and non-corporeal diners looked each other in the eye with no problem and some tables held larger parties consisting of many holo-customers alongside those that were physically present, all interacting naturally, as though nothing was unusual. Finch hadn't time to consider it properly, but somewhere in his mind he felt the image was the perfect illustration of the mainland – something about being present, but not quite.

Gracie greeted Finch warmly and mentioned that they were still awaiting Rex and Tyler, so he could relax, get a drink, do whatever he wanted. Freya and Otto were chatting among themselves and Isabella was using her device, so Finch looked to Caleb for the exchange of pleasantries.

'Hey, Frichard, so, how is the woman situation?' Caleb asked casually, responding to Finch's friendly approach.

'Oh, the same. I think the dog may be gone by now, though. Poor guy.' Finch was trying to sound easy about it but Caleb was no idiot. He shot a serious look at Finch.

'That's rough. What you don't need on top of a break-up is *more* grief. How are you handling it all?'

'Not so good, at times, but it helps, coming to these groups.'

'It's why we come. We've all been through it, Frichard. I'm divorced, so is Freya, and Tyler come to think of it, too. Otto's partner passed not long ago, sadly. There's room for some good news in this group, but we've all looked after each other through the difficult times. It does help.'

Otto and Freya suddenly laughed together. 'You can't have that!' Otto said, with an amused abhorrence at whatever Freya had requested.

'Oh, don't mind them. So, where have you come from, Frich? Monk Island, was it?' asked Caleb.

Finch dragged his attention back to Caleb and answered, before enquiring as to where everyone in the group had originated. It turned out that a few had come from the Isle of Wight, and Finch wondered whether that was the reason for his feeling that they were all kindred spirits.

Rex arrived, nonchalantly wearing a fez and a woman's vintage leather biker jacket. Finch admired Rex's ability to carry off the most random of sartorial combinations, and was reminded of his recurring air-fish dream. He would not have been surprised to see the fish swimming around Rex's head, too, for some reason. Maybe it was about creativity, or having some individuality, vibrancy present in one's world, or worlds.

Gracie started the meeting and began by welcoming Frichard back. Isabella confessed to being addicted to her device as she turned it off, sparking a conversation around the level of reliance on tech that they all experienced now, having been on the mainland for some time. Rex was unzipping his jacket as the conversation started and said, 'But even the clothes are tech, though. You can't actually escape it, even if you wanted to. This old jacket – it warms me up if I'm cold. It cools me down if I'm hot. I could keep it on forever and remain at a good temperature. And I do nothing – it just responds to me. You can't negate tech, even if you try. It's literally in the fabric of everything.'

At last Tyler appeared in the unexpected company of two bottles of sparkling wine and a thrilled expression. 'I have news. They cleared me of it – I'm free of any sign! It's over!' There was a cheer and many exchanged hugs. Questions followed, relating to how he was feeling. Everyone seemed overjoyed to hear the relief in Tyler's statements. They shared the wine and began chatting more freely.

'You know, we should get around to discussing some Leaver topics, soon. Poor Frichard has come to see us and we must be boring him,' exclaimed Gracie, but everyone was having too good a time with the wine and the long awaited good news. Finch had been chatting to Isabella about mainland food, so was not remotely bored.

'Oh, Frichard doesn't mind, do you, lovely?' asked Freya as she rummaged through her bag for something, causing some of the contents to escape. A toy plastic fried egg, a nearly life-size lemon and an equally fake frankfurter rolled out of her bag on to the table. Noticing the puzzled expressions on everyone's faces, she said, 'Oh, the kids I'm looking after – they love these vintage bits. Genuine plastic is such a rarity …'

'Random … Well, that's one for Grandad's fruit bowl,' said Otto, picking up the faded fried egg. You could've had *that*, but you went with the chastity belt of the

Loch Ness Monster. Amateur.'

'Well, that would explain its lack of offspring!' Freya said, laughing as she stuffed the fake food back into her large bag.

Finch was blinking, computing the importance of what he'd just heard said so unwittingly. 'I'm sorry?' he eventually managed, with a force that stopped everyone laughing.

'Oh, sorry, Frichard. It's just a surreal game we play,' explained Freya.

'Where did you learn it? When was Mia Henry here?' Finch asked with an urgency that seemed to alarm everyone.

'Mia? You knew her?' asked Otto, meeting Finch with an equal level of seriousness.

'Yes. I did. Do you?' asked Finch.

'I … did, too,' Otto said, as he stood up and walked over to Finch. He leant close and studied him, placing a hand near his jawline and scrutinising Finch's eyes. 'My God. Finch,' he said under his breath. 'Are you *Finch*?' he asked, astonished.

'Yeah. Yes. How do you know her? Where is she?'

'This is *Finch*? Mia's Finchiebobs?' asked Freya, coming close, examining Finch with new compassion and wonder.

'Come with me. We have a lot to talk about,' said Otto kindly, leading Finch out of the room. 'I have something for you.'

Otto and Finch walked. They were apparently headed for Otto's apartment, which was a few minutes away. 'Where is my mother?' asked Finch, no longer able to take his time with the subject.

'Let's just get to mine, then we can talk for as long as it takes. She's not here, Finch. But there's a lot I need to tell you.' Otto's tone was earnest and kind-hearted, so Finch accepted his suggestion. They arrived at the entrance of an enormous glass tower that seemed to be shaped like a jagged stalagmite. Otto greeted the robotic porter and they took the lift up to the thirty-first floor. A retinal scan and voice command unlocked the door and they entered Otto's vast apartment.

Finch's first impression was that Otto was an art lover. There were large modern paintings on most of the walls within the bright space. The furniture, though worn and old, was all splendidly stylish – a mismatch of neutral leather tones and exposed wood. There were interesting objects everywhere: piles of old books, sculptures, enormous houseplants and chunks of moulded plaster reclaimed from architectural salvage sites, along with carved wooden pieces clearly from the interiors of historic buildings. Otto even had what seemed to be an ancient gravestone leaning up against a plain white wall. It was eighteenth century with script so beautifully curled and ornate as to render it completely illegible to modern eyes. Some of the inscription was in deeper cut capitals and there was a skull and crossbones in relief above the text. Its shape was arched at the top, one arch at the centre flanked by two smaller ones either side. It made for a striking focal point.

'What's this? I mean, how come you have a gravestone?' asked Finch, diverted by its eerie presence.

'Oh, I know. It's not as macabre as it looks. I rescued it from a demolition site. They were flattening the churchyard for development.' Otto acknowledged Finch's bafflement and explained. 'That happens … the dead are viewed in a different light now – it's not as important to remember them or even respect them like people used to. Anyway, unbelievably, this was about to be thrown into a grinder, so I talked to them and they let me take it. I know, it's an odd thing to have, but it reminds me about life – to live it. I suppose it takes me back to before I heard about the Discovery, and how I valued life in a different way. I don't really expect people to understand but, if nothing else, it's incredibly beautiful.'

'It is, and I think I do. It keeps you grounded, maybe.' Finch was studying the engraved lettering, running his fingers over it. He could make out the dates 1711 and 1743. A short life, he thought.

'That's ... yes, I suppose it does. Here.' Otto handed Finch a glass of hot green tea. 'Please, sit down. Finch – I'm so glad you're here! I'm sorry about the chaos. So ... how much do you know about Mia's time on the mainland and why she left in the first place?'

'I know nothing, actually. Just that she left and she'd worked at SCI-PSY. We were told she'd died. We had a funeral for her. I still can't believe she was here all along and that she'd really left us.'

'Oh God ... well, *don't* believe it. This is exactly what she dreaded. Firstly, Finch, she absolutely did not leave you in the way you've been left to assume. They told her, originally, that she could return to the island after three months. The person who recruited her was, let's say, not exactly honest about the memory-wipe small print. They recruited her for her sensitive ability. She'd gone to the doctors, exasperated about her unusual experiences, and there was an undercover SCI-PSY recruiter who picked up that she had ability. She didn't care about being a sensitive, though – she left because of Hope. The death of little Hope broke her heart. Olivia, her, well, arsehole of a recruiter, promised her information about Hope, and in her deep grief, thinking she could return, she took the offer and left, temporarily as far as she was concerned. So, please don't think she simply abandoned you. She attempted five times to return to you, but kept getting caught and was eventually threatened with an enforced memory cleanse if she didn't desist. The island takes the threat of returning Leavers horribly seriously. She didn't want to forget you so she was completely cornered and forced to accept the situation.'

'So, how do you know all this? You two were, what – friends?'

'Married, Finch. I loved your mum very much. We met at the Leavers' group not long after she'd arrived.'

'And where is she now?' Finch asked, almost dreading the answer.

'Finch, no matter how much better your mum's life became, she couldn't live with herself for inadvertently abandoning you and her dad. She was tormented day and night. She was happy in our world, in a superficial sense, but the deeper trap she was in grew unbearable for her. She became gravely ill, Finch. I'm so sorry. The illness took her. She … let it, I think. She passed on about eleven months ago.' Otto could no longer maintain his composure and dropped his head in quiet, cathartic sobs. 'I'm sorry, I just … find it hard. But you're here! She would be – must be – so happy that you're okay and that you found me.'

Finch moved next to Otto on the sofa and put an arm

around his shoulders to comfort him as he cried. Finch's mind was taking in the many aspects of the news – good and bad – while aware that he needed time to process everything. So his mother had loved him, hadn't left them, but was, nonetheless, gone. It struck Finch that it was almost like being back at the beginning of his journey, as though he'd gone full circle, except at least now he knew the truth.

'Funny,' said Otto, blowing his nose, 'she always thought she'd see you again. She'd had this precognitive vision – of you. She said she'd seen you playing your cello as an adult, in a concert, and that you were wearing lipstick, all smudged. She thought she would somehow help by being there, that you would be nervous and needed calming, and she would be able to support you. That thought kept her going through the darker times. She was sure you'd appear on the mainland so this could play out.'

With that, Finch also melted into tears. The image of his mum's loving face blasting inner strength at him as he'd played on stage that night was with him again. 'She *did* that – she was there,' he said. 'It wasn't long ago – just before I left. She was there as I played. I could see her above the audience. She helped me get myself together. I had her lipstick on. I'd just punched Akton and I really wasn't coping.'

The look of astonished joy on Otto's face was a

wonderful sight. 'I've got something for you. I'll find it.' Otto disappeared into another room, shortly returning with a letter.

'It's from her – she wrote it to you, in case I ever found you.' He handed the letter to Finch. It was sealed and labelled 'To my Finch' in her familiar, crazy handwriting. Finch took it, brushing the ink with his fingertips. He didn't know whether he should open it now or wait until his mind was clearer. Considering that perhaps Otto would benefit from being included, he tore open the envelope to find many handwritten pages inside. He began to read.

My darling, Finchiebobs!

First of all – I MISS YOU SO MUCH, MY DARLING BOY!! I think about you constantly, hoping that you are well and happy in your life, and wishing with all my heart that I could be there with you.

I so hope you get to read this letter someday. I write this because I have no idea what they told you about my leaving, and I worry myself stupid that you and poor grandad have grieved for me unnecessarily. I'm so sorry if that's what I (and they) have put you through. I hope that you can forgive me for that – it is a crime to inflict that on anybody.

I was duped into leaving, Finch – I was a mess over little Hope, and Olivia, whom I thought a friend, said she had information – a way of helping me get in contact – to connect with Hope, and I trusted her in my grief. Hurting you both was never my plan. In fact, they told me I could return, and I never would have left if I'd known the truth – not in a billion years.

Well, you're here hopefully reading this, and you've obviously discovered that I'm not really gone – what with the Discovery, and all that ... I have wondered recently if you would find yourself recruited too, so thought Otto may find you at some point – or maybe you'd find him.

After arriving on the mainland, I came to suspect you have sensitive ability, too – I remember so many things you did as a child that I didn't understand at the time. As a toddler, you talked as soon as you could about your 'other, old life in the city', your family there, and your job as an architect! I found it odd, but thought you just had an active imagination. Then I came here – I saw the buildings – so much like what you'd described and drawn. And the detail – it was all there, so now I realise you must have remembered it. Then you used to talk to people that I couldn't see! Even my mother, it seemed. You sometimes called her name as though you were playing together! Anyway

– you clearly have it too, and I imagine that's how you've ended up tracking the wonderful Otto down and reading this, at long last.

I have tried many times to return to you, Finch. Five attempts, to date. Each time I can't get past those security drones – and now they are talking about 'removing the threat' by wiping my memory, so I have to officially cease my endeavours. I want you to know I have thought about you every minute of every day, and will do forever.

Now they tell me I am rather ill. I may well be leaving soon – I'm not worried about dying – I have seen the beyond in my work so I'm happy to go on, except that I will be leaving you again, in a sense.

I want to tell you to have A WONDERFUL LIFE, Finch. I know this mainland world is mind boggling and just so ridiculously complicated, but your life is precious and if you can value and enjoy every minute – every joyful and even miserable experience, you'll be living it well. Take opportunities and have adventures! I wish I could be there for you to help you along, through good times and bad, as mothers should.

Though it looks like I'm not going to be here physically, please understand that I will be at your side spiritually, always. I will love you more than anything else in the world for as long as I am a conscious being – so, pretty much eternally, then!

Love, always! (you'll never get rid of me, darling boy)

Mum
XXXXXX

Finch sat back on the sofa and closed his eyes. It was so wonderful to have the weight lifted. Without words, he handed the letter to Otto.

***

When Otto and Finch had both passed through the initial emotion of their encounter and all it had brought to light, Otto suggested they eat and started to busy himself in the kitchen.

'So, what I don't understand is why everyone I have spoken to at SCI-PSY thinks Mum was some kind of introverted, shy soul,' said Finch, pleased to have a source of answers after all this time and keen to ask anything and everything that came to mind.

'Ah, well – wouldn't you be? Imagine you'd left your child on the basis that it was just for a few months, only to find it was forever. Wouldn't you be utterly distracted and beyond miserable?'

'When you put it like that – yeah, definitely. But I got the impression she wasn't happy with the work, too. She got another job and left? It was all a bit vague.'

'Yes, she worried that SCI-PSY's intentions – harnessing the ability of sensitives – was not all good. I remember her mild concerns that they were all possibly being exploited, even weaponised, in preparation for some dreadful scenario, or to be used as spies. That was part of the reason she left. The other was to be with me. I am lucky in that I don't need to work any more. I could support her and we could live very well together – that's how she funded her many missions to return to you.'

'Did you not worry that she might succeed and you wouldn't see her again?'

'Yes, of course. We had five awful goodbyes, but I've been here long enough for some of it to sink in – that there's actually no such thing as a final goodbye. And yes, it would have been downright dreadful to lose her, albeit temporarily, but above everything I wanted Mia to be happy. She was so deeply troubled by leaving you both, the truth is, she was never completely present. She would get this look as though there was always part of her mind on the island, worrying about you and your grandad. Is he still on the island?'

Finch explained how his grandad had sacrificed

himself so that Finch would take the opportunity to leave and, before long, found himself conveying the whole story, which took some time. Otto listened intently and asked many questions about Finch's thoughts and well-being throughout the experience. They ate dinner together and Finch got the impression that Otto was a thoughtful soul, and a kind, intelligent one.

Otto went to make some coffee, leaving Finch to find some quiet relief from the intensity of the revelations. He took refuge in contemplating the apartment's many intriguing pieces of art. Though it was untidy in places, even the mess looked carefully curated. This didn't appear intentional; it was more a case of everything looking right together. Even piled up or thrown on a sofa, it all still, somehow, managed to appear visually harmonious. Otto clearly had many interests. In a pile next to Finch there were books on geology, art, psychology, stained glass, ancient Greece, street art, fashion, antiques, architecture, furniture, and multiple travel guides. A bust of Beethoven was balanced precariously on top.

'I thought actual books were redundant, now,' Finch commented, changing the subject, aware that he had reached his emotional saturation point.

'They are, but I still love them. It's great to have access, isn't it, after the appalling island library, if you could even call it that. There are only so many books on natural history that you can read.'

Finch thought back. He'd spent many hours there and read pretty much everything on the shelves. The Council's need to edit the available information had meant the subjects on offer were absurdly limited. There was, at least, a shelf of classic novels: works by Jane Austin, the Bronte sisters and some Dickens. Finch had enjoyed those. He now remembered that most books had the odd page missing and wondered if, like the Dead Parrot sketch, they had just been brutally edited by a demented Founder chimp with a flick knife.

'I liked the architecture books, though – funny, given Mum's comments about me as a kid, but I now see how out of date they were. This building – it's amazing. I've admired it from a distance. How long have you lived here?'

'Years. I had to wait a while for an apartment to become free. I became better known and suddenly I got a call – as though you had to be *someone* to obtain an apartment. It was worth the wait for the view alone, though.'

'Hang on – you're well known, Otto?'

'In a sense,' Otto confirmed, his tone conveying a very British sense of discomfort at the concept. 'I'm an artist. It's how I got off the island …'

'That's new,' said Finch. 'I've only ever heard

stories of leaving due to illness, or where risky escape or a particular talent were the catalyst.'

'Yes, but you'll find there are many things that can make you unwelcome on an island. My work while there was not well received. I was exploring concepts of existence, questioning things – you know, existential, sometimes transcendental stuff. It drew the attention of the Council. They asked me to go back to landscapes! I, in my fiery youth, refused. You can't tell an artist to stop doing what they must do, what drives them. So they eventually suggested I leave and a recruiter came to talk me into it. Artistic freedom sounded appealing so I agreed. It wasn't an easy choice. I left my sister behind, but I harboured hopes of her joining me later, not knowing how difficult that would be. I was naïve. But here, my roots as an islander have made my work all the more interesting to the art world, and thankfully I've known some success.'

'Is this all your work?' asked Finch, looking at the paintings hanging on his walls.

'No. Mia did that one. The rest are older – before my time. I've picked them up over the years.'

'Mum painted?'

'Yes – she was amazing at adapting and exploring her creative nature.'

Finch took a long look at the painting which was a

large square canvas, frameless and striking. It was an abstract featuring one bold black circle, off centre so that one edge had been slightly sliced off, and it was surrounded by many shades of palest off-white blocks that had been daubed on thickly. There were super-fine veins of bright orange mixed in with the white and kept to a minimum. A crackle or two of black paint escaped the circle to ease the perfection – almost a relief to observe.

'What does it mean? Does it depict something?'

'She said it was a self-portrait. But I think she was just mocking the art world.'

'Sounds like Mum.'

16 THE LOSS OF LOSS

Otto persuaded Finch to stay over and make use of his lavish guest suite, and Finch happily accepted. It was wonderful to spend time with someone who was so well acquainted with his mum and keen to undo all the wrongs, making Finch feel valued and loved again. After breakfast the following day Otto and Finch took a walk to the prominent modern art gallery that currently exhibited Otto's latest work. A rapport had developed between them during their long hours of revelation. Otto's calm and cerebral, openly analytical nature appealed to Finch, and Otto clearly enjoyed being a stand-in father figure; Finch got the sense that Otto had perhaps felt the absence of family as the years had progressed.

Otto took an interest in all aspects of Finch's world, and, having learned from Finch that he had genuinely stumbled upon his mother's widower and friends by chance, the subject moved to Olga, because she had been the cause of Finch's presence at the Vers and his more recent, unsolved turmoil. Finch explained the stalemate that'd developed between them over Sir, resigned to the fact that the situation was now immovable, a dead end. He still ached for Olga and would have done anything to fix their relationship, but knew that their many clashes indicated the harsh reality of incompatibility.

Otto thought for a while. 'But you can understand why a native mainlander would see it that way, I suppose?' he asked, referring to Sir's plight.

'Yes, I can totally understand why she comes to that conclusion from her perspective, but it just seems brutal, unnecessary. Cruel, even. He could have several more years.'

'But from her perspective?'

'From her perspective, she's just setting him free.'

'And, it's cruel because?'

'Because … because she's not valuing his time here.'

'You'll miss him, won't you?'

'Of course … God – am I being an idiot islander?'

'Of course – but understandably,' said Otto, with a glint of gentle humour in his eyes.

'I love her – I mean, seriously. We are connected,' Finch said, considering the balance, the argument about Sir set against the strength of his feelings.

'I can see that. But enough to understand her actions? To forgive them?'

'I don't know. I mean, absolutely, in a sense – in that she is doing the best she knows how to do, but I worry about how incompatible we are. I value life, the here and now, rather than the later and beyond, which seems to be her focus.'

'Perhaps you could meet in the *next week* and *just down the road*? A compromise?'

'I get your point, but it's over. She was exasperated with me. And I was angry at her.'

'Give it some thought, Finch. This world isn't going to go backwards, so we Leavers must move forwards. It's nothing to fear. That's all there is to it.'

***

Having spent two days enjoying each other's company, Finch and Otto said goodbye for now, while making plans to have dinner at Finch's apartment in a few days' time. Finch made his way home feeling different. His outlook had shifted with the news about his mother and as a result of Otto's perceptive insight. He felt lighter, easier with the mainland and elated for finally understanding the truth about his mother and her abiding love for him. He became conscious that there was a new, elevated part of his mind that was better able to comprehend and accept what he'd previously viewed as the somewhat jarring ways of the mainland.

As Finch entered his apartment, he didn't find the squalid mess he remembered leaving. The mom-tech informed him that Seb had ordered cleaners in and they'd made the place immaculate in his absence. Finch was grateful. He had been feeling uneasy about the idea of returning home to his previous mess and therefore walking back into his former mindset.

There were several messages from Seb, left over the course of the last few days, but Finch had neglected to look at them properly or reply. Guiltily aware that he must have worried Seb, Finch sat down to read the messages and relay the wonderful news of his encounter with Otto. The messages conveyed that Seb had become increasingly concerned about Finch's whereabouts:

> 'Hi Finch. How are you feeling now? Do you want to grab some food later? Let me know. Seb.'

> 'Hey – where have you gone? I have some info for you – get in touch. Seb.'

> 'Finch? Speak to me! I have tracked down a group your mum used to attend. They're called the Vers. Doesn't look like she's still a member though. Anyway, I hope you're feeling okay. S.'

'Please get in touch – I am worried about you. Seb.'

'Finch – where are you? Please get back to me urgently. Did you receive my message about your mum? Seriously, please call me ASAP. S.'

Finch immediately called Seb to apologise and explain, and heard the relief in Seb's voice as he relayed recent events. Seb expressed some heartfelt compassion for Finch at the news that Mia was no longer earthbound, and Finch told him it was okay, and in a sense, it was. Otto, an exemplar of enlightened and adjusted Leavers, had been a powerful influence on Finch; if Otto could have repeatedly said goodbye to his wife, knowing that it could have been for the rest of his earthly life each time, then perhaps Finch could give himself permission to adjust more to the mainland ethos. After all, Otto was an admirably enlightened character whose opinion Finch greatly respected. Finch decided to introduce Seb to Otto, so invited Seb along to the dinner he was planning, and Seb gladly accepted.

'Oh, Finch, do you remember that concert I mentioned back on the island when we discussed your leaving?' Seb asked. 'Well, are you interested? It's quite a well-known gig – at the Gunthorpe Chang. It's a huge venue. The concert's an annual thing – raises money for charity. I told them about you – a friend of mine organises it. They would love you to perform.'

Finch was pleasantly surprised, having assumed after leaving the island that the concert had been fictional, bait designed to recruit him. He was pleased to hear it had been a genuine suggestion and that Seb, unlike his mother's Olivia, had not duped Finch into leaving under completely false pretences. Finch agreed to perform and, as they said goodbye, he was uncomfortably aware that there had been no mention of Olga, confirming the low-level, ongoing dread in his mind that their relationship truly had been consigned to history.

Finch spent the evening alone, reflecting on the letter from his mother and his new-found friend, Otto. He thought about Sir, about his love for Olga and his own ever-shifting perspective on the mainland.

***

The morning was bright and Finch awoke feeling rested. There was a message from Seb on his device, which read, 'Meet me here for lunch – 1.00.' Finch opened the link to find a map and, with a single tap of his finger, ordered a drone cab timed perfectly for a one o'clock arrival.

When the time came, the drone landed outside Finch's apartment and he climbed in, checking the details on the destination screen and confirming the location before the drone began its vertical take-off. Finch enjoyed taking drone cabs. He loved the sensation of being alone in the sky with full, panoramic views of the city, other taxi, delivery or emergency drones being the only obstacles to hamper the view. Finch could understand why there had been controversy about the possible large-scale use of drones as domestic transport; it would have filled the airspace to an unpleasant degree. As it was, the drone cab network functioned as one system, making it safer. It worked in harmony with the emergency services and delivery drones so that they all talked to one another, and collisions were a thing of the past.

Each cab was painted individually so there were no two alike, and they added some playful colour to London. The artwork had been introduced to make them more noticeable among the visual clutter of the city, and had evolved into an art form. The cab Finch was riding featured a coral-pink background beneath a pen-and-ink sketch of a scrawled spider with cartoon googly eyes and eight shoes, each a different style. The door displayed a photorealistic painting of a giant pink hand forming a thumbs-up.

Sounding like a swarm of angry bees, the drone began its forward journey. As the ETA closed in, Finch could see a large body of water below him surrounded by trees. It wasn't the river – he'd just flown over the Thames. This was a large pond, it seemed.

The drone touched down on the grass. Finch emerged, baffled as to where Seb intended to eat. The place looked uninhabited – a rare, peaceful green space around a beautiful lake. Finch looked at his device. Seb had sent him a pin on a map, so he began heading towards it.

'Finch! Here,' shouted Seb, waving for Finch's attention, some distance away. Finch made his way over, wondering what Seb had in mind. As he approached, he saw a picnic laid out and two fishing rods set up next to the water. 'Don't be furious, Finch,' said Seb, 'but I've been involved in some subterfuge.' Finch was trying to decipher what Seb was referring to when Olga emerged from behind some foliage, looking remorseful.

'It was my idea, Finch,' said Olga. 'Sorry to completely ooderloop you.'

'I – er, think you may have just done it again by using that word … say-ooder-what-now?'

'Oh, ooderloop – bamboozle. Anyway – Sir, come on.' Sir came trotting out of the bushes, excited to see Finch, jumping up to greet him.

'Sir! God – it's good to see you!' Finch said, overjoyed to see his friend who seemed perfectly well, apart from a limp. 'You didn't go ahead with it, then! Oh, you are a sight for sore eyes, Mrs Danvers!' Finch said, as he fussed the dog vigorously.

Olga was standing back, allowing Finch and Sir some space for their greeting. As Finch glanced up, he found her watching through emotional eyes, close to tears.

'I'll leave you three to it, then,' Seb said as he left, barely noticed.

Finch stood up and walked towards Olga. 'You didn't go through with it?' He was curious to know whether Sir's release was delayed or cancelled, rethought.

'His hip surgery is booked for next week, and then he'll continue to live a long and happy life, hopefully. And no, I didn't go through with it. The things you said, they, well, I started to realise how you were right about some things. We *should* value life more. I've quit.'

'Quit what? Life?' asked Finch, in a sober tone.

Olga laughed. 'No. Impossible, I'm afraid. Smoking. I had hypnosis. I have no interest in it at all, now. It's amazing.'

'That's great, Olga, but all this?' Finch gestured to towards the picnic and rods.

She continued, 'I thought, well, maybe you'd like to do a bit of fishing? With me? We can sit here and not catch anything. Seriously – there are no hooks. We could just talk nonsense. Enjoy the moment. What do you think?'

'I think I'd love to.' Finch moved closer to Olga and

kissed her as they threw their arms around each other.

After some time, Sir grew tired of being ignored and managed to drag some attention his way, stopping the incessant kissing at last. Finch smiled at Olga. 'Something's changed,' he said.

'A lot's changed, my Finch. You'll have to be more specific.'

Finch stood back for a broader view of her. 'You – your energy – it's evened out. Your energy looks strong, balanced. That's amazing. How …?'

'Well, Sir and I have done a lot of thinking, and I'm here, now, with you – actually *in* the moment, and I think I understand – it's precious. When I connect with it, it feels, well, like I'm really alive – maybe even for the first time. I get it, Finch, about valuing life – every moment – and I'm sorry about how I was before.'

'Oh, you are more than forgiven. I've missed you, Olga. And I have news, too. I found my stepfather, Otto.'

'You did? I didn't know you had one.'

'Neither did I, and it turns out that Mum *is* gone, but somehow – that's okay. She's, she's still with me, I know.'

'Wow, Finch. That's amazing. You seem okay … considering.'

'I am. Will you come to dinner and meet Otto? Seb's coming. I want you all to know each other.'

'Of course. Will you … well, will you spend many, *many* decades with me, Finch, enjoying the … how did you put it? The luxury of now?'

'Yes. Definitely.'

***

Some fish were darting, some suspended, motionless. All were exquisite and precious, flashing iridescent light on to Finch's face as they swam past. He loved that he could see directly through the wall-sized aquarium into the sitting room where little Nova sat, busily building towers out of blocks. He stepped back from the fish tank and walked through to the study to find Olga sitting at her desk. She looked up at him with a warm smile, her hair long and her face beautifully aged. Finch was in paradise. He loved his blissful life with Olga and his little Nova … He awoke and gathered his thoughts after the dream. He rolled over to look at Olga who slept peacefully beside him. The sense of gratitude in Finch was overflowing. His world felt abundant, in bloom.

The feeling stayed with him as he made his journey to work. It was his first day back following his leave. Entering the psych lab, Finch had a new peace about him – a harmony within. A cluster of psychs who'd all been deep in conversation turned to see him as he entered.

'Finch! You're back!' exclaimed Nancy with a welcoming smile. She scrutinised him as he approached the group to the accompanying chorus of warm *hello*s from her surrounding team members.

'Hello, everyone,' he said, relaxed and smiling.

'Well, something's different. Did you find Mia?' asked Chikra, intrigued.

'Yes – and no … Sh-she's no longer with us. I did meet her husband, though – Otto.'

'Oh, Finch, I'm so sorry,' Nancy said, with a depth of empathy that would have had Finch dissolving into an emotional state just a few days earlier. Though he was aware of the likelihood of such a reaction, he didn't feel it welling up beneath the surface. Instead, he found a sense of peace. He felt secure, joyful, even. The bond of love between himself and his mother, the connection, even the humour, was all still there and she remained at the other end of it, conscious and present. He could even sense her relief and wonder that he had resolved his unhappiness at last and finally understood the truth.

'It's okay – no, really, it's actually okay. She's still with me,' he responded, aware that the statement couldn't possibly do justice to the inner healing he'd experienced, but hoping they'd understand, nonetheless.

'Well, we're glad to have you back! It's Chikra's birthday. We'd love you to come out for lunch with us.'

'Great – thanks. Count me in.'

'Ah, Mr Henry! Come hither into my space, young man,' Boff demanded, as Finch caught his eye across the lab.

Boff closed the door behind Finch and slumped down into his chair as Finch took the seat opposite and was forced to peer around a pile of white robes and general desk clutter in order to meet Boff's gaze.

'Hang on,' said Boff as he swiped the entire pile on to the floor. 'That's better. Ah, I wondered where those went. Meringue nest?'

'No, thanks.'

'So – what news? You found her?' asked Boff, showering the desk with meringue snow as he spoke.

'In a way. She was ill – she passed. She's in the next world. I found her husband and he told me the truth about what happened. She wrote me a letter. Turns out she didn't leave us – she was duped by the person who recruited her. But it's all okay. I feel like it's resolved … settled. I'm glad to be back. Thanks for allowing me the time to deal with it all. It really helped.'

'You're welcome, dear boy. Glad to have you back. And sorry to hear about Mia, but like you say – she's not truly left us, and it's good news that you've absorbed that fact now. So, shall we get started? You have a clearer mind, yes? I think you'll find it all easier. In fact, you'll probably connect with her now there's no emotional monolith standing in the way. Robe?'

'Why not?'

***

As days passed, Finch settled with ease into his new life. His work at SCI-PSY was enjoyable for his new sense of peace, which allowed him to perform with less resistance when exercising his abilities. The psych team were warm and accepting of him now they were allowed to discuss Mia openly, and he quickly felt part of a larger family.

Olga and Finch had spent a languorous Saturday morning in bed, each basking in the adoring company of the other. The afternoon drew in and Finch set about preparing dinner for Otto and Seb. Olga had taught Finch how to cook with meat subs and he was attempting a faux-chicken pie with mushrooms, tarragon, wine and cream.

Finch's guests began to arrive. Sir welcomed Otto enthusiastically at the door, leading Otto to raise a pleased eyebrow. Finch let Sir do the talking – The dog, whose plight Otto had heard so much about, was still with them so presumably therefore, Finch and Olga must have managed to resolve their differences. Otto greeted Finch with enormous warmth and, Finch sensed, an unspoken understanding about the significance of Sir's presence.

Otto and Seb, similar in age and outlook, seemed to connect instantly and conversation flowed freely between them. Despite the fact that the pie had collapsed in part during cooking, the meal was a success and was followed by coffee on the sofa with a background of Charles Mingus to keep them in good musical company.

Finch was soaking up the sheer joy of his situation. He loved Olga deeply and was so ecstatic to have her in his life on a more realistic footing. He turned his gaze to Otto, the closest person he had to family, a man so decent that Mia had agreed to be his wife, and on whom Finch could truly rely for balance and wisdom. Then there was Seb, who'd rescued Finch from a dreary and possibly short life on the island, and who continued to support him as a close friend. He felt exceptionally blessed. His world had arrived at a wonderful place at last and he planned to enjoy every moment, as instructed by his mother, whose presence he was ever more aware of at times like this.

The discussion had moved on to Finch's upcoming concert when the conversation was interrupted by a message from Rob. As he opened the contact on his coffee table device, Finch felt a sudden wave of dread. He had mentioned Rob's worrying tone and friendship with Grobert to Seb and Olga, but only recently, because his own tumultuous personal life had obstructed his good intentions. He sensed a new energy from Rob – a surge of risk, or danger. Whatever this was, it wasn't good.

The message was a link to a video channel that was a popular platform for users to stream live content. There was a note from Rob alongside the link that read, *'This month's grand showing'*. Finch opened the link. A movie screen appeared in mid-air. It was showing the title 'Monk's Entertainment' which was the introduction to all films that were shown on the island. The film title followed: *Summer Holiday*. There was some discussion about what they were actually looking at. Seb seemed concerned, and suggested they were watching the island cinema screen, live, but remotely.

'How can we be watching the island entertainment?' asked Finch. 'It's localised, isn't it? They have their own terrestrial system, don't they?'

'No. It's internet based,' was Seb's urgent response. 'The islanders don't know it, though. All their TVs were adapted years ago to simply pick up four permanently streaming channels that showed only the approved, massively edited versions of whatever entertainment the Council requested from the mainland. How else could they show that endless loop of drivel? God … Rob worked at TV House, didn't he? On the island?'

'Yeah – he said they had a computer they called the Machine.'

Seb was looking increasingly agitated. 'When they have a new showing – is that limited to the cinema or does it go into people's homes, their TVs?'

'Both,' responded Finch. The opening titles to *Summer Holiday* were abruptly interrupted by footage of Rob, who appeared to be live on screen, standing out in the open amid various forms of modern transport that continually rushed past him.

'Boo,' Rob said, as though sarcastically shocking the viewer, and adding hand gestures to emphasise the mock-eerie theatre of his opening line. 'That's right – it's me, Rob Duffy. Come back from the grave to … Oh, well, you've probably guessed – I'm not really dead like you all thought. In fact, there's no such thing, according to the mainland. That's where I am, by the way, everyone, on the mainland. I escaped. But listen, all you islanders, I have news for you. They've been keeping you all ignorant. Do you want to know why you are so shut off from the rest of the world? Why the Council made it policy to scare us all as children about the *terrifying* mainland? It's because here, they know there's no death. That's right – imagine it. We are energy – there's another existence after our bodies die. We go on – it's totally true. They've proved it: eternal life, my little islanders. And look, *look* at this place! Look at the technology here. The Founders, they didn't like this information so they chose to *deny* it. This, my poor islanders, is why you live so cut off from the rest of the world. And that's just the tip of the turd-berg, my friends. You know, they often take your loved ones to the mainland if they need medical help that the island can't cope with. Well, those people – they aren't allowed back. The island fakes their deaths. Nice, isn't it? Anyway … enjoy. I've sent some drones over – flying machines, that is. They have just dropped packages containing telescopes, binoculars, zoom lenses for your cameras. Have a look at the mainland for yourselves, yeah? Apologies for discomfuckulating your heads, but it needs to be done. Byesie bye.' The picture returned to a scene from *Summer Holiday*.

'Oh, holy shit,' said Seb as he picked up his device and held it to his ear. 'Island break code thirty-three, IOW,' he said. 'Robert Duffy.'

***

On the island, people put down their mugs. Trays of food were dropped. Knitting needles stalled and the eyes in the faces of the audience blinked, and blinked again.

ABOUT THE AUTHOR

E. Heroldbeck has spent the last two decades working as a professional fashion designer with absolutely no intention of ever writing a book. Work on this novel began after the concept of the living funeral presented itself in 2018, instantly becoming a new obsession. It seems that many more ideas are now demanding development.

If you have enjoyed spending time with Finch, first, please tell all of your friends! Then, hopefully, one day there may even be a sequel.

If you'd like to receive early information on new projects, please join E. Heroldbeck's mailing list by visiting

eheroldbeck.co.uk

Printed in Great Britain
by Amazon

27402985R00190